"Ellie, you need a husband."

"You're a fine one to think so."

Graham's downcast gaze cut into Ellie like a cotton hoe. "I've always thought so," he said, his voice quiet.

"I meant you have no room to speak, since you refuse to marry, too."

"With good reason."

"My reason is good, too."

"Then let's hear it."

She knew she shouldn't have told him how good her reason was, knew he'd take it as a challenge. And one thing she'd never seen Graham Talbot do was back down from a challenge. "I don't want to, that's all."

She couldn't explain to him the horror of being orphaned, of being taken in by strangers. Relying on her father to provide for her—and being disappointed—had been one thing. Depending on neighbors for daily food was another.

Never again woul⸻⸻⸻⸻⸻
to provide for her⸻
thirteen years to ⸻
planter's wife.

And a planter sh⸻

Christina Miller has always lived in the past. Her passion for history began with her grandmother's stories of 1920s rural southern Indiana. When Christina began to write fiction, she believed God was calling her to write what she knew: history. A Bethany College of Missions graduate, pastor's wife and worship leader, Christina lives on the family's farm with her husband of twenty-seven years and Sugar, their talking dog.

Books by Christina Miller

Love Inspired Historical

Counterfeit Courtship

CHRISTINA MILLER

Counterfeit Courtship

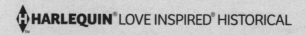
HARLEQUIN® LOVE INSPIRED® HISTORICAL

Recycling programs
for this product may
not exist in your area.

LOVE INSPIRED BOOKS

ISBN-13: 978-0-373-28369-9

Counterfeit Courtship

www.Harlequin.com

Printed in U.S.A.

I can do all things through Christ
which strengtheneth me.
—*Philippians* 4:13

To Jesus, the giver of dreams and gifts…

To my husband, Jan, my real-life hero
and man of God who has always believed in me…

To my mother, who taught me to read
as soon as I was big enough to hold a book…

To my father, who taught me that
I could do anything I set my mind to.

With gratitude to…

Miss Mimi Miller, Executive Director of
The Historic Natchez Foundation, for helping me
with countless historical accuracies and details
and becoming my lively new friend.

Mr. Terry Trovato, Dunleith Historic Inn docent
and storyteller, for brightening this book with his
tales and historic tidbits. What a delight it was to
write portions of this book in the parlor, dining
room and galleries of Dunleith, the house after
which I patterned Graham's home.

Dina Davis, my amazing editor,
whose expert skills made my book sing.
I can't imagine this journey without her!

Mary Sue Seymour,
the sweetest and wisest agent in the business.

Aunt Sister Sylvia Gehlhausen, who gave me a
quiet place to write in her ancient, enormous home.

Chapter One

Natchez, Mississippi
June, 1865

Colonel Graham Talbot slid from his mare and eased the reins over a live oak branch, the need for stealth and silence driving him. He crouched low to the ground and prayed that Dixie wouldn't whinny and give away his position.

As he surveyed the surrounding area, a gang of five appeared from behind the stable. How had they gotten there without him seeing them? And how had they known when he would arrive?

Crossing toward the imposing structure in the open air would make him vulnerable, but if he stayed where he was, they'd be on him in moments. He had to take the chance that they wouldn't look his way. Staying low, he rushed for the next oak. Just a hundred more yards and he'd make it—

"Colonel Talbot, is that you? Sneaking through your own backyard?" The shrill, syrupy voice brought him to a halt. "We've been waiting for you for days."

He stood and raised his hands in surrender. Just as he'd feared, he'd been captured by a force he dreaded more than a platoon of Yankees: a mob of husband-hunting Natchez girls.

As the gaggle of simpering females emerged from the side yard of his stepmother's town house, Graham held in a groan. Their exaggerated giggles and faded finery didn't improve his mood.

The girl who reached him first snapped shut her yellow-fringed parasol and leaned in close, taking possession of his arm in a way that made him want to head back to the army camp. She was pretty, even charming in her own way, but when had the hometown girls become so bold?

And why couldn't they have stayed away until he got a bath and a shave?

He sneaked a glance at the Greek Revival manor next door and caught a glimpse of Ellie Anderson waving out an upstairs window. Her honey-blond hair gleamed in the sun as brightly as her mischievous grin.

Ellie. His childhood chum, the instigator of most of his youthful calamities—and the reason he'd entered West Point, leaving behind his rejected heart. Even at this distance, the belle of Natchez brought back memories he'd worked hard to forget.

He stopped the thought cold. That had been eight years and a war ago. He'd been only seventeen at the time and still more boy than man. Things had been different in those days…

Ellie continued to smile in that maddening way of hers, a sweet, guileless smile, nothing like the cloying grins of the misguided maidens surrounding him—

"Our own war hero is home at last." The girl next to him interrupted his thoughts, and that was probably good since, as he now realized, he'd been staring at Ellie with his big mouth open. "You remember me, don't you, Colonel? I'm Susanna Martin, but an old friend like you can call me Susie."

"We've heard all about your war exploits," the redhead next to Susanna said. She looked vaguely familiar, but he couldn't place her. Then again, after eight years, he probably looked different too.

"What is General Robert E. Lee like? Is he as handsome as they say?"

Handsome?

"General Lee is a brilliant soldier and a fine Christian man. I was proud to serve under him." He started toward the house, wanting nothing more than a hot bath and a long visit with his stepmother.

But they sailed along with him, their giant hoopskirts swaying as the women jostled into each other, vying for position next to him. He was surprised they wanted to get that close. Having ridden all day yesterday and all night last night, he was bound to smell as ripe as fresh manure.

This sure wasn't the homecoming he'd looked forward to, but he extended an arm to each girl closest to him and let them carry him along. The South may have lost the war, and Andrew Johnson, the Yankee president, may have stripped Graham of his citizenship, his plantation and all his property, but he was still a Southern gentleman. And a gentleman didn't offend a lady. Not even five ladies who'd disrupted his plans and wearied his already-troubled mind with their chattering.

And with the war's end, being a gentleman was all he had left.

Climbing the stone steps to the breezy front gallery with its white columns and comfortable outdoor rockers, Graham hesitated. Surely these girls didn't expect him to invite them in—not in his filthy condition. But Noreen, like the lady she was, would welcome them into her home—his childhood home—and so should he.

"We haven't had many parties this year, so we can't wait for tonight. Miss Ophelia started planning your homecoming when Lee met with Grant." Susanna spoke in low, intimate tones, as if four other women weren't hovering about her, taking in every word.

"A party—tonight?" How was he going to get out of that without hurting Aunt Ophelia's feelings? Now that she was a war widow, she'd likely mother—and smother—Graham more than ever. Starting tonight, apparently. "Would you care to come in and tell me about it?"

Say no, say no...

"We'd rather hear about the war. All of Natchez knows about the hundreds of Yankees you captured." Susanna's drab green eyes turned hard as an artillery shell. "Although I don't see why you didn't just shoot them."

"I spared as many lives as I could." They reached the front door, and he saw it was shut. He hesitated. As hot as it was, why would Noreen not have all the doors and jib windows flung wide open to catch a breeze?

He grasped the brass doorknob. Surely his stepmother would entertain these girls and let him escape upstairs to a bath. Graham opened wide the cypress door painted to look like mahogany, and followed them inside the too-quiet center hall. He gestured toward the parlor. "Please be seated while I find my stepmother."

He barely had them in the parlor before he took off down the hall to the library. The room was empty. Where was she? It wasn't like her to leave the house unattended. Anybody could have walked in that door...

Something seemed amiss in the room, but he couldn't discern what. He ventured farther inside, toward the collection of poetry Noreen kept on the shelves between the windows on the east wall, and then he saw it. A nearly full teacup and a half-eaten slice of bread and butter sat on the table next to his stepmother's favorite fireside wing chair.

Food and dirty dishes sitting out—in Noreen Talbot's home? Something had gone wrong. He could sense it, just as he always could in battle.

Graham turned from the library and checked the dining room. He stepped through the breezeway to the kitchen dependency—nothing. He charged up the stairs. "Noreen?" Upstairs, he headed for her room at the end of the hall.

As he'd suspected, it was empty too, with both bed pillows fluffed and in place, Noreen's hairbrush and mirror at perfect right angles to each other as always—and the third drawer of Father's lowboy flung open.

The drawer where he hid his revolver.

Graham hastened to search the drawer. As he'd feared, Father's Colt Dragoon was gone, and the lid lay beside the open box of bullets.

What could this mean? He glanced down at his dirt-caked boots and the clumps of dried mud he'd left on the Persian silk and wool carpet. Noreen could have moved the gun, but she didn't leave drawers and ammo boxes open.

A wave of soprano giggles pierced the air around him, interrupting his thoughts. The girls.

He dashed into the hallway and toward his own room. He had to find out what had happened to Noreen, a mother to him since shortly after Mama and Graham's baby sister died in childbirth. But first he had to get rid of those girls. The thought of doing that made his stomach sick.

He could think of only one way to get them out.

Ellie Anderson pulled her head back inside the window of Uncle Amos's second-story bedroom, unsure whether to laugh at the scene below or feel sorry for Graham Talbot. For a moment, she fought the urge to send him their old childhood signal: a shrill whistle from between her teeth. But from the looks of things, he had enough noise in his ears as it was.

Would he even remember that signal, or had his war years erased the memory? It was such a childish thing, like the handkerchiefs they used to attach to wires and dangle out the windows of their rooms. A blue handkerchief was an invitation to an adventure, red for a picnic, and a white one was a distress signal. They had worked fine until Uncle Amos caught Ellie trying to fly hers from the weather vane.

She watched until Graham and the debutantes entered his home. Then she turned from the window in time to see Uncle Amos tip a spoonful of grits onto his lap.

She hastened to the bed, where he sat propped up by three pillows. "I'm not getting the hang of this," he said, the slur in his speech still unfamiliar, even two months after his stroke of apoplexy.

Reaching for a napkin, Ellie tried to smile some encouragement into his drooped face. "You will. Keep practicing." She wiped his chin and nightshirt front, and then she loaded more grits onto the spoon she had built up with a length of inch-thick dowel.

Uncle Amos reached for it, grunting as he spilled

the grits again, and tried to dredge the spoon through the bowl.

"Grab it like you would an ax handle, not with your Natchez table manners."

A twinkle appeared in his eye—the first one she'd seen since he took to his bed. "When did you last see me holding an ax?"

Ellie breathed a prayer of thanksgiving for this smidgen of humor. Surely it was a sign that he would recover. It had to be. Because if he didn't get better—

Light footsteps tapped down the hall, interrupting her thoughts. Within seconds, Ellie's maid poked her head in the doorway, a fringe of tight, gray-streaked black curls escaping her red kerchief. "That spoon you made working?"

"Better, Lilah May," Uncle Amos said in a loud voice of optimism—as always when anyone other than Ellie was around.

"Let me help him. Colonel Graham just got home. You best get over there and rescue him from all them women." Lilah May sat next to Uncle Amos on the bed and lifted a cup of no-longer-steaming coffee from the tray. "Besides, this man needs some coffee."

"Graham Talbot?" When she raised the cup to his lips, Uncle Amos held up one hand, stopping her. "What women?"

"Maiden women, that's who, from all over town. They got designs on him, for sure. One of them is going to wiggle her way right into that big mansion of his."

Her uncle's good eye widened, making the droopy one seem even worse by comparison. "Get over there, Ellie."

She glanced out the window, the hot midmorning sun streaming in and heating up the room, bringing only a breath of a breeze with it. At least today her uncle remembered who Graham was. "I'm driving out to Magnolia Grove to check the west cotton field this morning before it gets too hot. I want to see how well the plants are squaring."

"All you ever do is work. You're the best plantation manager a planter could ask for, but you're also a young lady. Go see Graham."

From the look on Uncle's face, this was an argument she was going to lose. "Make sure he gets more than coffee, Lilah May. If he had his way, that's all he'd take."

With Uncle Amos's snort ringing in her ears, Ellie headed downstairs. Her maid and uncle could imagine her running to Graham's side if they liked. But she had no intention of joining the fuss and flurry over the war hero's return. They'd been friends too long, and she knew him too well to think he would enjoy the festivities this town had planned for him. A Confederate colonel who'd served under General Lee was worthy of celebration, to be sure. But Graham would rather entertain General Grant in the parlor than attend all the parties, balls and dinners that were in his future—starting tonight.

The poor man. Surely all he wanted to do was rest after traveling all the way from Virginia.

Someone ought to warn him. He might need her help.

She hastened to the library and rummaged in her desk for stationery, then she dipped her pen in the ink.

Graham, old friend,
Maybe your welcoming committee has already told you this, but your aunt Ophelia has been at the ready for weeks, prepared to give you a coming-home party the night you arrive. If you need a quiet eve-

ning instead, I'll be at our old hideout and will bring you home for some of Lilah May's good cooking. Your friend, Ellie.

As she put away her pen, she noticed a letter addressed to her, propped against her walnut whatnot box where Lilah May always left the mail. Ellie pulled a pin from her hair and slit the envelope, then drew out the single thick sheet. Only three lines of large, bold handwriting scrawled across the page.

After my father's demise, I must put his accounts in order. May I call at your home Friday next at 8:00 p.m. to discuss the business he left behind? As always, Leonard Fitzwald.

As always? Surely that didn't mean Leonard intended to loiter here at their home as he had before the war. Honestly, if the neighborhood hadn't known better, they'd have thought Ellie and Leonard were courting.

The thought sent a cold chill down her back. Although not necessarily bad-looking, Leonard had an almost frail demeanor and, worse, some undefined, underlying peculiarity that made her uneasy. She'd have to find a polite way to discourage him from visiting, especially now that the cotton fields were squaring. Between supervising her new workers, keeping track of cotton prices and watching for the right time to sell the portion of last year's cotton harvest that she still had stashed away, she had no time for Leonard. However, since his father had been their cotton broker, Leonard no doubt had legitimate business to discuss.

But for now, Graham needed her help, so she tossed

Leonard's letter onto her desk and headed for the back door. Maybe her old friend would take her up on her offer of escape from the party, and maybe he wouldn't. Either way, she'd have an excuse to miss it too. Some girls never grew up, like that silly Susanna Martin, who'd all but thrown herself at Graham in the yard. And Miss Ophelia, who seemed as excited about Graham's return as the debutantes were. As much as Ellie loved Miss Ophelia, she'd welcome a chance to forego the festivities.

As Ellie neared the back door, Sugar got up from the rug and let out a sharp bark. Ellie grabbed the braided leather leash from the nail she'd hung the dog's leashes on for the past ten years. Fastening it to Sugar's matching soft leather collar, she gave silent thanks to God for allowing them to keep their ancestral home, as stately as Graham's and even larger. Others around them had suffered much more than she and her uncle had, but now the war was over, and they could all make a new start.

Everything would be fine—if Uncle Amos recovered. And if Magnolia Grove returned a profit this year.

The thought took her breath. As the only father she'd known since the age of twelve, her uncle had to get well. But he had shown little improvement since the early days of his affliction, and she had to face that fact.

Magnolia Grove stood an even smaller chance of improving—and now it was up to Ellie to make that happen. At least she still had ground to work. Graham, on the other hand, had little to come home to.

If things had been different, he might have come home to her.

She brushed aside the thought as always. Their world had changed—they'd changed—since that summer night when he'd come calling, a bouquet of white crape myrtle in his hand and his heart in his eyes.

If only she'd been free to accept his offer...

The black-and-white-spotted English setter barked again and tugged at the leash. Ellie made her sit, then she scratched behind the dog's floppy, curly ears and opened the door. With Sugar nearly dragging her toward Graham's home, she let her gaze drift over the white house with its two-story columns and Doric capitals.

A white handkerchief hung from his bedroom window, fluttering in the gentle breeze.

Their distress signal?

She picked up her pace, Sugar trotting ahead of her. He'd been home ten minutes. What calamity could have happened in that time? And why ask for help from her, of all people?

She caught sight of him in the stable and hastened toward him. "Graham, welcome home."

He turned toward her from the horse he was brushing. If she thought earlier that he'd changed, she now saw how much. Once the best-looking boy in Natchez, today he could turn every woman's head in Mississippi. Of a stronger build than she remembered, and still in his uniform, he looked at once both powerful and intimidating— and yet she felt strangely safe with him. His dark hair brushed his collar, needing a trim, and he wore several days' growth of beard, but the lack of scissors and razor couldn't detract from his stunning looks.

His eyes had changed the most. She'd dreaded this day in the past weeks, not wanting to see cold, war-hardened eyes. But instead, she found gray-green eyes that had surely seen the worst of horrors—horrors he had commanded—and yet had become even softer than before.

They no longer held his heart in them—at least not for

her. At the thought, she drew a long, slow breath of thanksgiving that held a pinch of bitter disappointment as well.

"Ellie." He dropped his currycomb onto a low table. Then he bowed from the waist, a little too formally, considering their long friendship. "Perhaps you'd rather I call you Miss Ellie, or Miss Anderson."

"That would be silly." Equally silly was her sudden pleasure in hearing his deep, velvety voice. "Why did you hang the distress flag?"

He drew a ragged breath and glanced toward the house, his eyes intense, as if he was heading into battle. "I'm in trouble."

"You?" Ellie couldn't help laughing. "The hero of Natchez needs my help?"

"It's female trouble."

Female? "Well, you do work quickly. Don't expect me to get you out of a hasty engagement or any such nonsense."

"It's nothing like that." The intensity in his eyes lessened a bit, so maybe her teasing had lightened his mood. "A whole flock of women was here when I got home. They came inside with me, but Noreen's gone."

"Is that all? All you have to do is put on some water for tea. Noreen keeps a few cookies in the pantry, so put them on one of her Spode dishes—"

"I don't want to serve refreshments. I want them out of the house so I can find Noreen."

The man must have been too war-weary to think straight. "She'll be back. You can surely tolerate an hour with a few pretty women."

"You don't understand. Something's wrong. I know she left in a hurry, because her half-eaten breakfast is still sitting in the library. And Father's revolver is missing."

Now, that was different. "In that case, tell them you

need to go. If Miss Noreen left dirty dishes, something has happened."

"They're not going to listen."

She thought for a moment, watching Sugar inch closer to the horse.

"Don't worry. I have a plan."

Chapter Two

I have a plan. How many times in his life had Graham regretted having heard those words? He had a feeling he was going to regret it again. "All I want you to do is go in there and ask those women to leave while I look for Noreen."

"If that's all it takes, you do it," Ellie said in her easy drawl.

The sick feeling in Graham's stomach intensified to a burn. How was he supposed to tell her that, since he left her house that night eight years ago, he had spent almost no time with women and had no idea how to handle them? What was he supposed to say—that he'd led men into battle but couldn't lead a gaggle of women out of his home? After all his time at war, he simply didn't trust himself with the social graces. But the grin on Ellie's face told him she wasn't interested in hearing about it anyway.

Well, she was going to hear about it, whether she liked it or not. "Look, I've been three days without a bath and in the saddle the past day and a half, and I smell worse than a wet dog. I've been stripped of everything I own, plus my citizenship, and now to be disgraced in front of all those ladies— I still have my pride. I can't do it."

"My plan is brilliant. Trust me."

He blew out his breath, sounding a little like Dixie when she saw something she didn't like. "Don't even tell me about it. You're just like the Confederacy—full of great ideas that never quite work out."

"I'm honored to be compared to the glorious Confederate States of America."

To his dismay, she smiled her sweet smile. He'd wanted to make her mad, prod her into helping him. Why couldn't she just do as he asked?

Then he realized she was baiting him, as she had for years when they were young.

"Fine. Carry out your plan. But I don't want any part of it." He stuck his foot in the stirrup, swung himself onto Dixie's back and guided her out of the stable.

Just as he was about to tap the horse's flank and take off, Ellie slipped out of the stable and closed the door, leaving the dog inside. She climbed the marble carriage steps and then took him by the arm and started to hoist herself right up there in front of him.

"What are you doing?" Against his will, Graham helped her mount. He'd left this woman here eight years ago, and she'd gone crazy while he was away. Now he not only had to get five girls out of his house, but he had to get another one off his horse.

"Ride up to the front of the house and pass as close to the south parlor windows as you can. You put the girls in the parlor, right?"

"Where else would I put them? The cellar?"

She leaned back against him. "Get the horse moving, and act as if you like it."

"Ellie, we're not children anymore. This isn't one of your schemes. Noreen could be in trouble."

"The sooner you stop talking and ride up there, the sooner you'll be gone to look for her."

How did she always make everything sound so logical? But in his situation, what else could he do? He nudged Dixie with his heel and she took off.

"Slower. We're supposed to be enjoying this."

He gritted his teeth so hard, they might break, and he slowed the horse. When they were ten yards from the window, Ellie began to giggle.

She really had gone crazy.

Turning back to look at him, she stopped the laugh cold and spoke through her teeth as she smiled. "You're scowling like an old schoolmarm. Smile and act as if you like me."

After all those years of war and responsibility, he wasn't sure he remembered how. He tried a rather tentative grin but it felt like a grimace.

"Better but not good. Think of something pleasant."

"Be glad you get this much. I'm out of practice."

As they passed the windows, Ellie primped a little and giggled again. "They're looking right at us. Smile."

This was ridiculous. He urged Dixie across the side yard and to the front hitching post, although he didn't exactly want to advertise the fact he was home. He didn't need any more women showing up. "Now what?"

"Help me down." She gave Dixie a good pat on the head and then held on to Graham as she slipped to the ground, her white hoopskirts twirling.

He dismounted and secured the horse. Then they ambled up the walk, Ellie clasping his arm as Susanna had done earlier. "I'm surprised you can stand being this close to me," he said.

She looked up at him, her eyes blue as the sky and almost as wide. "You're not that bad."

"I was referring to my hygiene—or lack of it."

"I admit you don't smell like a crape—" She cut herself off and lowered her head, a flush across her cheeks.

But he knew what she was going to say. Crape myrtle. He'd wanted to cut down that tree eight years ago, and he would have, if Father hadn't stopped him.

She remembered too. And since he didn't know what to say to break this sudden, awkward silence, he let it remain.

Actually, after the first few seconds, it wasn't so bad. Quiet was a rare thing around Ellie.

On the gallery, he opened the door for her as he had for those girls. And the quiet stopped.

"Graham, how nice of you to give me a ride. I'd been counting the days until your return." Ellie tugged at his arm and pulled him along with her until they stood outside the parlor doorway. Then she looked up into his face and batted her lashes at him, smiling like a debutante. "I can't believe you're finally home. Now we can—"

She pulled her gaze from him and turned to the parlor. "Oh, dear. You have guests."

Graham ventured a glance into the parlor. If Ellie was trying to get their attention, she'd accomplished her goal. They all sat motionless as sharpshooters, and a few had their mouths open.

Then, before he could figure out what she was doing, she took his hand and nudged him toward the parlor. Now what? Holding Ellie's hand in front of these girls was more awkward than the silence had been.

"Graham was on his way upstairs to freshen himself after his journey." She looked at him with those big eyes again. "Go ahead, honey. I'll serve refreshments."

This time she pushed him toward the stairs. Whatever she was trying to do, at least he'd get a quick sponge bath. Nothing else was going the way he wanted today, so why shouldn't he take ten minutes to get cleaned up? It would have taken a lot longer than that if he'd had to wait for those women to decide to leave. Come to think of it, he couldn't very well go out to look for Noreen as long as he smelled like a horse. A dirty, sweaty, dust-covered horse.

Although it was hard telling what he'd have to deal with when he got back down here.

"Ladies, if you'll excuse me, I'll fetch some cookies and tea." Ellie started for the hall, knowing full well she wouldn't get out the parlor door, acting the hostess this way in Graham's home. Immediately, she caught movement out of the corner of her eye. She turned to see the group rushing toward her, hoopskirts dancing with the motion.

"We appreciate the offer, but we must decline," Susanna Martin said, making the decision for the whole group as usual. "We came to see the colonel, and since he will be occupied for a time, we'll come back another day."

Ellie moved farther into the room and perched on the edge of a gold damask settee. She took a white lace handkerchief from her day-dress pocket and flicked an imaginary fleck of dust from the gas lamp next to her. "Whatever you say, Susanna."

She needn't have wondered about the effect of her actions. The girls, all from her Pearl Street neighborhood, sat back down as well and began asking questions all at once.

The charade was rather enjoyable, and Ellie let them

answer their own questions for a time. Then she held up one hand. "Ladies! Your mothers would be appalled at your manners."

"Colonel Talbot was right here in this room with us just minutes before the two of you came in. How did you end up riding with him?" Not surprisingly, Susanna took the lead.

"He sent a message for me. A white flag, so to speak."

"While we were all in the house?"

"It would seem so."

"But you never allow a man to come calling."

Ellie cast her gaze out the parlor door and toward the staircase. "Of course not."

"How long have you had this understanding with Colonel Talbot?"

"Understanding?"

"I heard years ago that he proposed marriage to you. Is that true?"

Ellie turned her face to the floor in what she hoped looked like a demure gesture. "It's true."

"Something's not right about this." Susanna stood and made for the door. "I don't believe you and the colonel are courting at all."

"Believe what you like, Susanna. It makes no difference to me." Ellie walked with her to the entrance, and the other girls trailed in their wake. "See you at church on Sunday."

When she'd shut the door behind them, Ellie fetched Sugar from the stable and brought her back to the parlor. Although she still wanted to go to Magnolia Grove before the heat of the day, she probably needed to stay until Graham came downstairs.

She went to the library to collect the dirty dishes he had said were there, and she washed them in the kitchen dependency. This area was as clean as if Miss Noreen still had a staff of twelve servants. How she kept it that way was beyond Ellie. If Lilah May and Roman hadn't stayed on after the others left, the Anderson home would be in sorry shape.

Moments after she had dried and put away the dishes, she heard Graham clambering down the stairs. Ellie hastened through the breezeway to the dining room and then the center hall.

"They're gone?" he asked, freshly bathed, shaved and dressed in what must be his father's suit—a good idea, considering all the Union troops still occupying the city. "How did you manage it?"

"I didn't manage much of anything." Ellie moved to the sunny spot Sugar always chose on the faded runner extending from the front entrance to the back door. The dog ignored her until she picked up the leash. Then she came to life, prancing in anticipation of going outside.

"I told nothing but truth, but I let them come to the conclusion that we are courting."

"But we're not courting."

"Lands, no. But since they think so, they got out of here in a hurry. You're free to go and look for Miss Noreen."

The look of dismay on Graham's face was not what she'd expected. "I can't believe you did that. Don't you realize why they left in such a hurry?"

"Of course. They wanted to leave us to our happiness."

He sat down hard on the wooden settle bench along the hall's east side and dropped his head into his hands. Just the way he always had when one of her childhood schemes had gone wrong. "No, they didn't. Have you forgotten who you're dealing with? Susanna left here to spread the 'news' all over Natchez."

"I'm not sure about that..." Or was she? What if he was right?

"The entire Pearl Street neighborhood will know by the time the party starts. Maybe the whole town." He raised his head and impaled her with his gray-green eyes. "You did it again, Ellie."

"What did I do?"

"You trapped me in another of your great ideas without thinking it through. That's why these plans of yours don't work out. You don't stop to think."

"I thought about it—"

"You never think beyond the present. You have to start considering the consequences of your actions."

Hadn't she heard that all her life? First from her parents, then from Uncle Amos and the tutors he'd gotten for her. "I can't help it if the consequences surprise me, can I?"

He groaned. "We're going to have to figure out what to do. After I find Noreen."

"Graham, I'm sorry—"

"You say that every time too."

Well, maybe she did, but that was better than not saying it.

Graham got up and started for the door. "I'm going to see if the neighbors know anything about Noreen. This afternoon, we'll decide what to do about this. And how I'm going to get out of going to Aunt Ophelia's party."

The party. Ellie retrieved her note from her dress pocket and handed it to him. "I was going to slide this under your door, but then I saw your signal."

She grabbed Sugar's leash and followed Graham outside as a carriage pulled up near the spot where his horse snitched mouthfuls of grass from the yard's edge. Within moments, Miss Noreen stepped unassisted from the conveyance. She turned and faced the carriage door and held out her arms. Someone placed a bundle into them.

A bundle that squirmed and cried…

Chapter Three

Graham's eyes misted over at the sight of his step-mother, and that surprised him more than anything else that had taken place this morning. What had happened to the soldier, the commander in him? He'd apparently been replaced by a nose-wiping ball of mush who hadn't even realized he was homesick.

He also hadn't realized he'd been running toward Noreen, but his slightly elevated pulse told him he had. He reached for the slender, gray-haired lady to give her the hug of her life—

And was met with a tiny fist to the gut.

"What? What is this?" In his relief and joy at seeing Noreen, he'd noticed but paid little attention to the white blanket he'd thought was merely wadded up in her arms. But there was something in that blanket. And that something was raising a fuss. So the crying hadn't come from the baby buggy Mrs. Lemar was pushing up the walk as he'd thought. "What's going on?"

"Graham." She laid one hand on his upper arm and leaned toward him. "I thank God you made it home."

He bent down to receive her kiss on the cheek. That

alone would have made him start to bawl right here in the street, along with the baby, if he hadn't been so shocked by his—or her—appearance.

"Everyone please come inside," Noreen said. "Ellie, you too, dear, and Joseph."

Joseph? Graham shot a glance back at the carriage. Their attorney, Joseph Duncan, climbed out and stretched his long legs. His suit was somewhat shiny from age and his stovepipe hat faded, but his famous, magnificent mustache was groomed to perfection as always and white as the clouds overhead.

Graham was about to offer his hand when the old gentleman gave him a snappy salute. "Welcome back, Colonel. I was a captain in the War of 1812. I know how pleasant it is to come home."

Although it felt rather silly to salute a civilian more than three times his age while wearing a borrowed suit, Graham returned the gesture. "What's going on? Whose baby is that?"

Joseph ambled down the walk with him. "We'd better let Miss Noreen tell her story."

Noreen and Ellie—and Sugar—were halfway to the gallery by now. "I should carry that baby for her." Graham started to pick up his pace, but Joseph clasped his arm.

"I wouldn't. Let her hold the child."

Inside, Noreen seated everyone in the parlor—Graham in his favorite leather wing chair, Ellie in the old-fashioned writer's chair in the far corner and Joseph on a comfortable upholstered settee. Noreen chose the gold damask settee for herself. "In a few minutes, I'll ask Ellie to prepare refreshments for us. We'll all need strength by the time I've finished my story."

She unwrapped the quieted baby from the blanket and

cradled him—or her—in her arms. "This is my granddaughter, Noreen Elizabeth. She's eight months old. Her mother called her Betsy."

Ellie gasped, and until that moment, Graham had forgotten she was in the room.

"Yes, my daughter-in-law named her after you, *Elizabeth*." Noreen smiled a tiny smile. "Apparently, she called her Betsy instead of Ellie to avoid the confusion of your shared name."

Just what Graham needed—another female with Ellie's name. What were the chances that her namesake would be as maddening as Ellie? "Why do we have Betsy?"

"I learned of her existence only this morning. You know that my son, Stuart, died of dysentery in Tennessee a year ago last March. Shortly after dawn, Joseph brought me word that his widow, Francine, succumbed to pneumonia." Noreen's always-soft, always-gentle voice was now edged with a sorrow Graham had never before heard. "A neighbor cared for Betsy overnight, and at first light, Joseph took me to Harrisonburg by ferry to fetch the child."

"I didn't know Stuart had a child." But he'd had a furlough shortly before his death, so it made sense. And now the poor little girl was fatherless. And motherless. That mist threatened Graham's eyes again. He swallowed hard to choke it down. He must have been more exhausted than he thought, as blubbery as he was.

"Neither did he. Stuart had just gotten back to his camp when the sickness swept through it. And Francine didn't know Betsy was on the way until after she learned of Stuart's death." Noreen caressed the top of the baby's head and then kissed it. "Now I'm her only relative, besides her step-grandfather when he gets home from war. And you, of course, Graham. I've always considered you my own."

Graham put his head down and pinched the inner corners of his eyes with his thumb and forefinger. If he didn't get control, he was going to embarrass himself. He cleared his throat and searched his stepmother's eyes. "Thank you, Noreen. I feel the same."

He stood and went to the window, not to see what was out there but to hide the fact that he had to wipe a bit of moisture from his cheek. What was wrong with him, anyway? He hadn't cried in eight years.

Turning back to Noreen, he rubbed his face hard and focused on keeping that stupid huskiness out of his voice. "I've been your son for the past twenty-two years, and Stuart was like a brother to me. I'll take care of you and his child as long as you need me." Although he had no idea how he was going to do that, since the government had confiscated everything he owned.

"I'm sure we'll hear from your father soon, and he'll return with his own troops. Between the two of you, and with God's help, we'll all be fine."

Did that little quiver in Noreen's voice mean she harbored some doubt? Well, so did he, so he could hardly fault her.

"I'll help you take care of Betsy, Miss Noreen." Ellie got up and rushed to the older woman. "I don't know much about babies, but you can teach me."

Seeing her mistress crossing the room, Sugar did too, and gave the baby a tentative sniff. Betsy reached out her impossibly small hand and grabbed the dog by the ear. Sugar stood still as the baby pulled her ear and giggled.

"Sugar won't bite, will she?" Graham sprang to his feet.

"She's never even snapped at anybody in her whole

life, and she's ten years old. She's not going to start now," Ellie said, but Graham noticed her moving in closer too.

Betsy apparently grew bored with Sugar's ear and released it, and the dog lay at Noreen's feet, facing the baby as if guarding her.

Joseph laughed his rich, deep laugh. "I'd say this is going to be the best-protected baby on Pearl Street."

As Noreen smiled at him, Graham drew in a huge breath. Ellie had certainly lightened the mood for them and helped them through this hard time, or rather, her dog had. But that didn't mean she had to help care for the child. He and Noreen could manage that just fine.

"Would you like me to watch her this evening and give you a chance to rest?" Ellie said as Noreen handed Betsy to her.

"No, you and Graham have a party to attend. Betsy and I will be fine by ourselves."

"I'm not going," Graham and Ellie said simultaneously.

Noreen gave Graham her mother-knows-best look.

He ignored it. "I'm going to take a hot bath. Then I'm going to the train station and sending a telegram to General Lee to ask if he has any news of Father's whereabouts. I'm going to write a letter to Andrew Johnson, asking for pardon and amnesty, and then I'm going to bed early."

"Graham, you have to go to the party. Ophelia has gone to great trouble and expense, more than she can afford, to give it for you. You'll break her heart if you don't go." Noreen turned to Ellie. "You too, dear. She thinks as much of you as she does of Graham."

He held in a groan. This was already the longest day of his life, and it was only noon. Did the women in his life have to make it the longest night too?

"Would you like me to come tomorrow afternoon and help?" Ellie asked.

The little minx, changing the subject like that. Sure, she didn't like the Natchez social whirl any better than he did, but if he had to go, so did she. He'd just sit back and wait for the best time to break that news to her.

"You can come back as many afternoons as you like, when it's too hot for you to be at Magnolia Grove." As the baby began to fuss again, Noreen took her from Ellie and bounced her on her knee.

"Noreen, you'd be better off without her help. If you let her hang around, you'll end up engaged to somebody." Graham started for the center hall, beckoning Ellie to follow. "But for now, we have some things to discuss."

He strode to the door and out to the front gallery, not bothering to see whether Ellie—or her dog—followed. Outside, he eased himself onto one of the old rockers. It still felt as good as it had before he left.

Within moments, Ellie came outside and chose the rocker farthest from him.

"Sit over here by me. I don't want to have to yell so the whole neighborhood can hear."

She took her time in complying, which was no surprise, but she eventually sat next to him.

"We need to talk about this party," he said, using his colonel voice.

"We already did. You're going. I'm not."

He should have known it wouldn't be easy. "Oh, yes, you are. You cooked up this courtship idea, and you're not leaving me to explain why you're not with me on my first night home. You owe it to me after causing this fiasco."

She huffed out a big sigh. "It's not that bad."

"It's not?" He leaned forward in his chair. "What happens when time goes by and there isn't a wedding? Did you think of that?"

Her wide eyes and surprisingly silent mouth told him she hadn't.

"You're the big plan-maker. I hope you have a solution for this." As soon as the words were out of his mouth, he regretted them.

"Now that you mention it, I have thought of something—"

"No!" The word came out like the howl of a man falling off a cliff. He sprang from his chair and headed for the door. "No more plans! I'll call at your house at eight. Just don't think between now and then. Please do not think!"

But he could see from her dreamy-looking eyes and the angle of her cocked head that she was, indeed, thinking.

Another orphan.

After dark that evening, Ellie leaned against one of the massive white columns on Miss Ophelia's back gallery and waited for Graham to return with her cold drink. Since he'd left her at this secluded corner, she'd discouraged eight hopeful suitors, from around age seventeen to over sixty. Now she finally had a moment alone to think, with the gentle strains of orchestra music wafting out all six of the floor-to-ceiling jib windows. If only a cool breeze would come and blow away the fog in her mind. In wartime, one heard of orphans all the time, but to have held one in her arms this afternoon—it made her want to cry.

As Graham had.

He'd tried to hide it, didn't want to admit how that baby had affected him, but she'd seen him wipe the tears.

And that might be a good thing, after four years at war. Perhaps he was starting to heal from its horrors already.

If only Ellie—and Magnolia Grove—could also recover from the war. Her visit to the plantation this afternoon hadn't eased her mind. The cotton was squaring nicely, but the fields were full of weeds, and the workers were few.

And what of that cryptic note from Leonard Fitzwald? What could he possibly have to say to her that she didn't already know? It was no secret that Uncle Amos owed Leonard's father fifteen thousand dollars, due after this year's harvest. She didn't like the fact that they'd borrowed money from their broker. But they'd had little choice, and nearly every planter in the Natchez area, plus across the river in Louisiana, had to do the same.

Magnolia Grove had to do well this year. They couldn't sustain another year like the past three. And with Uncle Amos laid up, Ellie had to make the ground profitable. If only she could be sure she could do it…

You can do anything you set your mind to.

Her mother's voice drifted back to her from the past.

I married an Anderson, but remember that I am a Stanton, and therefore, so are you. Stanton women have pulled their families through Indian raids, fires, death and destruction. God may call you to hard things too, but you'll come through, because you can do anything you set your mind to.

She twisted Mother's pearl ring, the one Ellie had worn on her right hand ever since Mother placed it there on her last day on earth. Yes, her mother and grandmother had been strong, but it would take more than the Stanton backbone and the Anderson name to keep Magnolia Grove in the family this year.

The tall case clock chimed the quarter hour in Miss

Ophelia's center hall. Ellie glanced at her timepiece—a dainty little brooch from Uncle Amos last Christmas—and realized Graham had been gone nearly half an hour. Had Susanna or one of her friends cornered him? Did he need help escaping?

Just as she was about to go in and look for him, he strode out the jib window, open tonight to extend the dancing to the back gallery, and handed her a silver cup. "Just as I thought, everyone in Natchez has heard about us."

Ellie turned from the view of the formal gardens and gazed into the crowded ballroom as the quartet transitioned to a sweet rendition of "Aura Lea."

"Who are they gossiping about? You and me? Or you, Miss Noreen and Betsy?"

"All of us. We're the talk of Natchez tonight."

Susanna and a man Ellie didn't know, dressed in a Confederate officer's uniform, whirled across the brightly lit room, her emerald hoopskirts sweeping the expanse. The woman seemed to think it was her responsibility to dance with every former Confederate soldier at the party. Ellie had to admit it was nice to see a few gray uniforms again after two years of occupation by the Union army.

Susanna's cloying smile turned to a frown as she caught Ellie's gaze.

"She's going to cause trouble." Ellie kept her own smile intact until Susanna and her partner danced across the room and out of sight.

Graham's grimace might have meant he thought any trouble Susanna could cause would be minor compared to Ellie's plan.

She snatched his arm and pulled him closer to the gaslight to see his face better. "I know what that look meant.

I'm doing only what you asked me to do—helping you get rid of the girls. They aren't bothering you now, are they? Think what tonight would have been like if I hadn't done as you asked."

In the brighter light, his eyes blazed like the flame. "I shouldn't have hung the distress flag. I should have camped out in the old hideout until the party was over."

So much had happened that day, it seemed she had seen the signal last week rather than twelve hours ago. Just this morning, she'd had no idea Graham would come home, that she would enter a fabricated courtship with him, that a baby would enter her life—

"The baby… What did you learn about her this afternoon while I was out at Magnolia Grove?"

"For one thing, I found out why the baby is your namesake." Graham swirled the punch in his cup as he used to when in deep thought. Then he looked up and met her gaze, the trace of an undefinable emotion in his eyes. "I didn't know how much you did for Francine before she and Stuart got married and moved to Harrisonburg."

Ellie sipped her punch, a little tart for her taste. "All I did was show kindness to her, a girl I liked, at a time when others in this town did not. She was a Ballard, and you know how most people in town viewed that family."

"Outlaws, thieves, drunkards—but I think most of that was exaggerated. Your friendship apparently meant a lot to Francine. And I appreciate it too, for my stepbrother's sake." Graham tasted his punch, and then he swallowed another big gulp. "Want me to get rid of yours?"

After all these years, he remembered that she liked her punch as sweet as her coffee. "Don't let Miss Ophelia find out."

"This isn't the first time I've rescued you from having to eat or drink something you didn't like." Moving nothing but his eyes, he scanned the gallery and gardens, then turned his back to the house and drank her sour punch as fast as if it were the best raspberry cordial. "Lilah May never knew that you didn't eat a single pea the entire time you and your uncle stayed in town."

She laughed at that. "Yes, I owe you for eating many a helping from my plate when no one was looking."

Graham set both punch cups on the wrought iron table in the corner. "Noreen told me what happened when Stuart announced their engagement."

"It was shameful. She was a good girl, no matter what kind of family she came from." Ellie unfolded her fan and waved the effects of the humidity from her neck. "I don't understand why Francine never let Miss Noreen know about the baby."

"Francine's father disowned her for what he thought was shameful behavior on her part. He thought Stuart, a man far above her station, was toying with her, using her for nefarious reasons. But he was wrong. According to Noreen, Stuart loved Francine and intended to marry her from the day they met."

"That's how I saw their relationship too. Francine lived by her Bible."

"She was afraid her family would try to take Betsy from her if they knew about her. So she continued to run the store Stuart's father left him, just as she had after he went to war. Harrisonburg is far enough away that no one in Natchez, including Noreen, found out she'd had a baby. I guess she never knew her father and brother were killed in the war."

Poor Francine. To have found love, had a child and then lost that love—it had to have been the hardest thing imaginable.

The only thing worse was never to experience love at all…

Where had that thought come from? She pushed it away. Romantic love was not for Ellie. And here at this party, with the man who knew her better than anyone else, was not a safe place to explore such a notion. Family love was enough for her, and she had that with Uncle Amos and even Lilah May and Miss Noreen, in a way. And she could love Francine's child like a niece. In fact, since Betsy was her namesake, she owed her as much love as she could give.

"Aura Lea" drew to a close, and Graham offered his arm. "Stroll in the garden?"

As they descended the stone stairs to the lawn, Ellie had to admit that the moonlight made him even more handsome, as every unattached female in the city had surely noticed tonight.

Since he seemed to want to talk of other things, Ellie decided to ask the question that had been nagging at her since he came home that afternoon. "Graham, why are you so opposed to spending time with a woman? I know Susanna isn't your type, but Natchez, and especially the Pearl Street neighborhood, has lots of nice, pretty girls."

She could feel the tension build in his arm—but why? "Did something happen during the war to make you leery of women?"

"If I tell you, will you promise not to think up a solution to the problem?"

Ellie had to laugh. "I promise."

"A promise is a sacred thing." His voice deepened, lowered to a near whisper.

She held her breath, waiting for what she sensed was close to his heart.

"I can't marry. I can't support a wife."

"Graham, just because Ashland Place and Ammadelle are gone—"

"You don't understand. None of those girls in there do either." He gestured toward the brightly lit house. "It's not just our plantations. I have no livelihood. I have no money. I'm not even a citizen anymore—of any country. I've lost everything."

"Why are you not a citizen? I haven't heard of that happening to any of our neighbors."

He let out a noisy breath. "Andrew Johnson has decreed that all West Point graduates who served as officers of the Confederacy must apply individually for our pardons and the restoration of our citizenship. Since Father and I are both West Point men and served as colonels, we lost Ashland Place, Ammadelle—and everything else."

The full moon revealed a fresh line between his eyes—a line that hadn't been there before baby Betsy arrived that afternoon.

The baby. His orphaned niece. No wonder Graham's worry showed on his face. He had a child to support now, and no way of doing so.

And Ellie's fear of marriage—fear that a husband would fail to provide for her as her father had failed—had driven him to West Point all those years ago. That meant she was to blame for Graham's dilemma. The thought made her weak, and she eased herself to the iron bench next to them.

But she couldn't let him find out about that. She blurted the first thing that came to her mind. "Well, that's what you get for going to a Yankee military school. You should have gone to Charleston—to the Citadel."

"Here we go with that again. Do you know that, at the time, I heard those words from everybody in town except

Father and Noreen?" He sat beside her, keeping a good distance between them. "But that's why I can't marry. I have nothing. If our town house didn't belong to Noreen from her first marriage, I wouldn't have a place to live."

Graham gazed off into the distance, in the direction of Ashland Place. "I can't buy or sell property. I can't vote or run for public office. My military career is over, my plantation is confiscated, as is Father's, and I have no other skills. Everything is gone. And now I have Noreen and a baby niece to care for. There's no room in my life for a wife."

And it was her fault. Above all else, she had to help him somehow... "Listen to my idea. I think it will work. I can keep those girls away."

He let out a moan that must have come from his toes.

"Let's continue the courtship arrangement. It would help me too. Dozens of discharged soldiers are coming back to town, and they're at my door every day, wanting to court me."

"Why don't you let them?"

"Well, just as you can't marry, I won't."

"Why not?"

"My reasons don't matter. Let's keep up the courtship ruse in order to discourage each other's would-be suitors and belles. But we have to promise to remain friends—nothing more."

He paused so long, she was sure he would say no. Then he took her hand and leaned in close. "I'll have to think about this. Something about making up a courtship doesn't feel quite right to me."

"But you'll consider it?"

"I'll consider it. And I promise to remain just friends with you. That suits me fine."

She should have felt relief, knowing Graham wouldn't

attempt a true courtship again. But something in his tone made her wonder, for the first time, if maybe her great ideas weren't so great after all.

The thought startled her as much as the rustling of leaves directly behind her.

She spun in the direction of the sound and faced a uniformed man, his left eye covered with a black patch and a scar across his left cheekbone. Ellie sucked in her breath. In the flickering gaslight, his gaunt face and form looked as if he had come back from the grave.

"Ellie," he rasped, reaching for her hand. "I'm glad I lived to see you again."

She instinctively pulled back from him. Then recognition hit her like shrapnel. "Leonard Fitzwald…"

Chapter Four

Graham's fists clenched at his sides as his memories of this man brought out every fight instinct he'd developed during four years at war. Of all the men he would have expected to die of sheer cowardice on the battlefield, Leonard Fitzwald would have topped the list.

"I trust you received my letter," Fitzwald said, his wheezy voice sounding like an eighty-year-old man's.

This weasel had dared to communicate with Ellie? The thought ignited a searing flame deep in Graham's gut. Fitzwald had no right to correspond with any decent woman. "Why did you send Miss Anderson a letter?"

Fitzwald took a half step back and ran his finger over the edge of the eye patch. "Business. With the potential of a social visit afterward."

"You're mistaken, Fitzwald. You're not visiting Miss Anderson, and you're going to do your business now, in front of me." He looked the man over. The Confederate uniform on his back did nothing to make him look like a soldier. "And no more letters."

"Graham!"

He was aware of Ellie's high-pitched voice, but all he

could see in his mind was Leonard Fitzwald calling on Ellie in the months before Graham laid his heart at her feet. "I know things about this man that you don't know, Ellie. You have to trust me."

"Colonel, let it go." The weasel turned to her. "I'll call at your house Friday at eight, as planned."

"Stay away from her, Fitzwald. I haven't forgotten how to fight."

Ellie wouldn't know he wasn't talking about the war. Her gaze snapped from Graham to Fitzwald and back again, her mouth open as if she didn't know what to say or whom to say it to.

But Fitzwald remembered the incident Graham referred to. He could see it in the man's weasel eye.

"Tell me your business now, Leonard," Ellie said, her voice quivering a bit. "Graham is an old friend, and you can trust him with whatever you have to say."

"Fine way to treat a veteran."

He had to be joking. "You're no veteran. You're a coward—at home and at war. I know what you did at Antietam." So did every Confederate from colonel on up. The story had spread fast—how Fitzwald had crumpled on the battlefield, whimpering like a baby crying for its mama. Even Betsy didn't act that way. Only Fitzwald's father's money and political influence had gotten him a desk job instead of the firing squad.

"Let him speak his mind," Ellie whispered, still the peacemaker.

Graham let out his breath with a low growl. He crossed his arms in front of himself and waited.

The weasel drew himself up to his full height. "I've inherited my father's property and investments. Ellie, your uncle—"

"Call her Miss Anderson."

Fitzwald glared at him as if he was a Yankee. "Ellie's uncle owed my father thirty thousand dollars. The loan comes due two weeks from today."

"Two weeks?" Ellie's voice turned shrill. "That's not true. Uncle Amos was careful to set the due date a month after harvest. And he owes fifteen thousand, not thirty."

"That was before he took out a second loan and attached it to the first. If you doubt my word, I can arrange a meeting with my lawyer."

Graham had had enough of this. "Fitzwald, it's time for you to go home."

"My attorney will come with me on Friday."

As the weasel retreated into the darkness beyond the gas lamps, Graham sat down again and motioned for Ellie to join him. The bench that had seemed inviting and comfortable minutes ago now felt rigid under his still-tense body. He took a few deep breaths in hopes of calming his jangling nerves and slowing his heartbeat.

Ellie eased onto the bench beside him, keeping as much distance as her hoops allowed. "Why are men as hateful as Robert Fitzwald allowed to have children?"

"I've wondered that for years." After Fitzwald's shocking news, it probably would have been appropriate to comfort her in some way. But wouldn't that add to the awkwardness already surrounding them every time they were together? He scooted a little closer to the end of the wrought iron bench and away from her, but that felt strange too, so he reached over and patted her hand. But that only made his discomfort worse. He'd better just talk and not touch. "Noreen told me about your uncle's illness. I was sorry to hear about it, but now I'm even sorrier. You shouldn't have to deal with Fitzwald's buffoonery."

"It's part of doing business. But I'd be glad to hand

this over to Uncle Amos if he was able." She glanced to the right and the left, and then she leaned toward him. "He had a stroke of apoplexy when he heard Lee surrendered to Grant. He refuses to get out of his bed. I think he could, with help, but he's so melancholy, all he wants to do is lie there."

That news was the biggest surprise he'd had since coming home. Seeing her downcast eyes and the way she bit her lower lip, he thought it might be best to change the subject. Courtship was one thing, but he had no idea how to deal with a crying woman. "Do you think there's any truth to Fitzwald's story?"

"None at all."

"Good. Then he'll have no reason to continue bothering us."

He had barely rested his hand back on his thigh when the sound of chattering females once again assaulted his ears. What now? He turned toward the offensive noise. The full moon revealed a bevy of hoopskirts and curls flouncing down the stone steps toward them. He wasn't sure, but they may have added a girl or two to the original pack.

He stood as dark-haired Susanna led the girls to the bench, although he would rather have hidden behind the giant live oak to their left.

"Colonel Talbot, Miss Ophelia requests your presence in the ballroom." Susanna eyed them in the moon's shadowy light. "I won't apologize for intruding, because it doesn't look as if we interrupted much of anything."

She was probably right. Ellie had kept a rigid distance from him and, other than the moment he'd made his friendship-only promise to her, he'd done the same. Anyone watching would have thought they were cousins or siblings, not a courting couple.

This charade wasn't going to work—not with Susanna around.

Ellie rose with as much dignity as he'd once seen in Mary Custis Lee. "Please tell Miss Ophelia that we will be in momentarily."

Susanna stood speechless for a moment, which was almost as much of a surprise as Ellie's sudden poise. The silence didn't last long, though. "You'd better do as she says."

Graham rested his hand on the waist of his "intended." "As Ellie said, we'll be along. Please give us a moment alone."

"If you're brave enough to defy Miss Ophelia, that's your business. And I still say this is the most peculiar courtship I've ever seen." The leader of the gang glared at Ellie for a moment and then stalked away, her troops following her as always. Apparently, his colonel voice worked better on Susanna than it did on Ellie.

As soon as they were out of earshot, Graham leaned in close to whisper. "I'm sorry you have to endure this party after receiving such upsetting news from Fitzwald. Would you like me to take you home?"

"No, because I don't think he's telling the truth. I'm not going to give this any more serious thought until I've had time to find out. And I won't run out on Miss Ophelia now that we're here." Ellie began to pace the path in front of the bench as if in deep thought. Finally she stopped and faced him. "But one thing we have to think about is our arrangement. Susanna could make a lot of trouble, so we have to be more careful. Even when we think nobody's around, people could be watching us."

"That's another reason I didn't want to fabricate a courtship."

"We can do it. We have to. If we stop now, neither of

us will be able to turn around without enduring a marriage proposal."

He had to laugh. "You're the only one who has to worry about that."

"Don't be too sure Susanna Martin won't try to make you propose."

The thought turned his insides cold. Ellie was right.

"Here's what we'll do…"

The chill in his gut now turned to fire. How did this woman manage to keep him in such turmoil? Was this what life was going to be from now on?

No, it was not. She'd helped him out of a jam, that much was true, but it didn't mean she could control him. He'd been a colonel in the Confederate army, commanding thousands of men, and no woman was going to give him orders.

Especially this woman…

"Whatever your new idea is, you can forget it. I'll think of something."

She smiled that smile that used to keep him awake at night—sweet, effortless, with a hint of amusement, as if she was going to let him talk his own neck into a noose. "That's fine, Graham. What do you want to do?"

"Easy. We're going to stop this nonsense."

"How are we going to do that?"

"We'll go into that ballroom and…" And what? Announce that they weren't courting after all? While that seemed like a good solution, common sense told him it would make a laughingstock of Ellie. He studied her eyes in the moonlight—clear, unselfish, innocent eyes. Eyes that had kept watch over him in childhood and still looked after him today. Eyes that saw right through him to the man he was inside. Could he do that to her, offend her this way? No Southern gentleman would treat a woman in such a fashion. He looked over her head, to the east, toward Ashland Place.

"What's your plan?" He ground out the words between clenched teeth.

Ellie took his arm and snuggled against him in a most convincing manner. "To go into the ballroom like a couple in love and let Miss Ophelia draw her own conclusions. She probably wants to honor your service to the Glorious Confederacy, so let her do that. Then just act natural and she'll spread the word that we're courting. But you have to make it look more realistic than you are now, or nobody older than little Betsy will believe it."

At once he realized they'd been ambling back up to the gallery. "Courting doesn't come naturally to me. I don't know what to do."

"Nobody here knows that. Just do as I do."

Now how in blue blazes did Ellie know how to act "in love"? She'd never treated him like that, and according to Noreen this afternoon, she'd not courted with anyone in all the years he'd been gone.

But as they climbed the steps to the gallery and the gaslight there shone on her face, he saw that she did, indeed, know how to look that way. Those big blue eyes of hers, gazing at him like liquid love—he cleared his throat and swallowed hard to get rid of the lump that somehow formed there.

"That's it!" Her lowered voice brightened with enthusiasm as they stepped through the window. "Now you look the part."

Somehow, that didn't make Graham feel any better. Pretending to be in love with the girl who had once ripped out his heart and then stepped on it—he couldn't go along with it. "Ellie, we have to talk about this. I can't— I won't—"

Ellie's adoring look vanished for an instant as something like an ache etched itself between her eyes.

She must have thought he found something distasteful about her.

How far from the truth that was. What Southern gentleman went about hurting women that way? And why did this whole situation have to be so complicated?

Holding in the groan that wanted to escape from his gut, Graham clenched his jaw and stepped aside to allow her to enter his aunt's home. If Ellie and Susanna were right, their friends had many more events planned for him in the near future, and he had to learn to deal with that. He'd give it some thought when he was alone.

If he ever made it out of this house and away from this party.

Graham wanted to talk about the courtship ruse? Ellie was thinking the exact same thing. It wasn't going to work unless he agreed to it with his whole heart.

The poor man. Ellie released his slightly trembling arm and stepped through the jib window and into Miss Ophelia's home. He hadn't seemed this uncomfortable even at their first "grown-up" party at Susanna's house years ago. What could frighten this war hero so much—the party itself or the thought of an imaginary courtship with her?

"Colonel Talbot!" Miss Ophelia called in her exaggerated, singsong voice. She sailed across the vaulted-ceilinged ballroom toward them, wearing more yellow ruffles and bows and longer ringlets of red hair than even the debutantes had. Of course, Ellie would never have expected Miss Ophelia to wear mourning clothes for more than six months. And, being Ophelia Prescott Talbot Adams, she got away with it in Natchez.

When she reached Graham's side, she enveloped him in a hug only a woman who had been like another mother to him could give. "You look stunning in that uniform, Colonel."

Miss Ophelia's matronly embrace brought a look of relief to Graham's eyes, clearly comforting him more than Ellie would have thought possible. When his aunt finally released him, he gave her a peck of a kiss on the cheek. "If you call me Colonel again, I'm going to march right out of here and take all these troops with me."

"Only in public, Graham," she said, blinking her long eyelashes as if trying to keep from shedding a tear. "I'm too proud of you to pass up any opportunity to boast about you." Then she gestured for the orchestra to stop, and she pulled both Graham and Ellie to the front of the room.

"The whole town has been waiting for this day." Miss Ophelia raised her voice and commanded the room's attention. "My nephew, Colonel Graham Prescott Talbot, war hero and defender of the great Confederate States of America under the celebrated General Robert E. Lee, has returned to us at last."

True to form, Miss Ophelia led the crowd in genteel applause. As she'd requested, Graham wore his freshened uniform and polished boots, and Ellie noticed at least a dozen other former soldiers in cadet gray as well. They all carried the hardships of war in their faces, as Graham did, no doubt having seen and endured things they'd never be able to forget. But what about their futures? Were these men's days to come as uncertain as Graham's, their prospects as dreary, their responsibilities as heavy? Were their burdens as great as his: no occupation, no potential for marriage and family in the near future, no means to support the stepmother and baby in his care—

And a counterfeit courtship with Ellie, who had once laughed at his proposal?

At once, she understood his discomfort with the courtship arrangement she'd suggested.

Miss Ophelia's pointed stare snatched Ellie from her thoughts, and she realized the room had gone silent. She nudged Graham in the side. "They're waiting for you to speak."

He cleared his throat as if summoning his colonel attitude. "Thank you, Aunt Ophelia, for the kind words. It's good to get home to Natchez, where the Spanish moss sways in the breeze, the catfish wait for us in the Mississippi River, the grits are always hot and the punch cold. I pray none of us will ever leave her again."

The men murmured their agreement, and Graham paused a moment. "As I told my troops in my mustering-out speech only months ago, 'May we all discharge the obligations of good and peaceful citizens at home as well as we have performed the duties of thorough soldiers in the field.' Always take comfort in the knowledge that, although we lost the war, your courageous men in gray did perform their duties well."

Miss Ophelia began another long round of applause, seemingly understanding his discomfort and distracting the crowd from the huskiness of his voice and the pain in his eyes. He turned aside for a moment, but his mouth quirked a bit as if he were trying for a more cheerful expression.

"That was a beautiful speech," Ellie said, sensing his pain. "It must have been hard, saying goodbye to the men who served under you for four years."

"I worry about them, how they'll fare now, what will

happen to them." He swallowed hard as if pushing back his tears.

This man had been through enough, even without her courtship idea. "We could go home now, if you like."

"No, Noreen was right. Aunt Ophelia spared no expense for this party, from the roast beef and smoked ham on biscuits to the pecan and sweet potato pies," he whispered to Ellie. "If nothing else, I need to show her some appreciation. Even though all I want right now is to get home and have some quiet time to rest and think—"

"Colonel Talbot, I haven't danced with you all evening." Like a machete through a cotton stalk, Susanna's shrill voice cut through the murmur of the crowd as she drew near Graham. "We have much to talk about after your long absence."

Six other neighborhood girls gathered in a semicircle behind their leader as if waiting in line for their turn to snatch up the handsome soldier.

Miss Ophelia's gray-green eyes, a mirror image of Graham's, turned a shade darker as always when she disapproved of the way someone treated her only nephew. "Let's all dance to 'Aura Lea' again, in honor of Colonel Talbot's own maid with hair as golden as Aura Lea's. Graham, Ellie, please start this dance."

"Dance? In front of all these people?" Graham's low voice sounded less like a colonel's than Miss Ophelia's had. "Aunt Ophelia, I've lived the military life for eight years, with no frivolity to speak of. Not tonight—"

"We'd love to." Ellie could hear the hint of challenge in her own voice.

"Ellie, you've gone too far."

The poor man. He'd commanded the entire room's attention with his wonderful speech, looked like the beau of Natchez in his uniform and had the bearing of a warrior. Yet the prospect of a dance clearly frightened him more than a line of cannons.

And it was up to Ellie to put him at his ease.

She swayed toward him and lifted her hand, then let it rest on his shoulder as she gave a tiny nod to her right.

He looked in the direction she indicated. Susanna stood a mere three yards from them, a knowing smile on her face.

Ellie knew Graham hated this charade and, in a way, so did she, but letting Susanna destroy it seemed even worse. He took Ellie's other hand and stepped out with one foot, sweat dripping down his brow as if the room was lit with blazing fires instead of mere crystal gaso liers.

Ellie moved with him. Seeing that he had forgotten even the most basic steps, she guided him with a gentle touch on his shoulder, pressing this way and that to help him remember which way to step. "Act as if you know what you're doing, and nobody will know the difference."

His grip on her relaxed a fraction. "At least other people are dancing now too."

"Including Susanna. Miss Ophelia and I saved you from her, you know."

"Not to mention the rest of her mob." Graham executed a graceful turn, and Ellie smiled her approval. "How many more parties did you say I have to endure?"

"Plenty. And all those girls will be at every one of them." Not to mention dozens of former soldiers. She lowered her voice. "That's why we both need our arrangement."

He wrinkled his nose as if Sugar had trotted right by him, soaking wet. "I'm still not convinced about that."

Ellie was, and not only because Susanna and her friends seemed ready to pounce on Graham, waiting for the moment Ellie would leave his arms. And not because of all her would-be suitors, either. From Graham's more natural steps and more relaxed hold on her, she knew she was helping him through more than a mere awkward moment. No, he needed her. And since she had caused many of the problems he now faced, she would help him all she could. That was what friends did.

For that reason alone, Ellie smiled her sweetest at him as she came into Susanna's line of sight, her mind grasping for a new plan that would solidify this faux courtship.

Chapter Five

An hour later, having seen Ellie home, Graham sank into one of the deep fireside wing chairs in the parlor, his thoughts racing as they always had before a battle. With Noreen at his side, rocking and singing softly to little Betsy, he sipped his tea and gave thanks for this peaceful home. Although common sense told him the baby would likely disturb that peace before morning.

Noreen paused in her humming. "You have a lot on your mind tonight. Your silence gives you away."

"You'd think with the war over, a soldier could simply come home and pick up his life where it had left off." Graham shifted in his chair, its plushness not sufficient to keep him as comfortable as it used to. But that probably had less to do with the chair's quality than it did his own melancholy mood. "Life never turns out the way we'd planned, does it?"

She pulled the baby closer. "Not in the least."

"I'm going to stay in Natchez with you and Betsy until Father gets home. But this afternoon, after I sent my request for amnesty to the Yankee president, I wrote to Major James White, superintendent of the Citadel. I inquired about teaching there, maybe starting this fall. Federal troops still occupy the school, but that surely won't go on much longer." He gulped the last half of his tea and set the cup on the cloth-covered walnut table at his side. "If I'd gone to the Citadel instead of West Point, I wouldn't be in this mess."

"Nobody should fault you for choosing the school your father attended." The dimmed lighting couldn't hide Noreen's smile of encouragement. "And I'm sure he will be home soon."

Graham wasn't so certain. It was probably time for him to tell his stepmother all he knew of Father. "Because he and Father were classmates and close friends at West Point, General Lee graciously met with me after the surrender and tried to pinpoint Father's whereabouts. I didn't know he had been transferred to the Trans-Mississippi Department, which didn't surrender to the North until May 26."

"Then he could come home any day."

"He was not on General Lee's list of casualties. I sure wish the Confederacy hadn't passed the new conscription law last year, raising the age limit to fifty. Father was a year too young to remain exempt."

"Ellie's uncle Amos escaped by only one year. He served in the Silver Grays instead."

"Silver Grays?"

"The home guard. I declare, I wish James could have done the same."

Betsy began to fuss then, as if she could sense their concern about her step-grandfather. Noreen jiggled the baby on her lap, but that didn't seem to help. A new weariness lined Noreen's delicate features, and she stood more slowly than usual. "She must want to be walked."

Babies wanted their mothers—or grandmothers, in this case—to walk about the room with them at this hour of the night? The mantle clock looked nearly ready to chime one. Noreen had always been early to bed and early to rise. How was this going to work out, especially at her age? Sure, she was a spry fifty, but it had to be harder than when she'd cared for her own child at age twenty-one.

At once, he left his cushioned chair and laid aside his musings about his father and his own future. Until Father came home, Graham was needed here, and he'd care for his family with an undivided heart, no matter the sacrifice. He crossed the room to Noreen and held out his arms. "You've been looking after Betsy all day. Now I want you to go to bed and leave her to me."

The baby let out a great howl, startling Graham into dropping his arms. Noreen shook her head. "You don't know the first thing about quieting an infant."

The howl grew to a shriek.

"Well, Noreen, I'm not sure you do either, at the moment." He tempered his words with a grin, raising his voice to be heard over the racket.

Her eyes widened, and then she smiled. "I am a bit out of practice. But I'll be all right."

Graham reached for the child, and this time, he took her in his arms. "Sorry, Noreen, but I'm the man of the house now. Until Father gets back, I'm taking care of both her and you."

Noreen pushed back a lock of hair that had fallen from her pins. "Maybe I'll lie down for ten minutes."

She climbed the stairs toward her room. Good thing it was in the back of the house, overlooking the gardens, while he cared for Betsy in the front. Otherwise, the little baby with the big lungs would keep Noreen from getting any rest at all tonight.

He looked around the parlor. What kind of atmosphere

would a baby like at bedtime? Maybe less light. But dimming the room meant he'd somehow have to hold Betsy in one arm while turning the gasolier knob with the other hand. Could he manage that without dropping her? No, he should set her on the floor instead.

But the moment her set her down, she howled all the louder. With a sheen of moisture forming on his forehead, he dashed to the gasolier and turned down the light.

That was better. He picked up the baby again. Too bad she didn't appreciate his effort.

Perhaps she was tired of being walked. He knew she wasn't hungry, as Noreen had been feeding her when he came into the room a half hour ago. Graham eased himself onto the wing chair, first holding Betsy tightly and then a little looser. Jiggling her didn't help either.

He had to get this baby to sleep, or Noreen would be right back down here, and she needed to rest after her exhausting day.

Fact was, Graham was beyond the point of exhaustion himself, and he couldn't hear his own thoughts over Betsy's howling. He shifted her in his arms and looked into her pretty little face, tears pouring from her eyes.

Did she miss her mother?

Heavenly Father, I can't do anything about that. Please show me how to comfort this baby.

No ideas came to him, other than shutting the two massive parlor doors to keep Noreen's room quiet. When he'd done that, he moved to the window, where he saw that the fog had obscured the Andersons' gaslight. He closed the windows so the baby's cries wouldn't wake the whole neighborhood.

About five minutes later, as Graham began to despair of ever getting the child to sleep, the front door opened and closed quietly. Then the parlor door eased open, and Sugar trotted in, followed by Ellie holding the leash.

He ran one hand over his eyes, his fatigue making his head pound. He hadn't the energy to spar with Ellie tonight. Why did she have to come over here? "Ellie, please…"

She unfastened Sugar's leash, her smile as bright as if she'd just risen from a full night's sleep. "I heard Betsy crying, and I came to help. I have an idea."

He groaned like a cadet on his first ten-mile hike. "I'm not letting you involve this helpless child in one of your schemes. No baby, not even a Yankee baby, deserves that."

"I'm a better nursemaid than you are." Still in her ball gown after her short visit with Uncle Amos, Ellie sat on the edge of the gold settee. She had to admit that she came here to do more than help with the baby. The moment she'd glanced out her window and seen Graham's silhouette in the parlor, pacing the floor with Betsy, she'd known how to calm her. This was the perfect opportunity to show him that not all her schemes went wrong. If she could somehow get that baby to stop crying, maybe he'd believe the courtship ruse would work out too.

Graham's square jaw clenched, and it made him look all the more commanding in his Confederate grays. "I'm not a nursemaid at all. I'm relieving Noreen so she can rest."

"She'll never fall asleep as long as Betsy is crying so hard. Let me try. You haven't done a great job thus far."

"Fine. Have it your way." He carried the squalling baby to her and placed her in Ellie's arms. "What can you do that Noreen and I haven't already done?"

She sat Betsy on the floor in front of her. "Nothing. But watch this. Come, Sugar."

Sugar ambled up to Betsy and licked her toes. After a few moments, the baby's cries began to taper off until she quieted. Then she reached out and grabbed a tiny fistful of black-and-white fur on the dog's neck.

"How did you know that would work?" Graham no longer looked as if he were ready to fire a cannon at someone—namely, Ellie—but she also didn't see the amazement she'd hoped for in his face.

"I remembered how calm Betsy got this morning when she grabbed that long, floppy ear, so I thought Sugar might settle her down tonight too."

"I have to admit, it made her happy again."

Graham Talbot—acknowledging that Ellie was right? That was momentous, and she needed to seize the moment. "My plan worked, and so will my courting idea. Give it some time, and—"

"Wait a minute. That's not the same. Just because a dog came over here—"

"She didn't come here on her own. I brought her. On purpose, so she could distract Betsy from whatever was wrong with her." Surely even Graham couldn't argue with that.

Sugar's high-pitched whine drew Ellie's attention. She looked down to find Betsy grabbing the dog by the tail.

"Not the tail, Betsy." She gently pried the little fingers away, and Sugar retreated to a far corner.

Betsy's face wrinkled, and she let out a long, low wail that sounded as if her heart had broken.

"Sugar, come," Ellie coaxed, but the dog did her ceremonial dance of three circles and then flopped onto the floor, curling herself into a ball.

Ellie lifted the baby and held her against her shoulder, patting her back. "A wagon ran over Sugar's tail last winter, and she can't stand to have it touched."

Graham strode to Sugar's corner and bent down as if examining the tail. He must not have touched it, though. The dog would have let her know.

"Don't you see that your schemes don't work out because they aren't based on logic? You have to think things through. You can't expect a dog to sit with a baby all night long so the people in the house can sleep."

Betsy's sobs had dissolved into shallow, fitful breaths now, and Ellie lowered her from her shoulder and cradled her instead. The baby's eyes drifted shut.

"Success," Ellie whispered.

"Don't forget how it went the last time she stopped crying."

"I remember that Sugar quieted her, just as I thought she would. I wanted you to see that so you'd realize what a good idea my courtship plan is."

"That's not how it happened at all. Yes, Sugar momentarily distracted her, but that's not what put her to sleep." She could feel Graham's exasperation in the air. "We're not children anymore. I'm a grown man with a grown man's responsibilities, and I can't go along with you and play your silly games like I used to. This courtship of yours has to end."

"Being an adult doesn't mean you have to be gloomy all the time."

"I'm not gloomy."

Bless his heart. He didn't begin to realize how much the war—and military school too—had changed him. "You used to be a lot of fun, but now everything is serious to you. The war's over, Graham, and it's time to stop fighting."

A look of pain crossed his face, and although she used

to know him better than anybody, she couldn't understand that look or what had caused it. Was it her complaint about his seriousness? She couldn't imagine that. Was he remembering the war, the suffering?

When he dropped his gaze to the floor as if unable to look at her, she knew. This powerful man, this war hero, had his mind on the past—their past—and she'd caused his pain with her careless words: *You used to be fun.* Her subconscious, underlying message spoke her truth: he wasn't fun anymore.

But was that true? Considering how he'd spent the past eight years, was it fair of her to compare him to the carefree boy who'd proposed marriage to her?

She twisted the ring on her right hand. She'd give Mama's best pearl if only she could take back those hurtful words. She wished she hadn't said them, wished they weren't true, wished she could somehow comfort him as she'd managed to comfort Betsy. She opened her mouth to say so, but he lifted one hand and shook his head.

"I can't think about it tonight. I wasn't this tired even after Chickamauga." He strode to her side and took Betsy from her. "Let's talk about it later. I'm going to put her in her crib."

When he'd disappeared up the stairs, Ellie leashed Sugar and started for home, the mist of regret heavier in her mind than the settling fog.

Chapter Six

The next afternoon, Ellie straightened the piece of wire she'd found in the stable. She tied a rag, one of Lilah May's old, frayed red kerchiefs, onto one end. Then she set the other end on the windowsill and weighted it down with *Pride and Prejudice*, flying the kerchief out her window like a flag.

Dear God, I'm putting this flag out here like Gideon's fleece. Despite what she'd said to Graham, she realized during her sleepless night that she didn't know whether Leonard Fitzwald had told her the truth about their debt. She needed advice—and help in searching Uncle Amos's library at Magnolia Grove.

If only her uncle would get well again, she could tell him about her conversation with Leonard and get his opinion. But since Doctor Pritchert told her uncle to avoid the exertion of business, Ellie was on her own. Besides, Uncle Amos had sounded so confused this morning, he couldn't have helped her anyway.

Her childhood Sunday school teacher used to say Gideon sinned by putting out his fleece to seek an answer from God. But Ellie didn't see it that way. Gideon needed to know whether God was going to deliver his enemies into his hands. And in a way, that's what Ellie needed to know too. She'd never thought of Leonard as an enemy before, but after last night, she wasn't sure.

"If Graham sees the red flag and comes over by the time I'm ready to leave, I'll ask him to go with me to Magnolia Grove. If he doesn't, I'll go alone," she whispered to the Lord. "Above all else, don't let me get outside Your will."

Ten minutes later, she went to the dining room and poured herself a glass of sugar water. She sipped it as she watched out the window for a sign of Graham. If he hadn't come by the time she finished her drink, she'd have to go.

When her drink was gone, she took her glass to the kitchen and then returned to the center hall. She tied on her plain, wide-brimmed straw hat in front of the mirror at the back door. It was time to go, and Graham hadn't arrived. With a pang of disappointment, she pulled on her gloves and gave Sugar a goodbye pat. "I'm riding Buttercup today, so you can't come along. We'll take the landau tomorrow."

At least tomorrow she'd have company, even if it was only her dog.

Pushing down the self-pity that wanted to rise up in her, she headed out the door. If God didn't want her to have help, that meant He would do the helping. Ellie learned long ago not to complain about that. If she didn't want to marry, she had to do things alone. Hard things. Hard work. Hard decisions.

She stepped into the stable, where Roman led Buttercup out of her stall, saddled and ready to go.

His eager service made Ellie smile. She wasn't alone, after all. "Roman, I hope our fortunes will soon be restored so we can hire a gardener. Then you can do only what you love—care for a stable full of horses."

"I'll pray with you 'bout that." The handsome older man held the reins in his mahogany-colored hand while Ellie mounted.

She spoke to Buttercup, and the horse started toward Commerce Street. As they turned onto Washington and passed the south windows, Sugar looked out and watched them go. Her throaty warbling let Ellie know she didn't want to be left at home.

Before Ellie reached Pearl Street, Graham raced toward her on Dixie. "I thought we were having a picnic. That's what the red flag means, right?"

He remembered. And he came. She didn't recall ever being so glad to see him.

Thank You, God.

She reined in Buttercup and smiled at Graham. "I didn't think you were coming."

"I came as soon as I saw the signal."

"I had a basket packed."

"Where is it?"

"In the kitchen."

"What's in it?"

"A whole chicken, biscuits and honey, and watermelon."

He spun Dixie around and cantered toward Ellie's house. "I've waited eight years for Lilah May's fried chicken."

Ellie laughed at his serious tone. She nudged Buttercup, urging her to follow. "I have an ulterior motive."

He groaned. "Not another plan…"

"Not like that. I couldn't find any loan agreements in this house, so I need to search Uncle Amos's library at Magnolia Grove." She didn't want to ruin the day by telling him she was in big trouble if she did owe Leonard thirty thousand dollars in two weeks. "I thought we could have a picnic and then look through the library together."

"That's not so bad. At least it doesn't involve dancing."

When they reached the stables again, Lilah May came out, their lunch in her hand and a grin on her face. "Goin' on a picnic and forgot the basket. That's love if I ever saw it."

Love. Her maid thought she and Graham were in love. Ellie's hand shot up and covered her mouth.

Lilah May handed the basket to Graham. As he settled it in front of him, Ellie noticed something she'd never seen before—his face and neck turning red.

Graham—embarrassed? Over the mention of love. It wasn't about her, that much she knew, so why had he colored so?

Then a distressing thought hit her. Did he already have a girl? Was that why he fought against their pretend courtship?

She should have thought of that. She'd assumed, without even thinking of it, that he was unattached. Somewhere, a woman could be waiting for him to return. Even—*oh, my word*—a wife!

No wonder he didn't want all those girls around—or want her at his house last night. It all made sense now.

But if he was married, or even courting a girl, they had no business riding out to Magnolia Grove together. "Graham, wait…"

He swung around in the saddle. "What for? I'm starving."

"We need to talk."

"Magnolia Grove is a twenty-minute ride. We'll have plenty of time to talk."

Ellie looked to Lilah May for help, but she merely shooed them away with a wave of her hand and headed back inside the house.

"We don't have to go if you don't want to." *If you're courting. If you're married...*

He looked at her as if she'd suddenly lost all her senses. "I said I wanted some chicken."

"But the picnic—we don't have to. You can take the chicken home."

He didn't understand. That she could tell by the way he gazed into the sky as if asking for divine guidance.

Finally he lowered his head. "Look, you invited me to a picnic." His voice dropped and he spoke each word slowly, as if she were too simple to understand normal speech. "Let's ride out to the country, and if you want to talk on the way, we will. I just want to get there and get something to eat."

Fine. He just wanted to eat. She tapped Buttercup's flank and they took off toward the street.

Within five awkward minutes, they were out of town. Graham reined in Dixie a bit, trotting next to Buttercup. "Ellie, I'm confused. First you ask me to a picnic, and then you don't want to go." He paused. "Did you intend to invite me? Perhaps I misunderstood the invitation."

"No, I'm the one who misunderstood."

"Misunderstood what? Ellie, if we're going to spend all this courting time together, you're going to have to start making some sense. I have no idea what you're talking about."

Afraid to speak, afraid her frustration would come out in her voice, she blurted her concern anyway. "It's about girls."

"What girls? Susanna and her mob? They don't know we're going out there, do they?"

"No! How can such a smart man be so dumb? I'm talking about girls and you. Do you have one?"

He looked at her as if she'd asked if he had a bale of cotton in his pocket. "Unless we're talking about you, and I assume we're not, then no."

"You're not courting anyone? Not married?"

He laughed the laugh of mockery, his handsome features clouded. "Not courting, not married. No opportunity for either. I've been at war, remember? And before that, military school. I've hardly been around women since I left Natchez."

Well, now, didn't she feel silly?

"Why do you ask such a thing? And why did you wait until now to ask it?"

"I didn't think of it until now."

"Well, think of it no more, because you're all I have along those lines."

And he hardly sounded pleased about that.

Where had Ellie come up with that foolish notion? Courtship—true courtship—was the furthest thing from Graham's mind. At this point, he was less interested in girls than he was in the basket of fried chicken he carried in front of him.

He glanced over at her, riding on the other side of the weedy road. Her hair shone like gold in the bright sunlight. He was wrong—the chicken wasn't as interesting as Ellie. But it would give him a lot less trouble.

He shifted his gaze, along with his thoughts, toward the plantation they passed on the left. The fields of Mansfield Manor, once as productive as those at Ashland Place and Magnolia Grove, now lay fallow. The charred ruins of its big house stood crumbling at the end of an overgrown lane, and when they passed the run-down Mansfield chapel, Ellie let out a sigh.

"I sometimes attended that little church with Amy Mansfield when we were girls. With more and more plantations confiscated and abandoned, these little chapels will soon fall into disrepair and eventually blow down in a hard wind." The crease between her eyes suggested that Ellie was thinking of Magnolia Grove.

"Have you been able to maintain your chapel?"

"It needs a new roof, but that will have to wait." She turned from the chapel and toward the road ahead of them as if pushing aside morose thoughts of her own future. "When we've finished our dinner and the search in the study, I thought we could ride the fields. I'd like your opinion on the condition of the cotton."

She was worried about more than just a chapel— Graham could tell it from the tone of her voice. "You suspect Fitzwald might be telling the truth after all?"

"He's changed since I last saw him. He seems more… callous. Harder."

They rounded a bend in the river road, Ellie's horse picking up the pace as they neared Magnolia Grove. How much should Graham reveal to her about the weasel? He hesitated, choosing his words carefully, determined to say no more than necessary. "He's always been that way. Selfish, greedy, cruel—you name the bad quality, he's got it."

"Don't be silly. He's not the beau of Natchez, but he's not that bad."

Ellie never could see the evil in a skunk. "You're going to have to take my word for it, unless you want me to tell you some sordid stories. I'll merely say I've had to intervene when he was on his way to mistreat a lady. I've also stepped in when he was cheating a man who couldn't afford to lose what the weasel was trying to take from him."

"Leonard behaved that way?" She turned those blue eyes on him, their innocence shining as brightly as her golden hair.

At her silence, Graham gave her time to think, to remember.

"I never felt completely comfortable in his presence," she said after several moments. "He was often disrespectful to Lilah May. Sugar doesn't like him either."

"This time, I agree with Sugar."

As they approached Magnolia Grove's lane, Ellie slowed her horse. "What did you mean when you told Leonard that you haven't forgotten how to fight? At first, I thought you were speaking of the war. But the surrender was only two months ago, and that's not long enough for a soldier to have forgotten how to do battle."

"You're better off not knowing."

"Have you ever fought with Leonard?"

"Fought hard and won."

"You were defending someone else?"

He hesitated. "Someone much like you," he said in a low voice.

They turned into the Magnolia Grove lane and stopped by the cypress bog. The still-magnificent big house hadn't changed, at least not that he could tell from this distance. But the weedy drive, the unmown lawns, the sticks and magnolia limbs in the yard, had turned the plantation shabby.

Graham worked to keep his dismay off his face. Magnolia Grove was Ellie's real home, where she and her uncle had spent the springs, Graham visiting nearly every day. This sprawling plantation was where she felt safe.

Now it looked less like a grand, productive estate and

more like an abandoned, run-down farm. The fact nearly tore his heart from his chest, so how must Ellie feel?

She winced as if seeing Magnolia Grove through Graham's eyes. "I'm ashamed to show you how much it's changed. We haven't even been able to keep up with the weeds in the fields, so we haven't done anything with the drive, the lawns, or the formal gardens."

He hesitated, searching for comforting words. "In wartime, cotton fields and vegetable gardens are more practical than flowerbeds. The time for flowers will come."

Ellie smiled, but for the first time, he saw doubt in her eyes.

Riding between the long rows of live oaks on each side of the lane, they finally drew near Ellie's ancestral home. The massive brick house looked as stately as ever, with its two-story, faux-marble columns and ornate entry, despite the spider webs on the gallery railing and sidelights. Her troubled eyes cleared a bit as she swiveled in the saddle and took in the house and lawns.

"This is still your favorite place on earth," he said. "I can see it in your eyes."

Ellie led the way behind and west of the house, toward the stables. "It seems too quiet. No sheep grazing in the lawn, no peacocks strutting about the gallery, no workers scurrying to and from the house. All the activity on the plantation takes place in the fields or at the cabins now, and that makes the house look deserted. Which it is."

Graham dismounted first and set the picnic basket in the shade of a nearby oak. Ellie maneuvered Buttercup to the marble carriage steps and slid onto them from her horse's back.

"I was coming to help you," Graham said, halfway to her side.

"Things have changed. I don't have the luxury of a groom out here. I get off and on this horse by myself, and I take care of her when I'm here." She led Buttercup to her stall and measured grain into the feed box. "You can bring some water from one of the cistern houses if you like."

He guided Dixie into the stall next to Buttercup and started out the door.

By the time he returned minutes later, carrying two buckets of water, Ellie had both horses fed and comfortable. She looked so embarrassed at the condition of the stable—and the plantation in general, no doubt—that he went ahead and said what he knew she was thinking. "When I was last here, this stable was full of horses, and you had three grooms to take care of them."

She looked over his shoulder, out the stable door and to the backyard, her eyes suddenly sharp as if she was searching for something just outside her grasp. "I drive up that lane every day, and it hurts as much today as ever. I feel bad for bringing you here to see how I've had to neglect this place. It's hard for you too, I know."

Graham sloshed water into the troughs. Then he straightened and looked around. "I'm sorry that I allowed my emotions to show. I'm sure Ashland Place looks far worse than this, so I'm not seeing Magnolia Grove with a critical eye. If anything, I'm envious that you have a plantation at all."

"Don't be jealous yet. If we owe Leonard thirty thousand dollars, we're in trouble. Not to mention paying the workers and property taxes and having something to live on until the fall harvest."

With the horses cared for, they made for the house. "It's still a beautiful home," Graham said, "and you have every chance of keeping it and living in it again someday."

"As soon as Uncle Amos recovers enough to travel. It's a pity we were in town when he took ill." Now that her initial embarrassment seemed to have passed, Ellie hurried him toward the house. "Let's open the windows and then have dinner under the live oak out front, where we might catch a breeze. I want to search the library as fast as we can. The thought of that loan is choking me more than the heat."

They left the basket under the tree and headed inside to the darkened library. When they pulled the blinds and opened the windows, a nice breeze wafted in.

"I should probably bring all of Uncle Amos's records to town," she said, "but for now, I come out here to do much of his bookwork."

"By yourself?"

"There's no one else. I told you, things have changed. We do what we have to." Ellie skirted past him into the great hall, where she opened the back door to let the breeze blow through the whole house.

There was clearly no point in arguing with her about that. He merely followed her to the parlor, where they opened more windows to create a crosswind.

Minutes later, under the oak's low-hanging branches again, Ellie spread her blanket on the ground. She set out the food and table service, poured glasses of lemonade from the crock and lifted the towel from the bowl of fried chicken. Then she bowed her head as if to pray silently.

Graham began a heartfelt prayer of thanksgiving instead, and Ellie glanced at him with eyes widened in surprise.

After his "amen," she sat still for a moment as he filled his plate. "I've eaten alone since Uncle Amos took sick, because he eats at odd hours, whenever he's hungry. Until now, I didn't realize how much I miss praying with someone else."

The wistfulness in her voice brought a lump to his throat as he realized he felt the same way. Words slipped from his mouth before he could sort them out in his mind. "Ellie, you need a husband."

"You're a fine one to think so."

Graham's downcast gaze cut into Ellie like a cotton hoe. "I've always thought so," he said, his voice quiet.

So he had.

When would she learn to think before speaking? "I meant you have no room to speak, since you refuse to marry too."

"With good reason."

"My reason is good too."

"Then let's hear it."

She knew she shouldn't have told him how good her reason was, knew he'd take it as a challenge. And one thing she'd never seen Graham Talbot do was back down from a challenge. "I don't want to, that's all."

He laughed, but it sounded short, sarcastic. "All unmarried women are looking for a husband. Look at that pack of wolves following Susanna around."

She couldn't explain to him the horror of being orphaned, of being taken in by strangers until Uncle Amos could get there to collect her. And little Betsy brought it all back again, stronger than before. Relying on her father to provide for her—and being disappointed—had been one thing. Depending on neighbors for daily food was another.

Sitting there with Graham, under her favorite live oak, Ellie renewed her childhood vow. Never again would she depend on anyone else to provide for her. Her uncle had taken the past thirteen years to teach her to be a planter. Not a planter's wife.

And a planter she would be.

Graham tapped her forehead. "Ellie, I can see there's a lot going on in there. Want to tell me about it?"

"Not if you plan to solve my problems by telling me to get married." She reached for a drumstick from the bowl. She'd let him help her look for information about the loan, and she'd even ask his advice about the crops, since he used to help his father. But that was all.

"Then what if I help you get rid of Leonard Fitzwald?"

He said it in a way that made it sound like an adventure. "How can we do that?"

"By first finding out if your uncle took out another loan from him. Then we'll go from there."

"I can agree to that."

They ate the chicken, biscuits and watermelon—and the pecan pie Lilah May must have sneaked into the basket. Then they headed to the house to begin their search for proof of a second loan.

At three o'clock, Ellie pushed back the hair that had fallen from her pins and over her eyes. "We've taken these files apart. There's nothing here."

Graham picked up the stack of documents he'd been reading and stuffed them back into their folder. "There's nothing in here either. I don't think anyone other than your uncle's attorney can help us. Let's call on Joseph Duncan on Monday and find out what he knows."

"You want to go along?"

"I want to make sure that weasel Fitzwald doesn't take advantage of you—or anybody else in this town."

Ah, so Graham's purpose was preventing Leonard from doing more harm in Natchez, not just to protect

Ellie. That was fine with her. Graham—always the soldier, ever the protector, even before West Point. The thought deepened her years-long admiration of him. "How about taking a tour of the fields now?"

He followed her to the stable, where they quickly mounted their horses. Within minutes, they headed to the nearest field—two hundred acres of cotton and close to the house.

"The plants look healthy to me." Ellie turned in the saddle to glance back at him. "No blossoms yet, but they could start anytime. The squares look good."

They crossed toward the field in the bottom land. "This is the best soil but the hardest field to get to because of the swampy ground south of it."

When they reached the bottom land, true Delta soil, Graham let out a low whistle.

"I know." Ellie took in the sight, over four hundred acres of cotton with thick weeds almost as tall as the crop. "We probably should have weeded this first, since it gives the highest yield of any field. But it's also the biggest field. Since we have a lot of new workers, I thought I should let them start with the smaller, more easily accessible ones."

Graham studied the area and then nudged Dixie to move ahead of her. "I'm not sure that was such a bad idea. The other fields are clean. What are you going to do with this one?"

She couldn't help the smile she felt blooming on her face. "Do you realize you just asked me to make a plan?"

"No, I didn't." Graham held up both hands, one of them still with the reins in it. "I merely acknowledged that you would have one, and I wanted to prepare myself."

"You're right. I do. I've been corresponding with Miss

Eugenia Middleton in South Carolina. The Middletons are in rice, you know." She pulled the reins, bringing Buttercup to a stop. "They use a different method there. We require our workers to keep set hours, so many hours a day and so many days a week. But the Middletons use the task system. They give each worker a task for the day, and when the job is done, they go home."

"How will that work with the few field hands you have now?"

"Starting next week, I'm going to pay by the task. When the task gets done, the worker gets paid."

"I don't see how that will get this field weeded any faster."

"Easy. The harvest around here is going to be plentiful, but the workers are few. Most of the freedmen left the plantations as soon as they could. But now they're trickling back, having discovered that jobs are hard to find in the city." She smiled at the beauty of the plan and the pleasure of having to explain it to him. Maybe now he would see that she could think things through. "Every planter in Natchez is trying to get the same few field hands. I'm going to entice them to work for me by dividing the labor into tasks they can complete in one day. And I'm going to pay for each completed task every day."

His smoky-green eyes turned gray. "Ellie, that's not going to work. Do you realize how expensive that will be? Do you have enough money?"

Did they know anyone in the South who had enough money?

"As long as we don't have to make a thirty-thousand-dollar loan payment to Leonard." As long as her property tax bill wasn't much more than last year's. As long as the bottom didn't fall out of the cotton price. And as long as she could get her stash of last year's cotton from its hiding places and ship it to New Orleans on just the right day, when the price would be the highest of the season...

Her idea of just days ago now hung limp in the air.

Chapter Seven

"Now that I think of it, we shouldn't have checked the fields this afternoon. When we didn't find anything in Uncle Amos's study, we should have gone straight to Joseph Duncan's office. I need my attorney here for this meeting." Ellie paced the front gallery of her home at ten to eight that evening, Sugar pacing right along with her. She'd turned up all the gaslights as far as they would go, wanting all of Pearl Street to see Graham here on the porch, supposedly courting her.

Which might have been fine if Leonard Fitzwald wasn't coming over. What would that look like? At any rate, it was too late to worry.

"Here comes Leonard in his father's surrey, racing the wind as usual." Graham looked every inch an officer, standing next to her rocker as if ready to cuff anyone who bothered her.

And if that person was Leonard, he just might do it.

The surrey came to a bone-rattling stop in front of the house. Leonard got out, accompanied by Joseph, his familiar brown leather satchel in his hand.

"I'm not riding home with you in that buggy of death."

Joseph's face looked nearly as white as his famed moustache. "You're going to kill that horse if you don't slow down. And he was your father's favorite."

Leonard strode up the brick walk ahead of the elderly man. "I pay you for legal advice, Duncan, not for a lecture on driving," he said in that annoyingly raspy voice.

As they drew closer, Sugar rumbled out a growl from deep in her throat and bared her teeth at them.

"What's the matter with the dog?" Graham asked, his brows raised.

"I don't know. I've never heard her growl at anyone before. And what's Joseph doing here?" Something was wrong, she could see it on her attorney's face. "Do you think he heard what was going on and came to help?"

Graham didn't answer but laid his hand on her shoulder in a strangely comforting manner.

Taking the gallery steps two at a time, Leonard scanned the area, especially the tray Lilah May had brought out minutes before. "I'm not meeting with you out here. Stand away from the door, Colonel, while we go into the house like civilized people."

"If that was the case, you'd need to stay out anyway." Graham's eyes blazed, igniting gratitude in Ellie's heart. After what Graham had said about this man, she wouldn't have wanted to meet with him alone, not even with Joseph here.

She stopped the thought cold. What was she thinking? Of course she would have met with him alone. That's what she'd vowed to do—be alone.

"Leonard, sit down. My uncle has had a bad day, and I don't want to disturb him. Joseph, would you please sit here by my side?" She tried to imagine what her poised, confident mother would have done in this situation. From what Ellie could remember of her, she would have taken charge of the men without letting on that she was doing so. *Dear Jesus, please help me to know what to do, what to say.*

"I'm here to discuss—"

"Mister Fitzwald, kindly remember that I am your counselor." Joseph impaled him with his gaze. "It would behoove you to keep your peace and allow me to speak."

Leonard's counselor? How could that be? Wasn't he here to represent Ellie?

She realized then that she hadn't served refreshments, so she poured a glass of lemonade for Joseph. As she lifted it to hand it to him, Leonard reached out and took it instead.

Sugar growled louder, then barked and began to circle him.

"Get this dog away from me!" Leonard kicked in Sugar's direction but missed.

"What is the matter with you, Sugar?" Ellie had no idea what Mother would have done about all this. "She's never acted like this before. Graham, please put her in the library, where she won't hear us, and shut the door."

When Graham left to carry out her request, she offered a glass to Joseph.

"None for me, Ellie," he said, rubbing his abdomen as if it wouldn't agree with him.

That was a bad sign. Her attorney, who was apparently also Leonard's attorney, was known up and down the Mississippi River as having the stomach of a billy goat.

Graham came back outside then, and Ellie poured a glass for him, but he waved it away and laid his warm hand on her shoulder again. She sipped the drink herself.

"Before we start, I want Colonel Talbot to vacate the premises," Leonard said. "This doesn't involve him."

"He will stay. Word has it that he and Miss Anderson

have an agreement, and with her father deceased and her uncle incapacitated, she is wise to have the support of her intended for this meeting."

"We'll see how long that lasts." Leonard gulped down his drink and poured himself another.

Even Joseph had heard of their supposed courtship? And believed it? Her respect for her uncle's friend caught in her throat. This felt wrong, so wrong. Maybe she should confess the whole scheme.

But in front of Leonard, and without Graham's approval? Then again, she'd started this without his consent, so perhaps it would be better to end without it too. But would it embarrass him in front of Leonard? She looked to Graham for some signal, some message that would relay his wishes.

He stood silent as the tomb.

Before she could decide what to do, Joseph opened his satchel and took out some papers. "We're here to discuss the estate of the late Mister Robert Fitzwald." Joseph's tone had turned businesslike, his eyes like flint as he watched Leonard. "Upon his demise, he left behind, among other things, a lien against your property for the borrowed sum of thirty thousand dollars."

The air grew thin, and Ellie's chest ached with the skipped beats of her heart. "Thirty thousand?"

"Joseph, are you sure?" Graham asked, his grip tightening on her shoulder.

"I was Robert's attorney and, I regret to say, I'm also Leonard's. For now. This is the last action I will take as his counsel."

No, this couldn't be happening. *Thirty thousand...* She clenched the glass in her hand. "I know only of a fifteen-thousand-dollar note."

"The first fifteen was for taxes and personal expenses," Joseph said, "and the second fifteen for labor and the new cotton gin."

"But I thought we paid our own taxes last year."

"The taxes were paid with this loan. This is the agreement. You'll see your uncle's signature, and mine, since I filed the note at the courthouse." Her attorney handed her the stack of papers he'd pulled from the satchel. "You'll see, dear, that the note is due in two weeks."

"I can't pay it." The fluttering in her chest intensified, and she leaned back in her chair and fanned herself with a rose-colored napkin until it abated. Even if she picked every boll on every stalk of cotton, she couldn't pay it. Not without a competent broker. Since the elder Mister Fitzwald passed on, Leonard was the only broker between here and New Orleans. And he had no experience.

She'd let the cotton rot in the fields and in her hiding places before she'd let this man sell it.

"Talbot, what are your circumstances?" Joseph interrupted her thoughts, his voice laced with anxiety. "I know you lost Ashland Place and Ammadelle. Do you have other property or money that I don't know about— that a hasty marriage would allow you to use to remedy this?"

She looked up at Graham. He hesitated, his shame palpable and acute. "I have nothing, Joseph."

"I feared so." Joseph slumped in his chair in a posture of defeat.

Leonard, on the other hand, sat on the edge of his seat, his one good eye wide as if he was watching a riveting play unfold. "And the rest, Joseph?"

"There's more?" Graham clasped both her shoulders now. She could feel the tension in his grip, and it both comforted and frightened her. If he was that concerned…

"Magnolia Grove, this home on Pearl Street and your

father's Louisiana–Texas Railroad are all tied into this loan. If you default, you will lose them all."

Her heart raced with the shock. Lose both properties? How could that be?

An instant later, she heard the tinkling of shattered glass and then realized she'd dropped her mother's crystal tumbler.

The light yellow of the lemonade made a puddle on the white painted wooden floor, and the glass formed a sharp design. Watching the puddle spread, she tightened her abdomen against the lacerating pain forming there—as if cut by glass…

"Ellie!" Graham's voice brought her out of her daze.

"I—I dropped the glass—"

Suddenly light-headed, she felt like a little girl again, a girl with no parents, no home—only an uncle she had never met. No comforting arms surrounding her, no kind words to soothe her heart—only loneliness.

Only the ache.

The ache gripped her now as it hadn't in years. Always hiding at the edge of her consciousness, it nipped at her occasionally, tripped her less often, but always let her know it was still there, had never left her.

But now it had control of her.

She began to shake, her breath coming hard and fast. Tears clogged her throat, wouldn't well up, wouldn't fall and release her from their grasp—

"Ellie, sweetheart…"

A strong voice from the past—or was it the present?—pierced the heaviness, brought her back to reality. She forced herself to breathe slowly. "This house—it's in danger too."

She'd never considered that possibility.

The ache began to lift, and her light-headedness subsided too. She couldn't give in to these emotions. Not if she hoped to keep their plantation and town house. She sat up straight on the edge of her chair again, as a proper lady would. "I'm fine. I was just startled for a moment."

It was more than that, and they all surely knew it. She needed time to think, to pray.

"There is one final point." Joseph cleared his throat and glared at Leonard. "This man—" he waved at Leonard as if brushing away a fly "—agrees to settle the terms of the loan on one condition."

Then she had a way out? "You'll give me more time, Leonard?" Had Graham been wrong about him after all?

"He will forgive the loan if, on the date it comes due, you marry him."

"Marry whom?"

Graham knew the moment Ellie realized the truth he'd absorbed instantly. The confusion in her eyes morphed into disgust, and her attorney's face mirrored that emotion.

As did Graham's heart.

Could Fitzwald be serious? The leer in his one good eye confirmed it.

"Marry Leonard?" Ellie said, her repulsion thick in her voice. "I'm to be the commodity that pays this debt?"

"It's your choice, Ellie." The would-be bridegroom's smug lips and sarcastic tone alone would probably have made her turn him down, even if she liked him. What was Fitzwald thinking? Ellie had never shown an interest in him.

Graham thought back to that fateful summer eight years ago. Despite Graham's warnings, Ellie had always thought nothing of the weasel's frequent visits. They'd been nothing more than two chums whiling away the evening together, she'd said.

But Graham had known better. Fitzwald had tried to court her, even back then. And when that hadn't worked…

The memory of a years-ago conversation, overheard in the shadowy alley Graham had cut through on his way to Ellie's, came crashing back to him. That fool Fitzwald had the nerve to boast about his plan of enticing her to go with him to a remote spot along the river. Then he would spread the word through town that they'd been out alone after dark—and would embellish the truth, as well. Her reputation would be spoiled, and she'd have no choice but to marry him.

He'd been as much of a weasel back then as he was tonight.

"Ellie, I'm sure we can come to an agreement." His lone eye wide with the power he obviously thought he had over her, Fitzwald leaned close. He reached out his hand as if intending to caress the blond curl that had escaped her hairpins and lay softly on her cheek.

By no means would Graham tolerate that. In an instant, he crossed the gallery and stood between them, his fists clenched. "If you so much as think about touching her—"

Ellie had shrunk back from the weasel's hand and now locked a firm gaze on Fitzwald as if she'd tolerate no nonsense from him. "Graham, it's all right—"

"No, it's not. Nothing is right about this. I told you back then, Fitzwald, and I'll tell you again. Stay away from Ellie." Graham yelled in a voice loud enough that the neighbors could surely hear, even the ones who'd retired from their porches early. "Remember what I told you last time, and remember how you felt after our conversation."

The rage heating up Graham's chest seemed to rush upward until it lodged itself in his eyes. If flames blazed from them, as it felt they did, Fitzwald had better take notice and back away from Ellie. Graham had protected her from this man once, and he'd not hesitate to do it again.

"Don't forget that you left Natchez the same day I did," Fitzwald rasped at him. "And don't forget why."

"I told you before—this is a bad idea, Leonard." Joseph pointed that long finger at Leonard like a gun. "I don't like it, and your father wouldn't either. He wasn't the most honest man in Natchez, but at least he never coerced a woman into marriage just so he could get his hands on her property."

On her property...

Joseph seemed to think Fitzwald's only motivation was Ellie's plantation, but Graham had always believed he'd been after her beauty. He thought back to the night in the alley. What exactly had Fitzwald said? Had he confessed love for her? Not that Graham could remember. Maybe Joseph was right and the weasel had merely wanted Ellie's ground all along. Seeing his greedy, beady little eye now, Graham could believe it.

"My father has nothing to do with this."

"Are we finished here?" Graham asked, glaring at Joseph.

"We're done." The attorney slid his documents back inside his satchel and made as if to stand.

"No, we're not." Fitzwald bounded from his seat. "Ellie hasn't given her answer."

Standing there, he looked so pathetic that Graham felt a twinge of—what? Sympathy? His patched eye and deep scar, his shriveled-looking arms and sunken-in chest surely did nothing to gain him favor with the Natchez girls.

Well, if he wanted to find love, he needed to start acting different. He couldn't buy it from Ellie.

"You know my answer. I'd let go of all I own before I'd marry you."

"But, Ellie, Talbot has nothing." His voice came out in a strange, abrasive whine. "You heard him say so."

That was enough. Graham escorted the spindly-armed imposter of a soldier down the steps. "Time to go, Fitzwald. You heard her answer. She doesn't have to explain herself."

As the weasel drove away, Ellie rang the bell for Lilah May. "I want that glass cleaned up so I don't have to look at it. As late as it is, I should do it myself, but I couldn't bear to throw Mother's crystal into the trash. Let's move to the other side of the gallery."

As soon as they were settled in rockers on the north side, Joseph let out a groan. "That was the worst thing I've had to do in all my years of law."

"It wasn't your fault," Graham said as Lilah May stepped outside, saw the mess and immediately went back in, presumably to get a broom and dustpan. "I've never heard more ridiculous terms. No woman should have to go through that, and no attorney either."

Ellie didn't look any happier than Graham felt. "What can we do? Does the loan have a loophole, anything that would help us straighten this out?"

"I spent the past two days searching for one." The lines on Joseph's face made him appear older than he had the last time Graham saw him—the day Noreen brought Betsy home. "The loan is perfectly legal. His terms of marriage have nothing to do with the law."

"Even so, he ought to go to jail for trying to force Ellie to marry him that way."

"Agreed. But that's impossible." Joseph crossed his arms over his chest as if ready to defend what he was about to say. "You could put this house on the market, but since the war, nobody is buying mansions in Natchez. As I see it, you have only once choice. Sell the rest of your property. That way, you'll still have this house."

"Perhaps, but it's not mine. Uncle Amos will have to sell it, but he's not well enough to do business. Besides, if he signed the papers tonight, he might not remember doing so tomorrow."

"He can't legally sell anything now because of his mental condition," Joseph said. "His power of attorney will need to do that for him."

Of course. Graham should have thought of that. Ellie would know who the power of attorney was.

But if he knew this woman the way he used to, she wouldn't let go of Magnolia Grove and still keep her heart intact. That place was her true home, her refuge. Finding a buyer wouldn't be easy, and letting go of the ground would be harder yet.

But what choice did she have? Graham certainly couldn't help her, as much as he wanted to. For their friendship's sake, of course, nothing else. At least that was what he kept telling himself. "Who is his power of attorney?"

"That's the problem, Graham," Joseph said. "It's your father."

Chapter Eight

What an agenda for a man to wake up to on a Saturday morning. First, he had to send another telegram to General Lee to find out if he had any more news concerning Father's whereabouts. Then he had to go to the post office to see if President Andrew Johnson had answered his letter, requesting pardon for the crime of treason against the United States of America.

Granted, he'd sent his letter to Johnson only a few days ago, but rumor had it that the Yankee president was trying to send replies as quickly as possible. Graham had never dreamed he'd write to a president, and he certainly never considered he'd be accused of treason. How his world had changed since he last lived in this house.

It seemed it had changed in every way but one: Ellie. She was still here, still the belle of Natchez, still the sweet, impetuous girl he'd fallen for on a summer night—in the garden, surrounded by white Natchez crape myrtle. In his mind he could smell them now, their fragrance mixed with her perfume to create the headiest of scents—

But she still didn't want him.

As soon as Father came home and this mess with Fitz-wald was straightened out, Graham was leaving.

But for now, he needed to find a way to earn a living in this new country that no longer felt like home. And he had to complete this list today, since tomorrow was the Lord's day. He threw back the sheet.

He rose then bathed and shaved in the tepid water in his white china bowl decorated with brown horses, the bowl he'd used as long as he could remember. When dressed, he knelt beside his bed. Here his knees had met the carpet from the time he was old enough to whisper "Now I lay me down to sleep" until the morning he left for West Point.

But his prayer today wasn't that of a boy with child-like faith. Today he prayed as a man with a stone for a heart. The words came fast, but he sensed no depth to them. He'd always prayed fervently before battle and given profuse thanks afterward. So why could he now not—

The ringing of a bell interrupted Graham's thoughts.

What was going on? It sounded as if it was coming from inside the house, but Noreen had never used bells, even back when they'd had servants. From an old but less prosperous family without domestic help, she always said she felt silly, ringing a bell and expecting someone to come running. He scrambled to his feet and headed downstairs, finding Noreen in the hall, carrying the laughing baby, and Ellie holding two ridiculously large brass bells. Ellie grinned, no doubt at the shocked expression that must have been on his face.

It was a relief that Betsy had laughed at that bell, considering how she'd cried about everything the night of Aunt Ophelia's party. Well, everything except the dog. He reached for her little fist. "Good morning, Betsy."

She smiled at him and made a cooing sound. Was she trying to speak to him or merely making a noise? Either way, she looked as if she might like him a little. Funny what that did to his heart.

"I'm sorry to surprise you so early in the morning," Noreen said, "but Ellie brought these bells over. She thought you and I could ring them when we need each other, to save me from climbing the stairs with Betsy in my arms."

Noreen and him, ringing bells in the house? That was absurd. Why did they need such a thing? They'd never done this before, and they didn't need to now. Ellie and her ideas…

"You can keep one on the walnut table on the upstairs landing, and the other down here in the hall." Ellie placed a bell on the receiving table by the stairs. "Uncle Amos rings his all the time."

"Or we could make it easier and just shout up or down the staircase."

Ellie's laugh tinkled like a bell, but not like those giant ones. "You've lived in army camps too long. One simply does not shout up the staircase in Natchez."

She may have been right about that, but—

"You have a letter, dear." Noreen held out an envelope. "That's why we rang the bell."

Graham took the letter from her and immediately recognized the handwriting. "It's from General Lee. He must have news about Father."

Noreen turned a shade paler and handed the baby to Ellie. "Let's all sit down. You too, Graham."

She swayed a bit, her hands trembling, and Graham took her arm. "Stay calm, Noreen. It's as likely to be good news as bad." He helped her to the sitting room and seated her on the stiff blue settee. As Ellie sat beside her, he pulled up an ottoman for Noreen's feet. Unable to sit, he ripped open the envelope and read aloud.

June 2, 1865
G. P. TALBOT:

I have received word of your father and my friend, James P. Talbot, on this date. For the sake of his health, he was detained at the home of Colonel E. W. Banwick, of Galveston. Colonel Talbot suffered much in the many battles in which he was engaged, and he collapsed after attending the surrender of the Trans-Mississippi Army in Galveston. Colonel Banwick, former West Point classmate of both your father and myself, notified me of your father's departure from his home, after having tried in vain to keep him there. The only clue Colonel Banwick has of James's intention is his repeated request to visit his daughter. That makes me wonder if James is headed for your mother's family home—River Bluff Hall, isn't it?—to see his daughter's grave. It is my earnest hope that you are able to locate him. Please inform me of his wellbeing at such time. May God be with you as I pray for his return to your home.

R. E. LEE

"Father—wounded in battle?" Now that he knew his father was still alive, Graham suddenly realized he'd always imagined him riding back to Natchez, unharmed. "I should have expected something like this, but I guess I didn't want to face the possibilities."

"Poor James." Noreen's eyes brimmed with unshed

tears. "He struggled so with this war and the issues behind it."

"I wish General Lee had given us some details about Father's condition." Graham studied the letter again. "This is dated June 2. He could have been on the road for weeks now."

"Do you suppose he's headed for River Bluff Hall?" Noreen asked in a tiny, childlike voice.

For a moment, Graham had to turn from the pain in her eyes. He felt a twinge of betrayal for her, as well. Why wouldn't Father want to come home to Noreen, his beloved wife since Mama and Daisy passed? It didn't make sense.

He raised his head and met his stepmother's teary-eyed gaze. "I've seen similar situations after battle. All the afflicted men wanted was to go home. Since Father was talking about Daisy, he might have gone to her grave."

Noreen's eyes cleared and took on a steely acceptance, the likes of which he'd seen in his men who'd seen their comrades shot in battle. "That's probably what he did. We'll remember to give thanks for General Lee's letter. Without it, we would still have no idea what happened to James."

"It's a three-hour trip to River Bluff Hall." Tentative plans began to take shape in Graham's mind. He couldn't ride Dixie as far as Texas, not after the hard ride home from Virginia, but she might manage the trip to River Bluff Hall. "We don't know if Father has a horse or is traveling on foot, so we need a carriage of some sort. What became of our conveyances?"

"I sold the barouche and the runabout last year and, of course, the Confederate army confiscated our horses before that."

Graham paced to the fireplace, his mind racing and his steps slow.

Ellie brushed her hand over Betsy's peach-fuzz hair. "Why not take our phaeton? It has two seats, so Mister Talbot can stretch out in the back if he needs to."

Graham stopped his pacing. Why was this woman still here? And why did she interject her ideas into every conversation? Especially this one, which didn't involve her. "Thanks, but I'll think of something. I'll rent a carriage."

"I agree with Ellie. James would be comfortable in Amos's phaeton. If he's injured, I'd feel better knowing he wasn't in some rented buggy."

Graham held back the tart words that wanted to shoot from his mouth. What happened to the days when he made a decision, gave an order and people obeyed?

In his moment of hesitation, Ellie handed Betsy back to Noreen, who looked better now with her color back and her hands no longer trembling as she held them out to the baby. "I'll go with you," Ellie said, as if Graham had no say-so in the matter. "Lucy and Buttercup have been skittish lately, and I know how to calm them."

No, no, no. "But what about Betsy? Don't you have to stay here and help Noreen with her? And what about your uncle—doesn't he need you?" He was grasping at any idea, anything that would keep her from tagging along with him today, and he knew it.

Her wide grin told him she knew it too. "Why don't you want me to go, Graham?"

"Yes, why?" Noreen asked.

"Because…because…" His stepmother's piercing gaze made him realize she, too, believed he and Ellie were courting. He had to set her straight, even if nobody else in town ever knew the truth. "Because things aren't as they seem…"

"In what way, dear?" Noreen asked, leaning forward as if to catch every nuance of every syllable he would utter.

"This is all for the sake of convenience. I needed to—"

He stopped the sentence cold and moved to the east window. Something nagged at his mind, just beyond his grasp, giving him the sense that he was on the verge of making a big mistake. He was overlooking some fact, some need. Everything in his life had changed in the past forty-eight hours. Unfamiliar emotions had assaulted him. He felt so unstable now, he had to collect his thoughts and discover what his subconscious mind was telling him before he could answer Noreen. On occasion, he'd felt this way during battle, and he'd always been glad he'd heeded the silent warning.

He turned to face his stepmother. "Please excuse me for a moment. I just realized I need to check something. I'll be right back."

Graham fled to the stable, praying silently that the two women would stay in the house until he had things sorted out in his mind. He'd spoken truth when he said he had to check something. He needed to check this strange, unrelenting sense of foreboding.

Inside the stable, he grabbed Dixie's brush and ran it down her back and neck. How had things gotten so mixed up since he came home? The methodic strokes helped him clear his mind and sort through his jumbled thoughts. "God, help me to see what I'm missing here. I don't want to do something stupid."

It was time to look at the situation objectively, as he had when forming battle plans. First, it was true that Graham entered into the "courtship" agreement to keep all the Natchez girls at bay. And although Ellie didn't know it, he'd secretly vowed years ago to help her whenever she needed it. But her need had now become much deeper, with Fitzwald acting as if he had no sense.

Second, as the temporary head of the family until Father recovered, Graham had the responsibility of providing for Noreen and Betsy.

Father couldn't be injured too badly, since it seemed he was able to travel alone. However, he may not be well enough to work and earn a living for them for several weeks or even months. And he was sure to have little or no money since his army pay, like Graham's, had been in now-worthless Confederate bills.

Therefore, Graham couldn't think of courtship or marriage now. But if he admitted that to Noreen and told her his courtship with Ellie was a ruse, she'd demand to know why. No matter what he'd tell her, she'd surmise that he couldn't support a wife because what little money he had would barely be enough to take care of her and Betsy. She had no way of knowing he didn't even have that much. He could never let Noreen think she was a burden to him. Better to let her assume he'd received enough pay to keep them comfortable.

Graham gave silent thanks to God that he had been able to change some Confederate money into gold last fall. He had only a double-eagle coin left, but if asked, he could honestly tell Noreen that he had some gold. Even though it was a mere twenty dollars.

It looked as if his future continued to be written in stone, just as it had been his whole life. It was time to face facts. What God meant to happen would happen, and that apparently included taking a certain blond-haired lady to River Bluff Hall. In her uncle's carriage, pulled by her uncle's horses.

It also included a temporary, make-believe romance with the woman he'd once hoped to marry. He had to do it, had no other choice. And Ellie was right—it would keep Susanna Martin and her gaggle of women away. At least he had that small comfort.

Women. Ellie's uncle seemed smarter than Graham, remaining a bachelor all these years and never courting at all, as far as Graham knew. The question in his mind now was whether he was smart enough to keep a distance that would protect his heart.

Smart or not, he had to do it. Her refusal of him eight years ago had driven him from his home, his family, his legacy of becoming the head of Ashland Place. Coming home, he'd found in Ellie the same sweet, pretty girl he'd once loved, but now she'd matured into a generous, caring woman. If she rejected him again, he'd have no means of escape—at least until Father got home and got well. A Southern gentleman didn't leave an elderly woman and a baby to fend for themselves.

Graham set aside the currycomb and made for the house. Following the chattering voices of the women and the baby, he found them puttering in the kitchen dependency.

If he had to endure Ellie's company, he at least needed to exert some control over her wild ideas, as a courting man should for his intended. Maybe that's where he'd gone wrong the other time.

As he crossed the threshold into the kitchen, he caught a snippet of Ellie's muffled conversation. "I've heard about the parties and picnics planned for Graham too. I've figured out a way for us to miss at least some of them."

Graham leaned against the brick wall. Another plan. This woman was harder to manage than a whole platoon of new recruits. Maybe he was foolish to think that would ever change. But he was committed to taking care of all these females until Father could take over the responsibility. *Dear God, please help me find him—today.*

"Graham Talbot sure knows how to make a girl wish she'd never agreed to help him." With a few minutes to visit with her uncle before she needed to leave with Graham, Ellie leaned back in the sewing rocker and debated how much to say. Something about her arrangement with Graham bothered her, but she wasn't sure what. Her uncle's mind seemed sharp this morning, so perhaps he would have some good advice. Rocking hard in the armless chair in a most unladylike manner, she decided to tell him everything and get his opinion.

"Made you mad, did he?"

"Not exactly mad, but he doesn't appreciate my help."

Uncle Amos smoothed down his bushy white beard. "A man doesn't like to depend on a woman for a ride."

"It wasn't about the horses and carriage. I had a great idea to help him out of a big problem, but instead of thanking me, he seems to resent it. Then this morning, as we were discussing his father and how I could help find him, Graham suddenly excused himself and dashed out to the stable."

Uncle Amos grunted. "That's what a man does when he needs some thinking time." Calm as always, her uncle used his clumsy left hand to drag the comb through his bedraggled-looking hair. He succeeded in making it look even worse. "Give him some grace. He's been through a lot."

For once, Uncle Amos didn't understand at all. Why

did he have to choose this day to side with someone other than Ellie for the first time? She bounded to her feet, glad for a chance to do something other than sit there and take out her frustration on the rocker. "I'm getting my scissors. You need a haircut."

"No, no! It's just now growing out from the last time you cut it."

"Let me even it up then."

"Get Lilah May to do it. I need you to do more important things."

He was humoring her as always. "She's making your breakfast. That's important, isn't it?"

Her uncle lifted his head and shoulders from the pillows he was propped up against, as if trying to see out the door, then leaned back again. "Tell me more about Graham before she gets here. What did you try to help him with?"

Ellie paced to the window, looking for Graham, then returned to the rocker. She raised the back of her hoops so she could ease herself onto the chair. "He's in turmoil. He says his money, his plantation and his citizenship are all gone, and he has nothing left."

"He's right."

"You should have seen how the girls acted at Miss Ophelia's party. Every unattached woman of marrying age in Natchez is chasing him."

He pointed the index finger of his left hand at her. "All but one."

"Yes, but I'm the one who caught him!"

Uncle Amos perked up at that. "You're courting with him? This soon?"

Ellie shifted in her chair. Why must he have that look of joy on his face? She was going to have to disappoint him as she had eight years ago, when he'd guessed that

Graham had proposed. Might as well get it over with now. "We're pretending to court."

He slumped back down. "How and why does one pretend to court?"

"Why? Because we both need protection from unwanted attention. You know how many men come calling here. And I'm protecting him from all those women."

"By telling lies?"

"We didn't lie. Not once. We merely let people draw their own conclusions."

"Including Miss Ophelia?"

His stern expression made her drop her gaze to the floor. Apparently, his apoplexy hadn't hampered his protectiveness of Miss Ophelia. "Including her."

He let out a puff of air. "My other question—how do you pretend to court?"

"Well, it's so new, we haven't worked out all the details yet. We went to the party together, and today we'll go to River Bluff Hall, as you and I discussed earlier this morning."

"What else?"

"I don't know. Whatever courting couples do." She hesitated. "With the war over, people are starting to have parties and dances and picnics again. So I suppose we'll go to some of them together. What else do you think we should do?"

"Courting involves more than where you go. You get to know each other, find out whether you get along well enough to marry." Uncle Amos gazed out the window, a faraway look on his face. "Or you might find out whether you care about each other enough to take a risk with your love."

Ellie had no words. Where had all this wisdom about love come from? Her bachelor uncle, who everyone said had been the beau of Natchez when he was young, had no experience with romance as far as she knew. Could he know what he was talking about? Had he learned this by watching others?

And was he right?

If only Mother were still here to answer all her questions.

But if Mother were here, everything would be different. If she had lived, Ellie would have stayed in New Orleans and somehow taken care of her. She never would have known Graham, never would have heard his heartbreakingly sweet proposal. And her fear of marriage, her fear of depending on a man to provide for her, never would have forced her to refuse him...

Uncle Amos turned his face from the window—and his mind from the past, so it seemed. "I don't like this, Ellie. Somebody's going to get hurt. I think it's going to be you."

"Me?" Ellie pointed to herself. "How am I going to get hurt?"

"It sometimes happens that way. When a man or woman pretends to be in love, love often comes unexpected, unwanted. The game turns into reality, but the falsehood gets its revenge. Love comes to only one. The other gets hurt."

A cold chill crept through her, but she tried to laugh it off. "That won't happen."

"You can't be sure."

"I am sure. The more I help him, the more he pushes me away. He'd rather have nothing to do with me."

"Don't believe it."

"I do. I know it's true."

"How long do you intend to continue this fabricated courtship?" He dropped his voice. "This false promise?"

False promise? "I didn't think of it that way…"

"It's always a mistake to play around with love. But you're old enough to make your decisions. Please promise me that, when one of you begins to take this joke seriously, you'll put a stop to the game." His voice grew more tender. "Hearts broken carelessly can't always be mended."

What if he was right? Could she ever care for Graham? Could he care for her? She needed the answer, because if love had a chance of blossoming between them, or in the heart of only one or the other, that would change everything. If love was even a remote possibility, she couldn't follow through with this scheme.

She'd wanted her uncle's opinion, and she'd surely gotten it. She clasped his hand. "If either of us begins to take the game seriously, I will call it off. I promise."

"That's good enough. Just one more thing. Lilah May!" He leaned forward in bed and shouted in the loudest voice Ellie had heard him use since he took ill.

Within moments, Lilah May dashed into the bedroom, her face damp as if from exertion. "What's the matter? You ain't never yelled at me like that before."

"I want you to take this girl to her room and have a long talk with her—the talk her mother would give her if she were still alive."

Lilah May's eyes narrowed. "You mean the courtin' talk?"

"Uncle, that's not necessary—"

"It is. Lilah May knows more about love than both of us put together. If you're going through with this, I want you to tell her everything you just told me." He pointed his finger at her again. "And anything else you might have left out. Does that suit you, Lilah May?"

"Suits me fine. I got a thing or two I been wanting to explain to her since the day the colonel got home."

She must have seen Ellie riding through the yard with Graham, putting on that show for Susanna and her cronies.

Could Lilah May be an expert on romance? Her features had softened when Uncle Amos mentioned love. But Ellie had never seen her maid look at a man that way.

As she thought about it, she remembered hearing rumors about a husband who had died before Ellie came to Natchez. She hesitated. It may be true—Lilah May could have all the answers Ellie needed.

She checked her timepiece. She had only a few minutes before Graham was to call. "Can we talk tomorrow afternoon instead? Graham won't want to wait for me."

He nodded. "Be sure you do it tomorrow. And I'm glad you had word of James. I'll pray you find him."

Ellie gave him a kiss on the cheek and excused herself to get her hat. In her room, she pondered her uncle's words. If he was right about romance, then Ellie was wrong. But what could she do about it at this point? She could hardly spread the word that she'd called off the courtship two days after Graham came home.

Besides, if she did, Graham would have one more reason to say she didn't think things through before acting.

Surely Uncle's poor health clouded his judgment. How could the courtship ruse not work? She had no feelings for Graham, and he'd made it clear he had none left for her. In a way, that was sad.

Graham clearly didn't like the courtship idea. Neither did Uncle Amos, and she was pretty sure she knew what Lilah May would have to say about it. The problem was knowing her own mind in the matter.

A bachelor soldier, a bachelor uncle and a woman who

may have been in love and married years ago—could she trust their opinions? But who else did she have to ask? Susanna? Never.

Sugar howled out her "my friend is here" bark as Graham, dressed in his uniform, crossed the side yard to her home. Ellie hastened to don her favorite hat, a sky-blue crepe bonnet that matched her dress and had a straw-colored feather and darker blue velvet loops. Graham's father had once remarked about how good the color looked on her.

If all went as planned, they would see the elder Mister Talbot today. Graham hadn't yet seemed to admit that his father might not be well. Illness, injury—it was hard telling what they would see if they found him. Ellie closed her eyes and whispered a prayer for the kind man. Her problems and Graham's would have to wait until they found Mister Talbot and discovered his condition.

Minutes later, passing Sugar in the downstairs hall, Ellie felt a twinge of regret for not paying more attention to the poor dog yesterday. On impulse, she snapped the leash onto Sugar's collar and called up the stairs to let Lilah May know she was taking the dog along.

What would her maid tell her about love tomorrow, and what would she think of their imaginary courtship? Would she say Ellie invited heartache, either for herself or Graham? Uncle Amos's words still rang in her ears until she decided to stop paying them any mind, at least for today.

Her uncle's reaction, especially his insight, had certainly surprised her, but she had a feeling she'd be even more astounded once she'd had her talk with Lilah May.

Chapter Nine

Graham had wished Ellie would stay home today, it was true. But now, as she sat next to him in the carriage, taking his breath in her blue dress and hat, she made him wish it twice as much. Why did she have to be so pretty? Blue-eyed girls with no intention of marrying should never wear blue hats that made the sky pale in comparison to their eyes.

On the other hand, who said he couldn't enjoy her company—and her beauty—as they traveled?

Heading south on Commerce Street, they met a half dozen Union soldiers on horseback, eyeing Graham and his Confederate grays. He held the gaze of each man as they passed, every instinct still honed to treat them as the enemy. When the troops turned onto Orleans Street, Graham relaxed a bit and realized his fists were clamped around the reins and his teeth clenched. With effort, he refrained from looking over his shoulder at the men. "I'm not sure I'll ever get used to seeing Yankees in Natchez."

"I admit they used to affect me the same way. But since the fall of Vicksburg, when the federal troops occupied Natchez, we've all become accustomed to seeing Union soldiers in the streets."

He hesitated, continuing to fight against the tension that kept trying to force its way into him. "Noreen tells me you're doing a great job of running the plantation," he said, trying to focus on something other than those Yankees.

"I've mostly been doing what Uncle Amos taught me through the years." Ellie's voice brightened as if she was trying to help him relax. "But I think we need some new methods. I have twenty-five hundred acres in cotton and, as you've seen, not enough workers to weed and harvest it."

"Pardon me for asking, but how do you plan to get that crop out of the field?"

"I don't have a plan yet. Nor do I have a plan for paying this loan or getting last year's cotton to market." She paused. "I didn't care for Robert Fitzwald, but at least when he was alive, I had a competent cotton broker. I know quite a bit about the market, but I have no experience dealing with buyers."

She turned her gaze to the sky, seeming to seek her answer in the clouds. "I may have to try to sell the cotton myself. But you know how those New Orleans and Texas buyers are. They'd just as soon deal with a rattlesnake than a female planter."

Ellie was probably right. With her gentle nature, she wouldn't stand a chance with the buyers.

If only he could fix her problems as he had when they were children. Only these problems were bigger and much more frightening. She shouldn't have to deal with them alone. "On Monday, we'll meet with Joseph again. Between the three of us, we'll think of a solution."

Ellie lowered her gaze, a smile forming on her lips. "A plan?"

He gave her a mock frown. "I intend to be in on all your plan-making from now on."

Her laugh tinkled much like the bells on Buttercup's harness. "Enough of my problems for today. Did you receive your invitation to Joseph's picnic Sunday evening? He's holding it in your honor. I hope your father will be well enough to attend too."

The complete change of subject surprised him, but it shouldn't have. Ellie had never been one to sadden others with her problems. Most women would take to their beds, doing nothing but cry about a dilemma as serious as the one Ellie faced. Instead, she loaned him her carriage and horses and came along to help him find his father. Graham breathed a prayer that locating him would also solve Ellie's problems.

He felt her gaze on him and shifted his focus to the picnic—and courting. A courting man would invite his girl to a party. His stomach churned as he formed the words in his mind. This was no easier than it had been back when he'd first realized he was in love with her. Best just to get it said. "Assuming Father won't need me at home, will you go with me?"

"I'd like that."

Her big blue eyes twinkled at him just as they used to when he'd suggest an outing. Except in those days, they went on outings because they were children having fun. Now they were adults and, as she'd so eloquently said, he was not fun.

Nonetheless, it was time for him to commit to the pretend courtship. And he dreaded finalizing that. It seemed crass somehow, a cheapening of the genuine.

And if he went along with it, the genuine might never happen...

Where had that thought come from? He sat up

straighter on the carriage seat. The genuine wasn't going to happen. Not for a long time, if it ever did, and not with Ellie. She'd turned him down once. That was enough.

Although she stole his breath when she looked at him, the bright sky and her bonnet intensifying those blue eyes.

He pulled his gaze from her and studied the road instead. They had serious business to attend today. Finding his father was crucial for everyone's sake. He couldn't spare the time or energy to concern himself with dreams that would never come to pass. Better to handle this courtship fallacy in a businesslike manner.

Out in the country now, and out of earshot of everyone in town, he might as well get it over with. Putting it off wouldn't make it easier. "I've made a decision."

"About what?"

As much as the courtship had absorbed his thoughts, it seemed almost unnatural that she didn't know what he was talking about. "Courting."

"Good. What do you want to do?" Her tone sounded light, as if she didn't care what he had decided, but the catch in her voice gave her away. And he couldn't blame her, considering the fact that Leonard Fitzwald pursued her as hard as Graham refrained from it.

"I think it's best for everyone involved if we continue the courtship and even intensify it a bit."

"Intensify?"

The anxiety settling in her eyes tore at his heart. "Don't worry. I don't mean in a personal way. I mean only that we should be seen together in public a lot, doing family things together. Act more like a courting couple."

"You would have to frown less."

He could feel her relief. He'd be a fool to expect anything else. "You'll have to annoy me less."

"I can't make any promises."

Her smile heated the summer morning to a sweltering level. He shifted an inch away from her. The woman still had more power over him than General Lee ever had, and she never knew it.

"Fitzwald is not going to sit passively by and let you sell Magnolia Grove without opposing you. He needs to know that you're with me most of the time and that I'm watching out for you."

Ellie's smile turned downright wicked. "And I'll let Susanna Martin know I'm watching out for you."

He laughed, a full, rich belly laugh—the first time he'd laughed that hard in years. Then he felt guilty for doing so. "Ellie, I'm sorry. You're in danger of losing everything you own, I'm looking for my father, whose condition is anybody's guess, and I'm laughing like an idiot."

"Stop apologizing. Laughing helps us feel better. Being gloomy would make it worse."

That was easy to say. "Laughing doesn't come naturally to me anymore."

At least, it hadn't until now.

When they'd traveled a good two hours, a cold drizzle began to pepper the carriage top. Moments after the thunder started, something large bumped against his foot. He looked down to see a white tail sticking out from under their seat.

"Ellie, your dog is right underneath me."

"She's afraid of thunder."

She had to be joking. "Sugar is a hunting dog. How can she be afraid of thunder?"

"Don't you remember how gun-shy she is? To her, thunder sounds like gunfire. During a storm, she always crawls under my bed, right under me, as she's doing to you now."

Fine—Ellie's dog liked him better than Ellie did.

"Thunder's getting closer. If we had much farther to go, we'd need to pull over, but if I remember right, River Bluff Hall is a mile past the next bend. My cousin's lane is over there, off to the right."

Ellie sat up straight, looking ahead. "When were you last here?"

He had to think about that as they rounded the curve in the road. "Both my grandparents died around 1855. The property was sold, and I haven't been here since."

Minutes later, they pulled onto the lane, and Graham reined in Lucy and Buttercup at his mother's family home—if one could call it that. Nothing remained except piles of bricks, two dozen fluted columns with their Corinthian capitals, some balustrades and iron stairs, and a giant live oak with resurrection fern greening up in the summer rain.

"When I was a boy and we visited here, the first thing I did was go up to the observatory on the roof. You could see the Mississippi River from there." As he thought back, looking at the ruins, those days seemed a century ago.

Ellie was out with her dog before Graham could secure the reins and reach her side of the carriage. They walked around the ruins, with Sugar on her leash and staying inches from Ellie's skirts. Not a wall of the house remained, and the columns revealed some of their brick structure where plaster had fallen off.

Burned. The home where he'd spent happy times with his grandparents was gone—eerily gone, its desolation complete.

Clearly, his father wasn't here. "Let's head home. We can stop at the houses we pass and ask if anyone's seen Father."

"Should we give up so soon?" Ellie turned in a circle, her hand shading her eyes. "What if he's right here somewhere?"

They were wasting time. "Look at the sky. This rain isn't going to stop. We need to get closer to home before it starts to pour. Besides, there's no place for a man to hide in these remains."

She started for the carriage and then stopped. "What if he's at the family cemetery?"

Ellie and her ideas. "No sane person would visit a cemetery in the rain."

"I'm going to look. Lots of family plots are by the river, so this one might be just through those trees."

She was right about that, but not about his father being there. "We need to go."

"I'll be five minutes." She took off through the woods, Sugar in the lead.

The wind shifted then. Within moments, the drizzle intensified to a downpour, and thunder crashed around them. Graham jogged toward the trees, then made his way to the cemetery, the old path barely discernible.

A hundred yards ahead, Ellie knelt beside a dark figure who embraced a tombstone.

It couldn't be. Father, out here in the rain? As Graham ran closer, he realized the man sat beside the stone, his arms wrapped around it, his head resting upon it. With Sugar beside her, Ellie knelt on the ground next to him in the tall, wet grass and the mud, her eyes closed and lips moving as if in prayer.

The rain now beat down on Graham and poured into his eyes, blurring his vision. "Father? Is it you?"

He didn't raise his head, didn't answer. Catching up to him and Ellie, Graham touched the older man's shoulder. "Father?"

The man looked up from the stone, his eyes empty, as if his mind and heart had deserted him. "She's gone."

Graham's blood turned cold as the headstone. Those hollow eyes had his father's shape and color, and the man had the same full mouth, strong chin and jaw. He had Father's thick, long beard and graying, dark hair, his tall, muscular form. But although the physical resemblance to his father was unarguable, none of Father's mind resided here.

"Who's gone, sir?"

"My Daisy. I couldn't find her, and now she's gone."

Daisy—Graham's baby sister who'd died at birth, taking their mother with her. The chill in Graham's body turned to a cold sweat and mixed with the cold rain.

"Father—Papa—it's me. Graham." He grabbed his father's arm and turned the man to face him. "Papa, don't you know me? It's Graham. Your son."

He looked into Graham's eyes, but the light of recognition Graham wanted to see wasn't there. Papa hesitated. "Where is she? Have you seen my Daisy?"

Graham swallowed hard against the fear lodged in his throat. He'd seen this before, always after battle. He'd never dreamed he'd see it in this man, the strongest man in his world, the most solid, the most stable.

Stronger and more solid than Graham, which meant it could happen to him too.

Papa pulled from his grasp and embraced the little granite stone. Then racking sobs shook his body as he mourned a girl he'd never seen.

Ellie laid her hand on his arm. "The Lord is my shepherd. I shall not want. He maketh me to lie down in green pastures. He leadeth me beside the still waters. He restoreth my soul. He leadeth me in the paths of righteousness for his name's sake."

His father joined her, his voice thick with his pain. "Yea, though I walk through the valley of the shadow of death, I will fear no evil, for thou art with me."

Graham opened his mouth to recite the psalm with them, but his throat felt so dry, he couldn't bring out a sound. The shadow of death. He'd often wondered what that was, but now he looked it in the face. His father—a shadow of his real self, looking and sounding like death itself.

"I will dwell in the house of the Lord forever."

Forever. The word was both comforting and chilling. Would his father suffer this way forever? *Dear God, I didn't think anything could be worse than war. I was wrong.* He knelt down and clasped his father's shoulders. "Papa, let's go home."

And never come back to this place.

An hour later, something nagged at the back of Ellie's mind, but she couldn't put her finger on it.

Having stopped for dry clothing and a hot meal at Graham's cousins' home, she tamped down the strange feeling. She'd fought with it all day, not wanting to burden Graham. He had enough on his mind, especially now, with his father wandering about Ambrose and Maria Cooper's house, still looking for Daisy. But the foreboding feeling seemed to have something to do with their meeting with Leonard Fitzwald and the danger of losing her property, so she couldn't shake it off.

With all of them now in dry clothes and full of grits cooked in cream, she'd told Graham's cousins about her problem with Leonard—even the marriage part. If only she could discern the source of her unease...

She glanced at Graham, sitting next to her in the parlor and paging through a month-old copy of the *New*

Orleans Daily Crescent. Even in Mister Cooper's too-large clothing, her pretend beau was as handsome as any man she'd ever seen. And he'd made sure Ellie had every comfort the Coopers could supply, living in their newly impoverished state in their white-columned mansion. He'd even walked Sugar in the rain so she could do her doggy duty in the yard, away from the house, and now had the dog at his feet. He'd certainly played the part of the attentive suitor.

Perhaps her unrest was due to the underlying tension of the loan. Or was it the loneliness of having a beau who was not in love with her?

That thought stung. After years of training herself to close off any sentiments or emotions about courting or men, had she come to that? Morose thoughts, melancholy words?

She'd have to take those thoughts captive if this courtship ruse was to work out. Of course, that would be easier to do if Graham wasn't so handsome. And she needed this courtship now more than ever, with Leonard determined to marry her.

Leonard. How could she not have seen what a scalawag he was? Sitting there with that smug grin on his face, listening to Joseph tell her they'd lose their plantation, their town house, their—

That nagging feeling pecked at her mind again. There was something else. Joseph had mentioned another property they would lose, but what?

"Graham, didn't Joseph list three properties at risk?"

"Magnolia Grove, the town house and the Louisiana–Texas Railroad."

"That's it—the information I've been trying to remember all day. I'm sure Uncle Amos doesn't own a railroad."

"He said it had been your father's."

Father? At the mention of him, her mouth went dry. No, her father had certainly never had a railroad. Or anything else of value, for that matter. If he had, she and her mother would not have gone hungry as much as they had. And Mother wouldn't have been reduced to serving in the saloon beneath their rooms. "That's simply not true."

Graham's eyes widened. "Joseph seemed quite sure. He wouldn't make a mistake about something so important."

"Sure or not, it can't be true."

Or could it? Could Father have somehow bought the railroad shortly before he died—without telling Ellie and her mother? She closed her eyes, searching her memory. How long had he been gone on his last binge? It had seemed like months, but she'd been so young, her judgment may have been off. And how much time had passed between his death and Mother's?

Of course, no one knew the exact date of his death…

At once she realized the room had grown silent during her musings. "Forgive me. I was gathering wool."

Maria reached across the table and laid her hand on Ellie's. "Are you all right, dear? I know this has to be hard for you."

"I admit it is. But I need to discover the truth. How could I have inherited a railroad without knowing it?"

"You were not of age when your parents passed," Graham said in a soothing tone. "Since your uncle was your guardian, he no doubt took care of all the paperwork for you."

"But I'm of age now, so why wouldn't I have inherited?"

Ambrose leaned back in his chair as if settling in for

a long discussion. "Perhaps it's in your uncle's name until you marry."

"And if I marry, who gets it?"

"I guess you do." Graham hesitated. "But if you married Leonard, he would no doubt control it."

"And benefit from the income, if there were any. But Sherman destroyed most of the South's rail lines. Our railroads are useless."

"Not the Louisiana–Texas line." Ambrose raised his gaze from the pipe he was filling with tobacco. "It's one of the few Sherman didn't get."

"I still don't think Leonard would care about that. He must want our plantation and the house."

"But his home is even grander than yours," Graham said. "And the plantation—it's large with a nice home, but he's never been interested in planting. His father owned a few Pennsylvania textile mills, and he came to Natchez to become a cotton broker. Besides, Fitzwald could buy any confiscated plantation outright if he wanted to plant."

"Textiles need to be shipped. Could his holdings have included railroads?"

Graham glanced toward the dining room door as if wishing his father would come back in and answer all their questions. "I've been away from Natchez too long to remember. Do you know, Ambrose?"

"No, but your father would, if he could tell us. He, Ellie's father, her uncle Amos and Robert Fitzwald were good friends in the early days."

Good friends? Not that Ellie had ever seen. "I can't speak for the others, but Uncle Amos could barely tolerate being in the same room with Robert Fitzwald."

Graham took a sip of his coffee. "I sure wish Father could give us some answers."

"Uncle Amos couldn't help either. He doesn't remember many people from his past except Miss Ophelia."

Ambrose laughed. "Nobody could forget Ophelia—apoplexy or not."

True enough. "You might be right about Leonard wanting the railroad. And if he wants it badly enough, he could do about anything to get it."

Graham set down his newspaper and took her hand. "Don't worry. I won't let him hurt you again."

His eyes revealed a hint of the devotion she'd seen in them the night he proposed to her, and her breath caught. She held his gaze, the memory sharp and somehow painful. How many times had she forced herself to stop thinking about that look? But seeing it again now, in his eyes rather than in her memory, made it harder to bear as he once again silently revealed his heart.

Graham looked away, breaking the moment, and glanced at the mantle clock. "And as much as I would love to stay and visit, we need to get my father home."

They all stood, and Maria touched his arm. "Couldn't you stay tonight? You could all get a good night's sleep, go to church with us and leave in the afternoon."

"You're kind to ask, but we need to get the doctor for Father. Besides, he might come to himself in his own home. Ellie needs to check on her uncle too."

All true, but Ellie also needed to get home and put distance between herself and that look in Graham's eyes. And so she could make sure Leonard Fitzwald kept his distance from everything that still belonged to her and her uncle.

Chapter Ten

This was not the homecoming Graham had envisioned for his father.

The rain having let up an hour earlier, he stopped the carriage in front of his home that evening and bounded out. Part of him wished to drive on, keeping the truth from Noreen. After the shock of Francine's death and the responsibility of raising Betsy, he dreaded seeing what this latest tragedy would do to his stepmother.

Noreen stepped onto the gallery, Betsy in her arms. Dear Noreen, always the Southern lady. She would die before she'd call out to someone in the street, even to find out if Graham had found her long-missing husband.

He opened Ellie's door and helped her out, then grabbed the end of Sugar's leash and let her scramble down the carriage steps, white tail wagging. He turned the dog over to its pretty owner as Father climbed down to the street.

Ellie moved in close to Graham. "Maybe it would be best if I take the carriage home and leave you two alone with Miss Noreen," she whispered. "Some people just want family at a time like this."

"If we're courting, then you're almost family. Better come ahead in."

Her smile and brightened eyes made Graham question his decision. But it was the first time she'd asked his opinion about anything, so he'd hate to tell her he'd changed his mind. Besides, Father seemed to take to her and her dog, so she might be a help, for a change.

But that thought was unfair. She'd been quite helpful today. He wouldn't have looked for his father in the cemetery without her suggestion.

When they reached the gallery, Ellie slid the leash's looped end over her wrist and took the baby from Noreen.

"James, you're home." In her own refined way, Noreen dropped a demure kiss on her husband's cheek, but tears ran down her face. "I've never been so glad to see anyone—"

"Do you know where my Daisy is?" Father pulled back from her and gave her that empty stare that chilled Graham to his bones. Then he peered into Betsy's small face. "This isn't Daisy."

Noreen covered her mouth with her hand. Her wide-eyed gaze shot to Graham, full of questions he had no answers for.

"I need to go for the doctor," Graham said. "Father doesn't recognize me or Ellie, and when we stopped at Ambrose and Maria's on the way home, he didn't know them either."

"I'll get Doctor Pritchert." Ellie gave the baby back to Noreen. "Mister Talbot will need something hot to eat. He had some grits at the Coopers' house, but he didn't eat much."

"Ellie, dear, you shouldn't drive about the city at this hour." Noreen's voice carried into the hall.

"Nonsense, Miss Noreen…"

Excusing himself from the conversation, and the decision he could tell he wouldn't be a part of, Graham guided his father into the house. Headstrong Ellie would win this confrontation and, truth be told, Graham was glad. Ellie was right; things had changed since the war started. He needed her tonight, and he didn't mind admitting it.

Noreen came inside, holding the baby and leading the dog. "Perhaps you two could rest in the parlor while I get some leftover ham for James. Will you mind the baby and the dog for me?"

Graham unhooked the leash and took Betsy from his stepmother's arms. They'd not addressed the fact that Father didn't recognize Noreen, and although it would be painful to talk about it, it somehow seemed worse not to. "I'm disappointed that the only person he remembers is my deceased sister. I was hoping he'd know you."

"This is harder than if he'd never come home at all." Noreen let a tear roll down her face, then turned and started toward the dining room and, presumably, the kitchen. "Sugar, you take care of Betsy. And James too."

Now, that was ridiculous. What could a dog do? Ellie must have put Noreen up to that. Although it would be nice if it worked. They could use the help.

In the parlor, Graham set Betsy on the blanket Noreen always used as a sort of rug for her. Then he seated his father on the gold settee beside the baby. Sugar ambled over and sniffed her. The dog lay down in front of her and licked her bare toes.

Betsy laughed and grabbed the dog's ear. Again.

Graham sat beside his father to watch the two on the floor. It felt awkward, sitting with Father and yet seemingly not relating to him in any meaningful way. As minutes ticked by, the silence grew more uncomfortable, and finally Graham said the first thing that came to his mind. "We have a good dog, Father."

Graham's father petted Sugar's head. "You're a good dog."

Those were the first sensible words Graham had heard him say. He shook his head. Ellie and that dog of hers.

Soon they heard a carriage pull up. The tinkling of those little bells told him it was Ellie and, he hoped, the doctor.

The front door opened, and Ellie's dainty footsteps, along with a heavier set, sounded in the hall as she called out to Graham.

She felt comfortable enough in his home to let herself in and bring the doctor with her. The fact warmed his heart in a way it hadn't when she'd let herself in after Aunt Ophelia's party. When they reached the parlor, he took her hand and started toward the door. "Let's sit in the library while the doctor examines Father. I'll meet you there in a moment."

"I'll take Betsy along." She crossed the room and picked up the baby. "Come, Sugar."

As the dog got up, Father followed her with his gaze. "You're a good dog."

Graham hastened to Doctor Pritchert's side as Ellie left the room. "I assume Ellie described his affliction to you. That's the second time he's spoken to the dog. It's the only thing he's said today that made sense," he whispered.

"Well then," Doctor Pritchert said in his drawn-out voice, "you'd better let the dog stay with him."

What kind of nonsense was that? "Surely having a dog in the room won't make a difference."

"This is a disease of the mind. I'll be honest with

you—I could tell what was wrong as soon as I entered the room. Actually, as soon as Ellie told me about him. I've seen case after case like this since the soldiers started coming home."

"Anyone can see his mind is affected. But what caused it?"

"Some traumatic event of the war must have done it. Many doctors think that seeing the horrors of battle affects the nerves in the body. The mind no longer knows what to do, even in ordinary circumstances."

Could it be that simple? If so, there should logically be a simple cure. "What can we do about it?"

"Every case is different. Some patients respond to rest, wholesome food and, eventually, some form of meaningful work. If a particular activity or person—or even a dog—seems to make him think and speak normally, it's usually good to encourage it."

As Doctor Pritchert sat next to Father and began talking with him, Graham left them to their privacy and started toward the library. Rest, food, work—Graham could understand how those could help. But a dog? Perhaps he should find a different doctor. This one had ideas as crazy as Ellie's. At least Ellie's ideas were more fun.

The thought shocked him as much as any of Ellie's schemes ever had. Was it true? Did he think Ellie was fun?

Of course he did. He always had. That was one of the things that had drawn him to her all those years ago. That, and those beautiful blue eyes, the ones that always saw him for who he was inside rather than who he tried to be.

Since he'd been home, he merely hadn't wanted to admit it. And he still didn't. But now it was getting harder to ignore.

The library, where he assumed he'd find Ellie, was empty. She also wasn't on the front gallery or in the kitchen dependency, where Noreen fixed a tray for Father.

Then Graham realized where she'd be—the backyard garden, her favorite spot. Arriving there, he found her seated under the crape myrtles, the baby in her lap. He crossed the yard and joined her on the grass, the dew beginning to fall and freshen the lawn.

He sat with her for a moment, not sure how to say what he felt. But it had to be said. "Ellie, I want to thank you. You're the one who found Father, but you did more than that. Without you there to help and encourage me, it would have been a much more difficult day—and evening." He took her hand and squeezed it for a moment—just a friendly squeeze.

"I didn't annoy you?" Her teasing tone comforted him somehow, tempered his seriousness.

He couldn't help the smile that came from his heart. "I'm getting kind of used to it."

Ellie, sweetheart...
That night, Graham's words during their encounter with Leonard floated back into Ellie's mind as softly as her white bed canopy fluttered in the breeze. She kicked off her sheet and gazed out the window at Graham's house bathed in moonlight. When he'd spoken those words, she'd been so distressed that they simply must not have registered. But now she heard them as if they came from Graham's mouth rather than her memory.

Ellie, sweetheart...
She knew he'd said that just to make Leonard and Joseph believe he was in love with her. But those words

sure had a way of convincing a girl that he wasn't pretending.

Lying here was useless, since sleep wouldn't come to her as long as those two words kept swirling around in her mind. And as long as her stomach ached as it did. She got up and donned her dressing gown, then made for the stairs and the dining room.

There, she lifted one of Mother's blue Baccarat glasses from the sideboard, left at Magnolia Grove when her parents moved from that house to New Orleans before Ellie was born. Or so the family story went. She measured a teaspoon of sugar as if it were the most potent of medicines, then sprinkled it in the glass. She filled the glass with fresh water Lilah May kept in the matching pitcher for her, in case Ellie needed it in the night.

She stirred the water with a long-handled silver spoon. Then she sat at the mahogany table and took a long drink of the sweet water, her stomach settling a bit.

Yesterday, Graham had said he wanted to intensify the courtship. What he didn't know was how his eyes had turned a stormy green when he said it. Was it wise to make their courtship look even more serious? Was there a chance he'd fall in love with her again?

Or that she would fall in love with him?

Nonsense. Their supposed courtship was a business arrangement—two old friends helping each other. It held no danger for either of them. Besides, he was right in saying they needed to make the courtship more authentic. She took another sip of her sweet water. It had to be past midnight. She closed her eyes.

Dear God, it's true, isn't it? We're in no danger?

The next morning, Graham knelt beside his bed, still in the nightshirt he'd borrowed from his father. Since he'd returned to Natchez, each day had brought new crises. First the girls scouting him like Yankees, then Ellie and her crazy courtship plan, then baby Betsy's appearance, then Leonard Fitzwald, now Father…

It would take a bigger man than Graham to deal with all this plus find a way to support them all. He needed work, needed an income, especially since Father would be no help anytime soon, if ever.

Holding his head in his hands, Graham forced his fear from his mind—fear that his prayer would again bounce off the ceiling as it had yesterday. By faith he began his prayer.

God, the only work I know how to do is soldiering. I probably could have succeeded as a planter, but I have no ground. I need Your help. What should I—

The crash of a metal object against his windowpane brought his head up. The sound was strangely familiar, one from long ago. He rose from the floor and hastened to the window.

It couldn't be.

Tied to a piece of twine strung twenty feet above the lawn, between his window and Ellie's, was the barrel of the old, broken fountain pen he'd scavenged from the trash heap twelve years prior. He looked up to the top sash. The twine was threaded around the small wooden pulley he'd nailed to the sash back then, identical to the one above Ellie's window. Graham reached through the open bottom half of the window and grabbed the barrel.

Their old secret-message vessel.

Although his fingers were bigger and clumsier than they'd been in his childhood, he managed to extract the slip of paper folded up inside the cylinder. Unlike in earlier years, this paper was a light plum color and smelled

of sweet flowers. He unfolded it with a sense of trepidation.

> Rise and shine, sleepyhead! Get up and spiff your-
> self up and get ready to beau me to church this
> morning. We need to get there in time to let ev-
> erybody, especially Leonard and Susanna, see us
> courting. Try hard to leave your frown behind.
> You could be a lot of fun if you tried. And you're
> invited to dinner at our house, and don't forget the
> sunset picnic at the river bluff tonight.
> "Sis."

Sis. So she remembered his old nickname for her—the
one he'd grown to hate when she'd laughed at his proposal and told him she was his sis, not his girl.

The old pain reared up in him again. How could she
have missed the change in their relationship back then?
Or had she missed it? Whatever had happened in her
heart and mind years ago, it was plain to see she had
no more desire for a romance with him now than ever.

And that was fine with him. He snatched a piece of
writing paper from his old desk and began a note of his
own.

> You may be just my Sis, but you have a role to play
> in this too. You'd better outshine Aunt Ophelia
> with fluff and feathers this morning. And don't
> make me wait on you to put them on.

If Ellie could keep up this charade, so could Graham.
He'd figure it out somehow. She didn't know it yet, but
she was about to get the courting of her life.

He hurried through his morning routine and dressed

in his uniform again. Tomorrow, as soon as the stores opened in Natchez, he had to buy some new clothes—

What was he thinking? For the first time in his life, he didn't have the money to buy something he needed.

As he sat in his desk chair, pulling on his boots, Ellie's giant bell rang. Looked as if Noreen had finally embraced the idea of using bells to call people in the house. Funny how quickly some people took Ellie's ideas and ran with them. What was it about Ellie that made people want to please her?

Everybody but Graham. At least, up to now. This morning, and every day until this mess was straightened out, he'd show her that he could court with the best of them.

Her note still bothered him. Signing it "Sis." Telling him not to frown. Hoping he'd be more fun. What made her think he would frown, wouldn't be any fun?

Then it hit him. He'd been frowning for the past three days.

He'd hardly remembered how to smile when he came home. And yesterday, he'd laughed—hard—for the first time he could remember. He got up and went to the mirror.

What he saw looked awful. He hadn't taken a good look at himself, other than to shave and comb his hair, for months. Maybe longer. Had he become the man Ellie thought he was? Had he allowed the war to make him hard? Judging by that scowl in the mirror, probably so.

Was that why God allowed him to have Ellie and that ridiculous dog of hers in his life again? Maybe, maybe not. But whatever the reason for the changes, he needed them.

What would it be like to enjoy life again? He needed

to find out. Now he wished he hadn't sent Ellie that sarcastic note through the pen barrel.

He looked in the mirror again and tried for a smile. *Pathetic.* This was going to take some time.

Graham sprinted down the stairs as Noreen rang the bell again.

"Good morning, dear." His stepmother kissed his cheek and set down the bell. "I thought you might want to help your father dress for church. Doctor Pritchert thinks he should go. I brushed and freshened his uniform last night. Breakfast in ten minutes."

Noreen made for the kitchen as Graham started back upstairs to assist his father. Then, on impulse, he stopped. "Noreen."

She turned to him. "Yes?"

Graham took a deep breath and smiled the best he could. "Good morning."

He thought he saw a tear in her eye. Then she gave him the first genuine smile he'd seen on her face since Betsy had come to their house.

"Good morning, Graham."

Half an hour later, those bells tinkled, signaling Ellie's carriage at their door. He stepped onto the gallery and saw her sticking her head out the carriage window, waving at him and pointing at the ostrich feathers on her hat. "Fluff and feathers—just as you requested."

She'd taken him literally? That was the gaudiest hat he'd ever seen. "You can't wear that. It looks awful."

"That's no way to win a woman's heart."

She was right. He'd already forgotten his resolve to court her for all he was worth.

And it looked as if he was in her debt again, this time for transportation to church. She'd done it for Father and for Noreen, who would struggle to carry Betsy to church in the late-morning heat. But it rankled against his Southern sensibilities to let her drive him around.

Nevertheless, Graham headed back inside to fetch Noreen, Father and Betsy. Within minutes, he had them settled in the landau's backseat. The only missing member of their families was Amos. And Sugar.

Graham got in next to Ellie. "Good morning. You look lovely in that hat."

She looked so startled, he must have done or said something wrong. When Noreen began to laugh softly, he knew he had.

"My grandmother apparently thought so too. She wore it to a Charles Finney revival in New York back in 1825."

Finney revival—1825? The harder he tried to understand, the more confused he got. Why was she wearing such an old hat—and why was Noreen laughing?

Ellie handed him the reins, then lifted a hatbox from the floorboard and pulled out a different hat. It might have been the one she wore yesterday. "It was just a joke, Graham. You told me to wear fluff and feathers, and this was the best I could do."

A joke. Laughing at him—again. He let out a puff of air that sounded like a growl. Try to court a woman, and this was what happened.

She tied her blue hat under her chin and blinked those big even-bluer eyes at him. "Is this better?"

"No, I like the other one." Which wasn't entirely true, now that he thought about it. Aside from the abundance of feathers, they didn't look much different to him. Both were too big and fancy.

"You poor man. Miss Noreen, you must have forgotten to give him his breakfast. He's as grouchy as Uncle Amos is when he's hungry."

"No, I fed him like a king. Grits with eggs, and biscuits with wild honey."

Graham shifted in his suddenly uncomfortable seat. He'd have to try again. "Ellie, you don't need a stylish hat to look beautiful."

Silence.

Apparently, that wasn't the right thing to say either. What was wrong with it? It was true, and it was complimentary. If these women couldn't appreciate sincere admiration, he didn't know what else to do.

"Thank you, Graham," Ellie said in a soft little voice. Her face held a hint of a dewy smile. Something soft glowed in her eyes, a womanly radiance so beautiful he could hardly breathe.

Betsy began to fuss in the backseat then, and the moment faded away.

"What gave you the idea to start up our message system again?" Graham asked, pulling his gaze from her.

"I remembered you banging that barrel against my window on Saturday mornings."

"And you did it to wake me up in time to play in the churchyard before Sunday school." Graham had all but forgotten about that. "I can believe the pulleys were still attached. But that twine should have rotted years ago."

"It did. That's why I came over yesterday morning, while you were grooming Dixie, and strung another length of twine."

"How did you do that?"

"Same way we did it before. I fastened the twine to my pulley, then I stood under your window and threw the ball up to the gallery."

A low chuckle from the backseat let him know who else was responsible. "You're in on this too, Noreen?"

"I'm afraid I am. I thought you needed a little levity in your life."

Levity? Why would he need that?

They arrived at church then, and Graham realized Father had not said a word the whole morning, even during the half hour Graham spent with him during breakfast. Would that get awkward in church? What if someone spoke to him, but he didn't answer?

He glanced at Ellie, who continued to chat with everyone in the carriage, even his quiet father. Did she understand how much they all needed that, needed her to encourage them? Today was Graham's first time in a church in at least two years. Sure, he'd attended camp services as often as his command allowed, but a ragtag meeting in a makeshift outdoor church was a far cry from worship in a Natchez sanctuary. Ellie seemed to know instinctively that his family needed the distraction from the awkwardness that could come.

However, the prospect of spending time with people who weren't soldiers or family felt less intimidating than it had when he first rode into town. A clean shave and the hasty haircut Noreen gave him before Aunt Ophelia's party had certainly helped. But his new calmness was due mostly to Ellie's easy friendship, and he knew it.

He also knew he needn't worry about the church's reaction to his father. As long as Ellie stayed by Father's side, chatting as usual, nobody would notice his silence.

They parked at the church, and Father exited the conveyance as soon as the wheels stopped rolling. He waited beside the door and helped Noreen and the baby out. That was progress.

Graham opened Ellie's door and took her hand while she stepped from the landau. The instant before he would have let go of her hand, he instead tucked it into the crook of his arm and drew her closer than he ever had.

She wanted courting? She would get it—as good as he could give it.

Chapter Eleven

"Is consulting our attorney considered work on a Sunday?" If not, Ellie might get some answers to the questions that had been nagging her since yesterday: Did she own a railroad? If so, why had she and her mother lived in poverty? And why did Leonard Fitzwald want it so badly?

Uncle Amos lifted the built-up spoon Ellie had made and tried to use it to scoop up some red rice and étouffée.

Ellie and Graham sat at the small square table at Uncle Amos's bedside. The older man had his Sunday dinner on the high bed table on wheels that Ellie had one of the Magnolia Grove workers make.

"Best not to defile the Lord's day with work." Her uncle's sagged features seemed to droop even more when he disapproved of something Ellie wanted to do—as they did now.

"Even if he does it as a favor?"

Uncle Amos frowned harder than Graham always did. "Ask…ask your young man here. He'll tell you the same thing."

"His name is Graham."

"I knew who he was, just forgot the name. He's the one you're in that imaginary courtship with."

She certainly hadn't expected that. "Only for the sake of convenience."

Uncle Amos fixed his one good eye on Graham. "I don't like it—not at all."

Graham hesitated. "It's nothing harmful. We're just like brother and sister, as always."

Her uncle snorted. "I know more than you think. Nobody should play around with love. It's dangerous, and somebody always gets hurt. Every time."

"Not this time, Uncle."

"Mark my words." His ominous tone sent a shiver up Ellie's back. "What do you want with the attorney?"

Graham looked as relieved as Ellie felt at the change of subject.

If she told Uncle Amos what was on her mind, he likely wouldn't remember the answers today even if he did know them. On the other hand, if she asked him and then he forgot, it probably wouldn't affect his health. She decided to take a chance. "Joseph Duncan told me that my father left me a railroad."

He frowned. "Joseph Duncan…"

"The attorney."

"Right. What did he say about a railroad?"

"That my father left me one when he passed."

He hesitated, frowning again as he did when trying to remember.

Perhaps Ellie could help him recall if she told him what she knew. "It's the Louisiana–Texas line."

"Louisiana–Texas…"

Just when she thought the memory was gone forever, Uncle Amos sat up straighter and shook his head. "No, no."

Graham leaned forward. "You don't remember?"

But he did. Ellie could tell. "What is it, Uncle? What do you remember?"

"Let it go. It's not worth it."

"Let what go? Do you mean I should sell it?"

"No." He raised his voice. "Just let Joseph deal with it. He knows what to do."

"But—"

"Let it go, Ellie." His face turned red, his chest heaving with every breath.

Graham touched her hand. "This is too hard on him. Forget it for now."

He was right. Ellie rushed to Uncle Amos's side. No railroad was worth endangering his already precarious health. "I'll tell Joseph what you said."

"You'll do what he tells you?"

"I promise."

"Good." He lay back against his pillow again and drew deep, slow breaths, his eyes closed.

"I'm sorry. I didn't know it would upset you."

He lifted his good hand then let it drop. His color had improved a bit, and his breathing had slowed to normal. "As long as you do what Joseph says, it will be all right."

If Uncle knew about the loan from Leonard, he would know that it was not going to be all right. Not all right at all. "I'll take care of it."

He opened his good eye and put all his uncle authority into his gaze. "Not on the Lord's day."

"Yes, sir."

"Take this food away." He closed his eye again. "I'm going to sleep."

"I'll get it." Graham rose from the table and collected her uncle's dishes. He carried them to the table and started to add his leftovers to the ones on Ellie's plate.

She hurried to his side and stopped him from scraping them together. "That's enough for our supper. I'll put it in the spring house to keep it cool."

"Or I could give it to Sugar for you." He looked at her with questions in his eyes. "Most people don't keep leftover crawfish. It'll spoil."

She hesitated. He might as well. Lilah May would feed it to the dog before the next meal, anyway, as she always did.

Within ten minutes, Graham had fed Sugar, and then he and Ellie moved to the parlor to explain to Lilah May about Uncle Amos's spell of nerves.

"Keep him as quiet as you can," Ellie told her maid. "Don't mention railroads."

Lilah May's brows rose, but she said nothing and returned to the kitchen, where Graham had stacked their dinner dishes.

"I can't wait until tomorrow to start getting money together to pay this loan." Ellie paced the parlor, her mind whirling with ideas she'd had while sitting up late last night. "I'm going to ride out to Magnolia Grove and talk with the workers."

"In this heat? Why don't you go in the morning instead? It's ninety degrees and humid as a thunderstorm. Nobody's going to be stirring out there."

"I have to go today. Tomorrow I meet with Joseph about that railroad and put my plan into motion."

"I'll go with you after I check on Father and Noreen. We can 'court' just as well out there as here in your parlor." Graham watched her from the rococo-style couch. "Why don't you sit by me while we make plans? You're wearing me out with all that walking. It's a day of rest."

"I can't rest. Let's start for Magnolia Grove, and I'll tell you about an idea I had."

Graham opened his mouth, and Ellie braced herself

for his snide comment about her ideas. But he closed it again and stood from the couch. "I'll meet you back here in a few minutes."

She watched him walk out, her plans somehow failing to capture her attention anymore. Graham Talbot had missed an opportunity to chide her about her ideas? What had happened to him?

Calling to Lilah May to ask for help in changing to an older dress, Ellie sprinted up the stairs. If her uncle knew she was going to Magnolia Grove today, he'd have something to say about her working on the Lord's day. But didn't Jesus say that if an ox falls into a pit, the owner would pull him out on the Sabbath? Well, if she didn't do something about this loan, she would be the one in the pit.

When she had changed, she leashed Sugar and headed toward the carriage house. Roman had the landau ready to go, just as she'd asked before dinner. As soon as Graham got there, she let Sugar climb into the backseat, and they took off for the plantation. She opened her parasol and held it over them both for shade.

"More than anything," she said as they turned onto the country road to Magnolia Grove, "I want to go to Joseph's house and find out why my uncle got so agitated about that railroad. But if Uncle remembers anything about our conversation, he'll ask me what we did today. If I say we went to Joseph's, I'm afraid his attack of nerves will happen all over again."

"Or something worse could happen. He had me scared for a minute."

"Me too. I hope he won't find out what I'm going to do out there."

"I'm not sure I want to know either, but you ought to let me in on the plan before we arrive."

For the first time, Ellie hesitated to tell him her plan. No doubt that was because she was unsure it would work out. Graham was right that her plans didn't always achieve what she wanted them to, but she'd never doubted before. Not until Graham had come home. And that scared her more than the loan did.

This was her last chance to back out. She drew a deep breath. "I'm going to put my plan of daily pay in place to keep them from moving on to some other plantation."

"I assumed you'd do that."

"That will not only retain our workers, but I think it's the right thing to do. Planters in this area are starting sharecropping programs, and I think they're a terrible idea."

"I don't know much about that, other than the planters leasing out tracts of ground to the workers."

"It's terrible because the laborer never gets out of debt to the landowner. The workers don't get paid until the crop is harvested and sold. Until then, they rack up credit at the plantation store. The workers have to buy their own tools and animals besides living expenses. So basically, they are still slaves."

"And by paying them daily, you'll eliminate the need for the workers to live in debt. I like it."

She might as well tell him the rest now, while he was impressed with her daily-pay idea. "Also, if anyone brings me a new worker, and that person stays on through the harvest, they each get a bonus of a double-eagle coin."

He looked at her as if she'd proposed giving away the entire plantation. "That's going to cost you."

"It'll cost more to leave cotton in the field to rot."

"You know that's going to make you unpopular with the other planters in the area."

"It doesn't matter." The humidity was turning oppressive; she fanned herself with her handkerchief. Maybe Graham was right and they should have waited until morning. "I have to get this crop in. Desperate times call for desperate measures, and this is about as bad off as I've ever been."

Graham leaned back into a comfortable-looking position, gathered the reins in one hand, pulled out his handkerchief with the other and dabbed his neck with it. He looked so much the part of the landed gentry that she didn't know whether to laugh or cry. "I'll give that some thought."

He assumed he was meant to be a soldier, but Ellie knew better. Even as a child, Graham had an eye for the crops, a way of kindness with the workers and an uncanny business sense. If he had ground, he'd be the most successful planter in the county.

They passed the abandoned chapel again, with its falling-in roof and rotting siding. Such a shame for it to go to waste…

Her new idea came to her as she mourned the loss of that chapel. She watched the plan unfold in her mind as if she were seeing it with her natural eyes.

"Graham, I just got an idea that will save our plantation and give you an opportunity to make a living for your family."

"Ellie, no—"

She interrupted Graham with a rush of words so fast, he had to concentrate in order to keep up. "I know this plan will succeed. It will keep your family going until your father gets better and can find something to do, and if he wants to, he can work here too. We'll start

with the cabins and then the chapel. It won't be long before we can—"

"Stop!"

She looked at him with eyes so big, he couldn't doubt
that she had no idea what she'd done. "What's wrong?"

"I know what you're going to say. You want to hire
me to help at Magnolia Grove."

Ellie all but bounced on her seat. "It's going to work
out wonderfully!"

Did she mean to strip him of what little pride he had
left? Or did that just happen naturally? "Look at me,
Ellie. I have nothing. I have no prospects. I'm already
driving your horses and carriage. I'm not going to let
you pay my way too."

"My idea is going to change all that."

"Your ideas change things, I'll give you that. But this
time, I'm not going along with your plan."

"Graham, don't be silly."

"Even if I would agree to do this, which I am not,
where are you going to get the money for all this labor?
And how much will you need to rebuild the cabins? What
shape are they in?"

"They can't be that bad."

Graham ran his hand over his eyes. How could he
make her see her mistake? He'd never been able to do
that before. But he could give her another idea. "Why
don't we wait and see if Father improves enough to sign
for the sale of the property? That way, you could pay off
the loan, and you might have money left over. I heard in
church this morning that Yankees are swarming down
here, buying plantations and thinking they're going to
get rich on cotton."

"Well, they're mistaken. Cotton is selling high now,
but I expect the price to plunge by the middle of Septem-

ber. And a high price doesn't guarantee a large profit. We have to pay laborers and taxes, do maintenance and up-keep. Cotton isn't the foolproof crop the North thinks it is." Her sweet smile looked like bravery shining through fear. "And that way we wouldn't have a livelihood either. This way, I can keep working."

She knew her cotton farming, of that much he was sure. In fact, she knew a lot more about the market than he did. "Why don't you sell half of the ground then?"

Ellie lowered her parasol and met his gaze. "Because we barely survive on twenty-five hundred acres. How could we live on less than that?"

He had no answer.

"How did you get the manpower—and money—to plant and cultivate that much ground?" He paused, realizing the Andersons' entire financial situation didn't add up. "What about taxes? Hardly anybody around Natchez has this much cotton planted, because no one had the money."

"Miss Noreen and my uncle were quite clever. Two years ago, they guessed how the war was headed, so they converted most of their Confederate money into gold coin. It wasn't the most patriotic move they could have made, but seeing how things turned out, I'm glad they did it."

As Graham had done in Virginia. "But Union troops occupy this whole city. How did they not confiscate the money?"

"We hid it in our matching mahogany sideboards—in our dining room and yours."

"But the Union soldiers would have known to look in the sideboard for valuables. We kept our silver in there."

"They did, but they didn't know the mahogany was a

veneer, and the sideboards are actually three-thousand-pound cast-iron safes with secret recesses in the doors."

That could not be true. "I lived in that house for years. I would have known about a giant safe that looked like a piece of wooden furniture."

"No one knew except your father and Uncle Amos. They ordered them together, from Philadelphia. Before your father left for war, he told Miss Noreen about it, and when Uncle Amos got sick, Miss Noreen told me."

Secrets. He didn't like it. But at least they'd had the money they needed. "I assume that's how Noreen kept the house. She paid the taxes with that money."

"Some for daily expenses too, but she's been exceedingly frugal."

He didn't allow himself so much as a moment to hope there was money left. "It's gone now, I'm sure."

"Miss Noreen used the last of it to buy several hams, sacks of flour and some laying hens. I have enough to pay our workers this week. Nothing more. And I have a gold dollar in my reticule for groceries when our hoard runs out."

Ellie gazed off into the distance as they turned into the Magnolia Grove drive.

He'd seen that look before. She was lost in her dream world, and there was no sense in trying to pull her out of it.

"I admit I haven't paid attention to the cabins all spring. Let's drive straight there and see them. Maybe we can talk to the workers too. It's so hot, everybody might have decided to stay close to home. Either that or they'll be at the river."

"You mean you'll talk to them. I have no part in this."

She smiled in a way that was downright calculating. "Of course you do. You're my beau, remember?"

He didn't bother to hold in his groan.

Then he remembered his vow to court her with all he had. "That's right. I am. And since I'm your intended, it's my duty to make some decisions to protect you. First, we're not paying double-eagle coins. Second, I'm not repairing any cabins. Third—"

Her giggle tinkled in his ears. "Graham, you always make me laugh."

Laugh? "I was being serious."

So much for courting. He had to get somebody to tell him what he kept doing wrong.

As they approached the cabins, the half dozen or so older men, lounging in the shade, stood and took off their straw hats. As soon as the carriage stopped, Graham bounded out of his seat, unwilling to sit in her conveyance a moment longer than he had to. He helped Ellie out, who helped Sugar out. The workers must have been used to seeing the dog there, since each one petted and spoke to her before she ran toward the nearest cotton field.

"Sugar always greets us before she takes off to do whatever dogs do." The Andersons' longtime overseer, a gray-haired man in a patched, rolled-sleeved shirt, ambled their way. "You remember me, sir?"

"Moses Lark. You used to keep us out of trouble in the old days."

"Colonel Talbot is now my intended, Moses," Ellie said. "And we have some things to discuss with all of you—things you will like. Could you get everyone together?"

"Yes, ma'am." He motioned for one of the younger men to ring the dinner bell by the big house.

"Ellie, let's look around the cabins to see what repairs are needed while we wait for the workers." Graham extended his arm to her, and they started toward the cabins.

They remained more or less as he remembered—small and hot, but now in poor repair. "Some of these roofs need shingles, siding needs paint."

Ellie took a small ledger and pencil from the handbag she carried, and they stopped while she made notes, starting with the chapel.

"The wood is rotting near the foundation on this one. You'll have to replace that."

They inspected each cabin until her page was full of her list of necessary repairs. By that time, the workers had assembled in front of Moses's house.

Ellie put away her book and pencil and gave them her attention. "I have some changes in mind that I think will benefit us all..."

A half hour later, Ellie had addressed all her issues and answered every question, except the one that kept invading Graham's mind. Where would the money come from?

"I will be here every morning as usual and will speak to anyone who wants to come to work for us." She brightened then, in that way that always meant she had another idea. And he could tell by looking at her that she was going to announce it now rather than thinking it through first.

"Ellie, wait—"

"If we pick every boll of cotton on this plantation, everyone who has worked here for at least thirty days will receive another double eagle. Tell your friends to be here tomorrow afternoon if they want to work for us."

Graham lowered his head, not wanting the workers to see what he was sure was in his eyes. What was she thinking? She could never pay that bonus. He started to say so, but the shouts and laughter of the workers would have drowned him out anyway.

When the roar quieted and the workers went back to their homes or the river, Ellie turned to Graham, her face flushed and her eyes sunny. "That went well. I think we gained all the workers' complete loyalty, and I'll be surprised if each of them doesn't bring a dozen friends along."

Graham cupped her elbow and guided her toward the carriage before she could give away anything else. "How will you handle it if they do? That's a dozen double-eagles for the friend and a dozen for each worker who brings a dozen more. You're going to have to sell the ground in order to pay this debt, let alone your other one."

"I have one idea left."

He should have known.

Ellie twisted the ring on her right hand, then pointed to the field where a white tail waved like a flag above the cotton plants. "Sugar explored that entire field during the meeting. When she plays in the fields, I see nothing but tail."

"Don't change the subject. If this new plan of yours doesn't work, you'll see nothing but Leonard Fitzwald standing at the altar, waiting for you."

"I will never see that."

No, she wouldn't, not if Graham could help it. But she needed to face reality. "Ellie, it's time to give up these schemes of yours. We need to find some way to sell this ground. I'm praying that Father will come around soon. If he does, you need to sell enough of your ground to pay off your debt to Fitzwald."

"Let me show you my plan, and then we'll see what you think about that." Her saucy tone almost gave Graham a shred of hope. Whatever that plan turned out to be, she believed in it, that was for sure. She started toward the carriage. "Get in and drive away from the river. Sugar, come!"

Graham obeyed, but the dog didn't. She headed toward the river instead. He'd never seen a dog with more of its master's personality than Sugar had of Ellie's. Stubborn, bound to go her own way, heedless of the words of others…and sweet. Heartbreakingly sweet.

Twenty minutes later, they left the edge of the field and drove into the woods. After another five, they stopped on the rutted dirt path and faced a barn of some sort, amid waist-high weeds and brambles. Its ridge sagged and its paint peeled, its huge doors closed tight.

"This rickety old barn is your secret weapon?" Graham tried and failed to keep the sarcasm out of his voice.

"You'll see." Ellie opened her door and descended the carriage steps before he could get there to assist her. She plowed through the weeds ahead of him.

"Ellie, wait. Let me go first."

She paid him no mind. Rather, she fought the foliage until she reached the barn, then shoved the wooden door on its track. It budged about ten inches.

Graham wrangled ahead of her. "Let me do that." His voice sounded like a growl, and he softened it as he tried to grab the handle. "Step to one side so you don't get hurt."

"How do you think I did this before you got home?" She gave his arm a little push. Then she put her weight into it and got the door open wide enough for them to walk through.

Stubborn woman. "Are you going to let me go in first to make sure it's safe, or can you do that too?"

"I can do it." She marched into the barn and crooked her finger for him to follow.

This was what he'd been reduced to—following a woman's orders. He stepped inside as she'd commanded.

The sunlight gleamed against what must have been fifty or more giant rectangles tied in jute. Cotton bales.

Graham took a step back. Dust motes floated in the sunshine, with little specks of cotton fluff in the stifling air.

"This has to be at least five thousand dollars' worth of cotton."

"If I sold it today, it would be worth seventy-five hundred dollars. If I sell through the Texas border to Mexico."

He moved closer to the first bale and then rubbed his fingers over the soft cotton. "I admit it—this is an effective secret weapon."

"I have four more loads like this scattered about."

"Five barns full of cotton?" He'd sure been wrong about this scheme of hers. "That's enough to pay your loan."

"And to pay the laborers. Of course, it leaves us almost nothing to live on until harvest."

Graham pinched a bit of cotton from the nearest bale and pulled apart the fibers. He tossed it in the air and blew on it. The fluff drifted to the rafters. "I can't believe you have this. Why didn't you sell it last fall?"

"I sold three quarters of the cotton and held on to the rest, because I thought the prices would rise about now. And they did."

"But your uncle was still able to work last fall. Why didn't he make that judgment call?"

"Because that's my job. I watch the cotton futures and trends and decide when we sell and to whom. Several years ago, Uncle Amos recognized that I have a bit of talent in that area, so he let me make those decisions."

She paused, glancing at the cotton bales. "Of course, I have to make all the decisions now."

And she shouldn't have to, at least not alone.

"I have a lot to do these days. I'm going to hire field help and contract men to work on the cabins. I also have to check the fields every day so I'll know when to start harvesting. Lilah May needs my help at home because that big house, plus Uncle Amos, are too much for her to take care of alone. And Miss Noreen needs me to help with the baby. So I have a business offer to make you."

"I'm afraid to hear it, but ask anyway."

"I want you to be my broker. I'll teach you what I know about price trends and markets, but I'd like you to negotiate and decide who we'll sell to—take care of all the details."

Graham—a cotton broker? He had to admit the idea intrigued him.

"You've always been interested in planting, and you have a mind for numbers. I can't help thinking how much more profit we'd make with you as our broker—someone with a personal interest in this farm."

He lifted his gaze from the cotton bales and took in the beseeching look in her eyes. She was right—he had an interest here. And he used to love working with Father on their two plantations. If he hadn't gone to West Point, he'd have taken over operations on his own ground, Ashland Place, and eventually Ammadelle, his father's property, too.

"I'll spend some time praying about it."

Her blue eyes glowed. "Don't wait long to decide. Prices are high now, and I want to get this cotton on a boat as soon as I can."

They exited the barn and Graham pulled shut the door as Sugar bounded up to them. Then she suddenly stopped at the door and growled at who-knew-what. Graham glanced around and saw nothing. The dog probably smelled a tortoise.

Ellie had been right about one thing—this hoarded cotton would pay for the labor, even enough to get the new crop in. Graham wasn't sure he would have been smart enough to have saved this much of the crop last year. But as sure as he was about this good move of hers, he was equally certain of another fact—that Leonard Fitzwald was not going to sit idly by and watch him ship Ellie's cotton down the river. If he sensed God leading him to take this job, part of his work would be to anticipate the weasel's next move.

Chapter Twelve

The river at sunset, a string quartet playing, a nice breeze—the perfect setting to court a pretty woman. As Graham and Ellie approached the gathering at Joseph's palatial home that evening, Graham glanced around at the other picnickers, especially noting the courting couples. This time, he'd get it right. He'd not give Ellie reason to laugh at his attempts again.

"I can't remember the last time we had a picnic at the river bluff." Her honey-colored hair glowed in the waning light—at least the part that wasn't covered by her little white bonnet.

He did remember. She'd worn a soft yellow dress that made her skin look creamy and her eyes sparkly. "It was the first weekend in September. Aunt Ophelia made me set up all those tables in that same spot under the oak."

Holding his arm, Ellie turned to look toward the tables. Graham dodged her white parasol to keep it from knocking into the brim of his hat. In so doing, he felt his elbow connect with someone's ribs.

Susanna Martin. With Leonard Fitzwald at her side.

Of all the people to jab. "Susanna, forgive me. Are you hurt?"

"Oh, I don't know…" Her syrupy voice sounded like that of a melodramatic actress.

"Colonel, you need to watch what you're doing." Fitzwald's scowl, along with the eye patch, made him look like a villain.

"I'd advise you to let this drop." Graham kept his voice as low and calm as he could.

"You're in no position to advise me about anything." Fitzwald stepped closer, edging nearer to Ellie.

As Graham stepped up to put a quick end to it, Ellie laid her hand on his arm, stopping him. "Leonard, we all know you're upset with me, not Graham, because I won't agree to your terms about the loan. This has nothing to do with that, so let's forget about it. An elbow in the side certainly didn't hurt Susanna."

Graham kept his gaze solidly on the weasel, although he would have liked to have seen Susanna's expression. Ellie shouldn't defend him—it was *his* job to take care of *her*. "Just move along, Fitzwald. Ellie, let's get something to drink."

He drew her closer to his side as they left those two behind. It was just like Fitzwald to ruin the evening for them. The evening he'd intended to show Ellie that he wasn't a complete chowderhead when it came to courting.

Well, he was a complete chowderhead about that, but tonight he wanted to rid himself of that description in her mind. "That man is determined to make us miserable."

"He tried, but he couldn't do it." She hugged his arm and turned her face upward, giving him that sweet smile of hers.

The combination nearly knocked the ground out from under him.

Oh, Ellie. She had no idea what she still did to him. No matter how he fought it.

She shifted her gaze to the table. "Since it's early, the punch might still be cold."

"Chatham Artillery punch as usual?" he asked as he tried to regain his composure.

"Yes, without the alcohol, of course. Which means it's mostly tea, orange and lime juices, sugar, and lots of citrus fruit and cherries."

Graham poured two glasses of punch. "I need to find a place where I won't have to look at Fitzwald's sorry mug for a few minutes." And a place where he could get all those emotions under control.

"The swing?"

"It must have rotted away by now." But he headed in that direction anyway.

"I was here last fall, and someone had painted it and repaired one of the arms."

If he remembered right, the swing was just upriver, hanging from a live oak branch. A short walk would do him good.

Strolling along the edge of the river bluff and upriver, they soon approached the swing. Sure enough, it was painted and looked big enough to hold both of them, plus Ellie's skirts. The tree was as he remembered, its Spanish moss swaying in the breeze and its branches stretched low to the ground.

Ellie settled onto the swing and arranged her skirts as he eased down beside her. She still held that renegade parasol over them, blocking both the sun's rays and his view of the party downriver. He leaned forward and gazed around it. From this distance, he could barely see the people, let alone tell which one was Fitzwald. He handed a glass of punch to Ellie and took a drink of his own. It tasted just as it had eight years ago at this spot. Well, not right at this spot. He hadn't been able to talk Ellie into sitting on the swing with him that night.

In the quiet of the river, the violin music carried along the water and played softly for them, flavoring the air with its high, poignant notes. "This is better."

"I'd rather have a restful evening on a swing than a boisterous one at a party." Ellie sipped her drink and then faced him. "It's a picnic. You didn't get anything to eat."

"I'm fine. Are you hungry?"

"No." She sat with her back straight and her skirts gracefully arranged around her like the belle she was. Just as a Southern gentleman didn't offend a lady, a Southern lady didn't sit like a man—or act like a man. Unless she was driving her carriage to the plantation she managed. Or checking the cotton fields. Or making plans to keep that plantation running…

Or providing work for her old childhood friend in a way that let him still feel like a man.

Graham chugged the rest of his drink. The wind shifted then and carried with it the sweet scent of her perfume, as well as an even sweeter strain of a song he didn't recognize.

Ellie continued to sip her punch, watching the river, then watching him. The breeze tickled his neck, and the cicadas sang their own melody as he caught his reflection in her blue, blue eyes. Eyes that saw straight through to his heart, and always had.

Something about the peaceful look on Ellie's face drew him as never before. She had to be terrified about the future—Graham sure was, and he had less to lose than she did. Her poise was as natural as a society princess's, and she had the beauty of a pampered heiress, but she chose to be neither. And at this moment, he'd give what little he had left in this world if he could take more of the burden from her.

He took her glass and set it with his at their feet. The violins hushed for an instant, then played the opening strains of "Aura Lea."

The song he and Ellie had danced to the first night he was home... The song of the maid with golden hair...

Not giving himself time to think, he cupped his hand behind her neck and let his gaze drift to her lips.

"Ellie..." He gently pulled her toward him and kissed her.

She tasted of cherries and sunshine, warmth and lemon. And when she slipped her arm around his waist and kissed him back, a portion of the stoniness of the years washed out of his heart. His finger traced her jaw, the smoothness of her cheek.

Ellie. Sweet, smart, generous Ellie, the girl he'd loved so long ago. The one face he always saw when he awoke in the night—the girl of his dreams and the woman of his future—

The future.

No. He pulled away. There was no future. He had no future. *No, no, no.*

Graham opened his eyes to see the shock on her face. He cradled her cheek in his hand. "Ellie, forgive me. I shouldn't have done that. I made you a promise."

"Graham—"

"I'm a bum. I'm worse than Fitzwald." He turned from her, suddenly unable to look into those big eyes that held—confusion. Not affection, not even surprise. Confusion. He heaved a sigh that came from his gut. "At least he's offering to marry you."

Standing, he kicked their empty glasses to one side. He turned his back to her, faced the river. The swishing of her skirts told him she had stood too. Then he felt her take his hand.

Ellie heaved a huge breath. "Graham. It's all right. We'll pretend it didn't happen. Just don't think about it."

Don't think about it. Like he hadn't thought about it at West Point, through the whole blamed war and every waking moment since he came back to Natchez? He'd dreamed of kissing her, longed to hold her, wanted to touch her face for eight years.

Don't think about it. He'd never kissed her. And now he had, and she wanted him not to think about it.

Why had he done it? He always said Ellie needed to start thinking things through before she acted. Well, she surely had the right to hang that over his head now. He'd kept his sanity through thirty-one battles during the war. Never lost control. But give him one golden-haired, blue-eyed beauty who was smarter than him and more courageous than him and he was a goner.

He turned to her, beside him, those big eyes of hers looking right through to his heart. "I'll leave town. I'll find somewhere to go, and I'll leave tonight."

"Who will provide for Betsy if you do? Your whole family needs you."

Why did she have to be right? "We'll sell the house. We'll move to the other side of—"

"Graham." Her voice was firm but soft. "You're talking foolishness. I know you can't marry me. You know I won't ever marry. We still have our promise, and we'll just call this a slipup. A mistake."

Did he imagine it, or were her eyes showing him that she felt as he did—that it was not a mistake? Had she enjoyed their kiss as much as he had?

"I didn't think I'd ever know what it was like to kiss a man. It was nice." Her eyes twinkled in the last rays of the sun. "It was—really nice."

She had never kissed a man? He'd look even more the fool to her now if he told her how many women he'd kissed—zero—since that fateful evening when he asked her to be his wife. She probably wouldn't believe this was his first kiss too.

"If what you're saying is true, Ellie, neither of us will ever forget this day."

The sad thing was, he knew he was right.

If only Ellie could get home and be alone with her thoughts. Thoughts of that kiss.

Leaving Joseph's party with Graham, she fought through a bone-weariness she hadn't experienced since the early days of Uncle Amos's stroke of apoplexy.

"Ellie, is that you?"

Leonard. At the sound of his raspy voice, she clutched her reticule tighter.

Graham drew her closer and turned toward the unwelcome sound. "What do you want, Fitzwald?"

"I couldn't let you leave the party before I had a chance to speak with you." His Confederate uniform clean and starched stiff, Leonard hastened toward them with Susanna Martin on his arm as if they were a courting couple.

What were they doing together? Had Susanna stopped pursuing Graham? And, more important, had Leonard given up his interest in Ellie?

"I told you to call her Miss Anderson." Graham gave him a look as hard as his voice.

"I only want to let Ellie know that my offer still stands. I assume you'll visit our attorney tomorrow to get the details about my proposed agreement. At least, that's what I would do in your position. When you're finished at his office, I'm confident that you'll want to visit mine." Leonard ran his finger along the scar on his cheekbone. "In fact, you might want to speak with me after you get back to the colonel's house tonight."

"I haven't changed my mind about your offer, Leonard." Ellie worked to keep her voice steady. Something about his words sounded ominous, dark. But she didn't want him to know how much he was scaring her.

"You will."

His tone now frightened her more than his words. She instinctively backed away from him.

"Fitzwald, stay away from Ellie." Graham pulled her closer, his eyes seething with his anger, every inch of him a warrior, every breath a threat.

"Colonel Talbot, must you speak so harshly to Captain Fitzwald?" Susanna batted her long lashes at Leonard. "He's a Confederate veteran and one of our city's wealthiest men."

"If he's got so much money, why doesn't he buy a suit? It's time to stop impersonating a soldier, Fitzwald."

"I'll have a lot more money two weeks from now." Leonard's smirk revealed the guile in his heart. "Yes, I'll soon be a richer man, one way or the other. I'm getting a real gem."

"The only thing you're going to get is a black eye. Ellie, let's go, before I'm obligated to give it to him."

They started down the sidewalk at a pace so fast, Ellie was hard-pressed to keep up. However, the faster they could get away from Leonard, the better. "We should have taken the landau instead of walking tonight."

"The last thing I need now is for that weasel to goad me about driving your carriage."

"Leonard knew we were going to see Joseph tomorrow."

"He merely guessed."

"No, I think he knew how confused I would be about that railroad. That's what this whole mess is about, I'm sure of it."

"It seems that way." Graham glanced behind them, no doubt to make sure Leonard didn't follow them. "If he's so set on marrying you, why would he court with Susanna? And why would she have anything to do with him? He's a coward, he's mean and he's not the best-looking man in town either."

"He's rich, that's why. Susanna is after a man, but if the handsome, poor man won't have her, she'll take the ugly, rich one."

Having left Leonard far behind, Ellie pressed Graham's arm to slow his stride. "I can't keep up with you."

Graham eased off into a stroll, giving Ellie a chance to catch her breath. When they reached a shady spot under a magnolia, he stopped and faced her. They probably looked like any ordinary courting couple. Except for the fact that Graham looked extraordinary in his uniform. No wonder Susanna had her heart set on him.

"I hope he didn't upset you too much," he said. "Are you all right?"

Ellie held fast to his arm, looking up into his eyes, and the tenderness there took her breath. How quickly he'd changed from fierce to gentle. If only things had been different, if she were different, she could let herself get lost in that gaze—

"Ellie!"

The high-pitched voice came from behind her, and Ellie jerked her hand from Graham's arm. She turned toward the sound and saw her old friend Lydia Sutton running up the street, her faded skirts twirling with each step.

"Lydia, what on earth…?"

Reaching Ellie, the woman clasped her reddened, work-roughened hands together, tears in her eyes. "Little Annie is sick with croup. Could you spare us some cherry pectoral? I can't get Doctor Pritchert because we already owe him so much money after Myron's war injury. His leg, you know."

"Of course." She took Lydia's hand and started home at a good clip. "This is Colonel Talbot. He went to West Point before you moved to town and then, of course, the war. Graham, this is Lydia Sutton. When we were girls, she and her family lived on the edge of the Pearl Street neighborhood."

Lydia heaved a huge sigh. "That was before things got bad in Natchez. We lost our house, and now Myron and I live along the river with our baby, Annie. And I'm acquainted with your stepmother, Colonel. Please give her my greetings."

"I'll do it as soon as I see her."

"How old is Annie now?" Ellie asked.

"Eight months."

"Oh, dear. That's the same age as Colonel Talbot's orphaned niece who is living with them."

"I heard she was here, and that she's your namesake, Ellie."

As they rounded the corner to Ellie's home, she realized she had given neither Lydia nor Annie much thought since they stopped attending church. From the haggard look on Lydia's face, she could use a friend.

Graham opened the door for them. Once inside, Ellie sent them to the parlor, with Sugar right behind them, while she retrieved her elixir.

Upon finding it, she hastened to the parlor. She handed the bottle to Lydia and then opened her reticule. "Take this gold dollar in case the elixir doesn't work and you need to get Doctor Pritchert."

"Ellie, I can't take your money. I had to swallow my pride and nearly choked on it just to beg medicine from you." The tears welled up in her eyes again. "And I wouldn't have asked for that if I hadn't needed it for my baby."

She pressed the money into Lydia's hand. "You'll take this for your baby too. I feel partly at fault for your predicament. I should have called on you when you stopped coming to church. I wasn't a good friend to you, and I hope you'll accept both the money and my apology."

Lydia's tears spilled over, and she pressed a kiss against Ellie's cheek.

"I'll help Roman hitch Lucy and Buttercup to the carriage so she doesn't have to walk home." With Lydia's face turned to the medicine bottle, Graham smiled and winked at Ellie.

The gesture made her heart flip and her mind turn back to their kiss. Her face warming, she pressed her hand to her chest. Well. He certainly must have approved of her giving away the dollar. "Good idea. Lydia lives a mile out, and she needs to get this medicine to the baby."

"Thank you. Mother is home with her, so I should get back. Myron heard of a man who's hiring, and he's at his house now to try for the job. On Sunday. I never thought it would come to this."

"Things are hard all over Natchez—for everybody." Then she thought of Leonard. Things were hard for… almost everybody.

"I never thought I'd have to beg. We weren't wealthy, not like your family or Colonel Talbot's, but we had a nice small home and decent clothes. Until tonight, I haven't been ashamed of our situation because I know it's not Myron's fault. I certainly never expected this." Lydia wiped her eyes on a tattered handkerchief. "Myron even asked for work with the Freedmen's Bureau."

Ellie sucked in her breath. Every Southerner hated that newly formed Yankee agency, established to rebuild the South after the war. Myron must have felt desperate if he'd taken such measures. "But he didn't get work with the Bureau?"

"No, not even after he spent an hour waiting for the Bureau agent in the parlor of that seedy old Mason's Boardinghouse. I declare, as soon as he got home, I made him change clothes out on the back gallery so I could boil the lice out of them." Lydia shuddered as if those lice were crawling on her skirt. "That Leonard Fitzwald got the job instead of Myron. I think he's selfish to take it when my husband needs the work so badly. Mister Fitzwald has enough money to keep him in tall cotton for the rest of his life."

That much was true. And Leonard never was known for generosity.

"We've all suffered from this war. I don't understand why God saw fit to allow us to keep our home this long, but I'm grateful for it. I don't take it for granted as I used to." She looked around the room, its familiar furnishings and pretty décor. "And there's no guarantee that we'll be able to keep it."

"I used to think that because we were Christians, the war wouldn't touch us. Then when we lost our house, I got angry and blamed God." Lydia turned toward the window as if ashamed to face Ellie with her truth. "I even refused to go to church. Myron wanted to go, but I wouldn't, so he stayed home too. Now I wish I could go back, but I'm afraid people won't want us."

Ellie clasped Lydia's hand. "I'm confident they will want you. But I think you fear God's rejection, not people's."

"That too," she said in a squeaky voice.

"The father was glad to see the prodigal son when he came home."

Lydia's tears started raining down her face. It was as if Ellie could see the woman's despair leaking from her eyes. "Do you think He would be glad to see me too?"

"I do."

She squeezed Ellie's hand. "Then we'll come. I've wanted to for so long."

A half hour later, having driven Lydia home and seen her safely in the house, Graham and Ellie headed for home. "I was proud of you tonight," he said.

"Proud of me?"

"You told me that you had enough money in the sideboard safe to pay your workers this week, plus a dollar for food. And I saw you give away that dollar tonight."

She felt her face flaming. "Thank you, but it wasn't that much."

"But it was. The widow gave her mite, and you gave your gold dollar. It was all you had."

"I have more than Lydia does. And we'll get by just fine. I still have some canned beef and some rice, and Roman has been picking green beans and digging some new potatoes. He fishes and catches crawfish for us too. We won't go hungry."

He smiled at her in the moonlight as they pulled into her drive. "Come over and I'll cook you some camp rations if you do."

She smiled back. "I will." Then she sat forward. "You made a little joke!"

"Some people think I'm gloomy all the time. I wanted to show them that I'm not."

"You're making progress." While she appreciated his lightness, she still fought the emotion that blocked her throat. "Lydia wants to come back to church when the baby gets better."

"Your gift opened that door." He helped Ellie out, his touch tender and his voice low, and he let his hands linger on her waist, drawing an extra beat from her heart—

The sound of sobbing, followed by Betsy's crying, tore through the open gallery windows. "That's not Miss Noreen. Who is it?" Ellie said.

Graham didn't answer. He bolted through the yard and into the house. When Ellie got there, she started for the parlor, where the crying seemed to come from.

She heard Graham's voice before she saw him. "Aunt Ophelia, what's wrong?"

Ellie entered the parlor, her heart heavy for the poor dear. For all her eccentricity, the older woman loved her only brother. Seeing him in this condition must have torn her heart out.

But Mister Talbot wasn't in the room.

Betsy sat crying on her blanket while Miss Noreen tried to comfort Miss Ophelia on the couch. Graham sat on his aunt's other side, so Ellie picked up the baby and paced the floor with her as she'd seen Miss Noreen do.

"What is it? What happened?" Although he'd been fierce as a warrior earlier this evening, Graham now held his elderly relative's hand and spoke as softly as a mother with her newborn.

"They can't do this." She laid her head on Graham's shoulder. "My late husband, Willis, was an Adams—the most prestigious family in Natchez. They even named this county after the Adamses. They can't take it away from me."

"What are they taking?" Graham asked. "Who's taking it?"

Miss Ophelia let out a heart-rending wail.

"It's Cedar Hills," Miss Noreen said in her quiet, soothing voice. "She was getting ready for evening services when she got word that it's been confiscated for back taxes. They're also taking her town house."

On a Sunday? Even the Yankees wouldn't be that cruel—or would they? "Who brought you the notice? Was it one of those Freedmen's Bureau men?"

"I could bear it easier from a stranger."

"Who was it?" Graham asked.

Miss Ophelia sat up straight and wiped her eyes. "It was one of our own. Leonard Fitzwald."

Graham looked as disgusted as Ellie felt. "I'd hardly call that weasel one of our own. What did he do—join the Freedmen's Bureau so he could serve confiscation notices? And still wearing a Confederate uniform?"

"He may look a little bit like a weasel, but his mother was from an old Natchez family, and Leonard was devoted to her. And his father helped us all establish our fortunes—" Miss Ophelia burst into tears again. "But mine is all gone now."

Betsy jabbered and flailed her arms, and Ellie realized she had been so engrossed in Miss Ophelia's problem that she hadn't noticed the baby had stopped crying. At least that was something to be thankful for. "What did Leonard tell you?"

"The federal government has taken all my land and my town home because I didn't pay the taxes. But how were we to pay taxes when we had no crops?"

That was the dilemma for every planter in the Natchez area—for all of Mississippi.

"How soon must you leave your home?" Graham asked softly.

She bent over and crossed her arms over her stomach as if she was in pain. "I have a week, but I wish I never had to go back. I wish I could remember it as it was before the war, back when we were happy."

"Graham…" Miss Noreen whispered the name, and when she had his attention, she gestured around the room, her brows lifted in question.

Of a sudden, Ellie understood Miss Noreen was asking Graham's permission to let her move here. Taking her in was the right thing to do—that was what you did for family—but another mouth to feed was the last thing Graham needed.

He nodded but held up one finger as if wanting to wait with that. "Do you have a plan?"

Miss Ophelia lifted her head. "I had one once. I'd planned to have lots of children to take care of me in my old age. But that didn't work out."

It didn't work out. Just as, according to Graham, none of Ellie's plans ever quite worked out. She pulled Betsy closer, hoping the child's body heat would drive away the sudden chill in her middle. But it didn't.

"Then you'll move in with us," Graham said, patting her ample arm. "We have plenty of room, and it might be good for Father too."

Miss Ophelia let out a halting sigh. "Graham, do you mean it? I wouldn't be too much trouble?" she said in a little-girl voice. "Leaving my home is the worst tragedy I can imagine. But I don't know where else I could go. And to live here with you, my family, in a gracious home like mine—it's more than I could have asked."

"You could help me take care of Betsy," Miss Noreen said.

Her eyes lit like the sunset over the Mississippi. "I could—yes, I could help." She reached out her plump hands. "Ellie, dear, do let me hold her now."

Ellie carried the baby to her, and the older woman snuggled her to her chest. "May I stay tonight, Noreen?"

"Of course. We'll send for your personal things tomorrow, and Graham and I will make a room comfortable for you tonight."

"And my horse, Handsome Boy, and my runabout. Bless you, Noreen. I always did say you were my favorite of all the in-laws." She looked around the parlor, floor to ceiling and wall to wall. "I've had tea here a hundred times since you married James, but I never dreamed this would be my home."

"I'll be glad for your company." Miss Noreen's tone said she meant it.

"I'm thankful you were able to keep this house. It's so elegant and beautiful, and I would have hated to see it leave your family." Miss Ophelia dabbed at her cheeks as if leftover tears still lingered there. "Ellie, I never did figure out how you managed to get Magnolia Grove planted. You were wise to find a way to keep planting."

"Thank you, ma'am." The fear of experiencing this moment for herself—losing her home as Miss Ophelia was—had driven her. But of course Miss Ophelia wouldn't dream of that. Then again, Miss Ophelia knew little beyond entertaining and Natchez society life. That blessed woman never had to. How would she get by if not for family? The fact that she and her husband were of the finest families in Adams County certainly hadn't spared her. All the money and prestige they once had, all their social and business connections, all their earthly assets, could not prevent Miss Ophelia from falling into poverty, relying on her relatives for food and shelter.

And if this calamity could happen to Miss Ophelia, it could happen to Ellie.

The knowledge stuck in her throat and lodged there as if she'd swallowed a bone.

The difference was that Ellie had no relatives to run to. In fact, she had her uncle who depended on her to provide for him now.

Suddenly, her previous chill gave way to a cold sweat that started at her hairline and moved down to her neck, her spine, until she couldn't tell if she was too hot or too cold. Just as it had when Leonard came to gloat about the loan. To coerce her into marriage.

Still standing next to Miss Ophelia, Ellie now made for the door. "Excuse me a moment."

She rushed through the center hall to the front entry and gallery. About to collapse in a rocker, she remembered it was Sunday night. All of Natchez seemed to be still out, promenading on the sidewalks of Pearl Street, stopping to visit on porches or lawns.

The last thing Ellie needed now was for one of them to stop her for a chat. She hastened to Graham's backyard, where she could hide among the myrtles.

Once in the garden, she collapsed on the grass, next to the smooth marble statue of Rachel at the well. As a child, she used to pick the flowering myrtles and place one in Rachel's hand every morning. Now she plucked a sprig and fastened it between Rachel's fingers.

Rachel still had a home, at least until the next time taxes came due. But Ellie was fooling herself to think she and her uncle were safe.

If only she could sit here in the quiet of the evening and think of the sweet things of life, mainly Graham's kiss and the promise it held. Could she ever again think of it without remembering how safe she'd felt, how cherished? But now, despite those moments, the whole world seemed to root against her. She could talk all she wanted of picking cotton, of offering daily wages, of rebuilding the cabins for more workers, even of selling her hoarded cotton—but it was all talk. Mere talk. She had two weeks to pay her debt. She had twenty workers already dependent on her, not to mention Uncle Amos, Lilah May and Roman.

Two weeks to save her uncle's plantation—her grandfather's plantation before him. Ellie's plantation after him.

If Miss Ophelia could lose her property, it could happen to Ellie too. Because like Miss Ophelia's, Ellie's plans never quite worked out.

Her fear of returning to the poverty of her childhood had driven her to defy society and learn how to become a planter. And that fear had served her well, had worked for her as she made the hard decisions since Uncle's illness. So why not now?

She had two weeks to pay her loan and harvest the crop—all while keeping both her outward promise and her inward vow to Graham. She had to do it in two weeks. If she didn't, she'd fail her family—her only living relative—in a worse way than her father had failed her.

She tucked the myrtle bud closer to Rachel.

That failure would be worse than death to her.

Chapter Thirteen

God, please stop me if I'm misunderstanding Your instructions.

The next morning, Graham stayed on his knees at his bedside even longer than he had the day before. Somehow, being the man of the house that sheltered an elderly stepmother, a man living in the past, a baby and a widowed aunt weighed heavier on him than his command of thousands of troops ever had.

Not to mention Ellie.

Last night had proved beyond doubt that he still had feelings for the one woman who would never become his wife. And he could do nothing about it. With that kiss, what little peace he'd had about this counterfeit courtship vanished like fog on the river.

Worse yet, the best he could discern, God was leading him to become Ellie's broker. And once he accepted the position, he'd have to work closely with her and spend even more time with her than before.

God, help me to keep my mind on business when I'm around her.

And off their kiss. He rubbed the ache that was starting in the back of his neck. Nothing less than divine intervention could bring that kind of focus to pass.

In order to shield his heart and do Ellie's business, these thoughts of romance needed to go. Yes, he'd keep his thoughts where they needed to be, concentrate on the cotton brokerage instead. If his arrangement with Ellie worked out and he thought he had some aptitude for brokering cotton, he'd offer his services to other area planters who wanted to get their ground productive again. These were new days and hard times, and old methods wouldn't work anymore. Planting—and selling—cotton would have a different face today. Graham would need Ellie's creativity and ideas in order to pull a profit from the old dirt of Natchez.

He glanced at the clock on his lowboy. Ten of seven. He needed to get up and get downstairs if he didn't want to hear that offensive bell this morning.

Aunt Ophelia picked up that bell just as Graham bounded down the last step. "No need, Auntie. I'm up."

"You're up, dressed and perky." She looked rather perky herself in her bright blue dress that pulled the blue out of her hazel eyes. "What plans do you have today?"

"Big ones." Graham crooked his arm at her, and she took it, letting him escort her. He turned left to head to the library.

"Not in there." She tugged him in the opposite direction, toward the back of the house. "I have reinstituted the tradition of high breakfast in the dining room."

"High breakfast?"

"That's what your dear, departed grandmother used to call it. She knew how to set a breakfast table. All of Natchez envied her."

Graham didn't know about that, but Aunt Ophelia certainly seemed to have made a place for herself in the household already. And that was probably a good thing. He could understand Noreen eating in the library when she lived here alone, but now they had four adults and a baby in the house. The dining room seemed a better option. And the aromas coming from that direction told him they had a feast waiting.

They entered the room where Father and Noreen sat, not at their usual places at the head and foot of the table, but across from each other at one end. Betsy sat on Noreen's lap, babbling and grabbing her grandmother's silverware. The room's yellow walls and white trim made it even more cheerful than Graham remembered.

"Good idea to eat in here again."

Then his gaze landed on the mahogany sideboard— the one whose contents had saved this house. Thousands of dollars' worth of gold coin, hidden nearly in plain sight. Too bad it was empty now and couldn't buy back Ashland Place or Ammadelle.

He seated Aunt Ophelia next to Noreen and then rounded the table to sit by his father, against the west windows. "Good morning, Father."

Father turned and fastened his empty-eyed gaze on Graham. "Good morning."

It would be easy to let his father's condition drag Graham into melancholy as well. But the women at the table needed his strength, so he forced himself to smile. Perhaps they all needed to talk to Father more, encourage him to participate in the family's chatter. It was hard to make conversation with a man who often couldn't or wouldn't speak back, but Graham decided to give it more effort.

The bowl in front of his plate caught his eye: scrambled eggs with onions and peppers from their garden. He glanced around at the rest of the table and saw hotcakes and thin-sliced ham. "Father, look how good breakfast looks. Where did all this come from?"

"Ophelia made it," Noreen said, giving Betsy her spoon to play with.

Graham couldn't help laughing. "Aunt Ophelia, your cooking skills are the best-kept secret in Natchez."

"My mother believed every girl of privilege should know how to cook and keep house." She puffed herself up to her full height and girth. "One never knew, she said, when one would find oneself without domestic help. And this war has proven her right."

"But you've gone to far too much trouble for us, Ophelia," Noreen said.

She sniffed. "Yesterday, I didn't know if I would have to find a job as a cook somewhere, just to survive. I can surely cook for my family."

"Let's make her happy and let her cook, Noreen." Graham breathed deep of the good aromas. "Father, would you like to pray?"

His father bowed his head. "We give Thee thanks, Almighty God, for home and food and family. In the name of Jesus, amen."

"Meh-men!" Betsy banged the spoon on the table.

Well, it wasn't Father's usual lengthy prayer, but his tight voice hinted that he'd meant it. That was a good start.

When they'd finished, Graham helped Aunt Ophelia carry the dirty dishes to the kitchen dependency. She stacked the plates and then turned to him, a motherly concern in her eye.

"Susanna Martin came to my home yesterday afternoon." Her expression suddenly clouded. "She was the last caller I'll ever receive in that house."

"I'm sorry." Sorry for her grief over her home, and sorry that he even had to talk about Susanna.

"She gave me some distressing news. It seems she saw you and Ellie riding out of town together yesterday."

That prying little husband-hunting snoop. "We drove out to Magnolia Grove, yes."

Aunt Ophelia took one of his hands, and hers felt soft as cotton. If she kept cooking and doing dishes, they wouldn't be that way for long. "Don't you see, dear, that such behavior compromises Ellie's reputation? I know you were childhood friends, but you're not children anymore."

"But our trip was for business."

"Doesn't matter. Now that you're courting, you must protect her virtue. At all cost."

Of course she was right. "But I've decided to become her broker. How will I advise her about her crops if we don't go to Magnolia Grove together?"

"I have the solution."

Ten minutes later, Graham dashed to his room and scribbled a quick note to Ellie.

Are you game for a visit? You're not the only one with crazy ideas. Now Aunt Ophelia has one for us.
Graham

He crammed the scrap of paper into the broken fountain pen barrel still outside his window. Then he tied it to the twine, pulled on the rope and sent the missile flying toward Ellie's window. With a satisfying clink, it hit the glass.

Within seconds, she reached through the open window, grabbed the barrel and gave him a quick wave. A few minutes later, her answer came sailing back.

Come in the back door and up to Uncle Amos's room. Don't be late! I'm meeting with Joseph this morning. Come with me if you like.
Sis

Well, it had been a fine morning until he read her signature. It was time to put a stop to this. He grabbed his pen.

If I'm courting you, then you're not my sis. I don't want to see that again.

He sent this note zooming over their yards with much more force than necessary. Her reply took only seconds.

Very well. Signed, your loving, faithful, devoted intended. Like that better?

He would have eight years ago. As it was, the mockery cut into his heart more than "Sis" had.

Go back to Sis. Or Boss, since I'm going to be your new broker.

This time, when the barrel hit her window, it sounded hollow. He stormed out and down the hall. He'd gotten what he deserved, sending messages to her house over a pulley as if they were still children. Why did she make him act so childish?

Or was it childish? Perhaps it was merely lightheartedness, as Noreen had said. How was a man to know the difference? He banged on the guest room door, which was now Aunt Ophelia's, and yelled that he was ready to take her to Ellie's.

She poked her head out the door, her eyes wide. "What's your hurry? Why are you shouting in the house? And what was that thunking sound I heard coming from your room?"

What was wrong with him? He'd never even yelled at his soldiers on the battlefield. "I was just thinking how I was being childish, and then I confirmed the fact by hollering at you."

"So you did." She patted his cheek. "That happens sometimes when you're in love."

In love. What would she say if she knew he had just demanded that Ellie sign her notes "Sis"? "If that's what causes childishness, I must have it bad. I've not been thinking straight."

She took his arm as they started down the stairs. "I don't like to drop in on people this early in the morning, but I suppose it's excusable since we're calling on your intended."

There was that word again. *Intended.* "She knows we're coming."

Aunt Ophelia came to a full stop on the bottom step, her brow furrowed. "How could she possibly know?"

"Because…" The ridiculousness of the situation hit him like a flying ink barrel to the chest. Why had he told her Ellie knew they were coming? Now he had to explain and bear the embarrassment. "I…sent her a note, of sorts."

She nodded and stepped off the staircase. "You delivered a note saying you'd be there in five minutes. You're right, Graham. You're not thinking straight. Her maid probably won't see the note until after we have left."

"It wasn't exactly like that." He didn't want to tell her, didn't want to confess his foolishness, but her uncharacteristic silence drove him to it. "All right, I admit to our childishness. There's a pulley above each of our bedroom windows, and there's a long piece of twine attached to them. We send each other notes by this system."

Her laughter rang out into the yard as they exited the back door and he pointed out the twine stretching above their yards. "That's not childish," she said. "That's child-like. There's a difference."

"What difference? A child is a child."

"Childishness is selfishness, greed, pettiness. Child-likeness is innocence, trust and faith."

Now, that was something to think about when he was alone.

They approached Ellie's back entrance. "We're to walk in and head upstairs to Amos's room."

"Amos." His aunt spoke his name as if he were a cherished friend, which he was. "I hope he's well. I haven't seen him since his misfortune."

"But why? He and Uncle Willis were great friends."

"Yes, my Willis and Amos were the best of friends. But after Amos had this spell, he didn't want me to come." She stepped inside as Graham opened the door. "I've never understood why."

They took the wide staircase to the second floor, then Graham knocked on the open door to Amos's room.

With a flurry of pink hoopskirts, Ellie ushered them in. As he stopped to catch his breath at the sight of her the morning after their kiss, she dropped her gaze, her cheeks rosy as her dress.

Perhaps she had as much trouble not thinking about that kiss as he did.

"Ophelia." Amos sat up straighter in bed—unassisted—and smoothed down his beard. "I didn't want…"

She hesitated, and then a knowing look came over her

face. At his bedside, she reached for his hand. "I know you didn't, Amos."

Didn't what? These people had a strange way of communicating, but they seemed to understand each other.

"Graham asked to come over and meet with us," Ellie said.

"What for?" The twinge of irritation in the older man's words surprised Graham. He wasn't sure he'd ever detected that in Amos's voice before.

Ellie pulled out one of the dining chairs. "Miss Ophelia, would you please be seated here next to me?"

When they had all taken their places at the table to the side of Amos's bed, Graham addressed the older man. "With your approval, sir, Ellie and I would like to put an idea into place."

He narrowed his good eye, making himself look severe. "I already told Ellie that I don't like it."

What? He didn't want Graham to be their broker? "I don't understand. I thought you would trust me to do this."

"Why would I trust you with something that precious to me, when I know you're just going to throw it away?"

Throw it away? "I admit that men sometimes have poor judgment and make bad decisions, but I would do my best—"

"Miss Ophelia, would you please join me in the kitchen?" Ellie sprang up from her chair and grabbed the older lady's hand. "I have great need of your advice."

What now?

"Ellie, dear, can it not wait?" Aunt Ophelia tried to pull her hand away, but Ellie didn't give in.

"It is of utmost importance!"

Probably seeing that Ellie had no plan of turning loose

of her, Aunt Ophelia slowly stood. "Very well, but I don't know why it must be now—"

"This is so gracious of you. I don't know of anyone else I can ask." Ellie stood back and waited for the older woman to exit the room, and then she closed the door.

"What was that all about?" Amos asked with that slur in his voice that Graham couldn't get used to.

"Who knows, with those two?" Should he talk to Amos about becoming their broker, or should he wait until Ellie's return? And what could be so important in the kitchen that she had to drag Aunt Ophelia down there before he could accept her offer?

"I'm not worried about them. I'm worried about you and Ellie."

"Us? Why?"

"Ellie told me about your plan to pretend to court. Believe me, that's going to cause nothing but heartache."

Pretending to court... So that's what Amos objected to. "I thought you referred to the fact that I am accepting Ellie's offer to become your broker."

"She told me that she asked you, and I'm glad. But this courtship deception is more important than business. Every day, I pray that God will give you and Ellie wisdom to be good stewards of everything He has given you. Including your hearts."

More important than business? Amos must have changed in the years Graham had been gone.

Or had he? In those last months, he'd often happened upon Amos and Father on their knees together, praying for their families. And for a solution to the problem of slavery that had pricked their hearts ever since they'd heard Charles Finney preach in New York.

Besides, it was a little late for Graham to become a good steward of his own heart. Eight years too late.

Ellie had apparently taken good care of hers. But maybe Amos knew that.

"Ellie's vulnerable. She tries to act as if romance means nothing to her, although I don't know why." Amos shifted his weight on the pillows, but whether from physical or emotional discomfort, Graham couldn't tell. "She has a woman's heart. Attention from you, either true or false, could lead to…an attachment."

If he knew about Fitzwald and his schemes, he'd think differently. And if he knew how Ellie had shunned Graham years ago, he'd see how safe she was. No, the man didn't understand, although he surely meant well.

"Thank you for the insight. I'll keep it in the forefront of my mind. I promise not to let it get out of hand."

Amos lifted one brow, then shook his head. Graham couldn't blame him for his doubt, since the man didn't have all the facts.

Or did Amos have a lot more wisdom than Graham credited him with?

Of a sudden, Ellie's hasty departure made sense to him. She knew her uncle disapproved of their "courtship," and she'd seen the direction the conversation had been headed. "Amos, I believe Ellie created that diversion to ensure that my aunt wouldn't hear us discuss the nature of our courtship. We want to keep that a secret."

"And Ophelia can't keep secrets."

Graham smiled. "Exactly."

Lilah May's soprano voice wafted into the room from down the hall as she sang her favorite hymn, "Blessed Be the Tie that Binds." Within moments, she poked her head in the door. "Colonel, Miss Ellie sent me to ask if it was safe for her and your aunt to come back."

"Please tell her Amos and I have discussed our courtship."

"Mmm-hmm. I'll tell her." Lilah May's cutting tone let Graham know she was also aware of their arrangement—and disapproved.

This was getting embarrassing. He turned his gaze from her probing eyes and used his handkerchief to wipe the sweat gathering on his brow. Did the whole town need to know that his romance was false? It was bad enough to be spurned. Now he still couldn't get the girl he'd wanted, even if he tried. Even if he wanted to. And this entire household knew, probably down to Roman, the groom.

"You okay? You look a little peaked."

Graham's head shot up, and he saw Lilah May scrutinizing him as a young girl's mother would pierce the heart of her renegade suitor. What was she looking for? What did she think he was going to do to Ellie? He was only trying to protect her.

Until last night, under the magnolia where they'd stopped to rest a moment and catch their breath. Problem was, it hadn't been restful. Hadn't been restful at all.

Those big blue eyes of hers, looking up at him with trust and respect, silently thanking him for protecting her from Leonard—they had nearly done him in. If anyone thought he was going to back away from her now, they were wrong.

"Don't you break her heart." Lilah May's voice brought him back to the present and to two pairs of probing eyes.

"I'd sooner break my own neck." And he found that he meant it.

As she left the room, her sideways glance made him think she'd be glad to help him do just that if he trifled with her employer.

* * *

If Uncle Amos gave Graham the same courting talk he'd given Ellie, today might be the last day of their courtship ruse. And her disappointment at the thought surprised her more than her uncle's outburst had.

Disappointment aside, she needed Graham to keep Leonard at a distance. Last night proved that. Oh, she could deal with him herself, but how much more effective was a supposed fiancé in a Confederate officer's uniform, his sidearm at his hip? Yes, she would always keep her independence, but why not use the most effective means to achieve her goal?

Not to mention how devastatingly handsome that officer was in those cadet grays...

"You knew I needed to talk, didn't you?" Miss Ophelia, her hair even more haphazard than usual, sat at the kitchen worktable writing a receipt for her Lady Baltimore cake. "It was kind of you to get me away from the men, under the pretense of learning how I make my cakes."

No, she hadn't, but it was no surprise. Besides, Miss Ophelia's chattering usually required no answer, which gave Ellie plenty of thinking time. "It wasn't pretense. Lilah May has been pestering me for this receipt."

"We're so much alike, I'm not surprised that you knew I had troubles."

So much alike. That chill came to Ellie again, driving away the false sense of security she'd talked herself into last night so she could fall asleep. Truth was, she and Miss Ophelia were alike in many ways. Flighty at times, talking too much a lot of the time, but thinking all the time. Planning. Making a way for themselves. And praying always.

If only Ellie didn't have the paralyzing feeling that Miss Ophelia's fate would also be her own…

But in reality, she wouldn't have that fate. If she couldn't make it on her own, she had no relatives to take her in. And she had Uncle Amos to care for. So, no, Ellie would not wind up a poor relation living on the charity of her family.

She'd be married to Leonard Fitzwald.

Nothing could be worse than that.

If she were all alone, she'd find a way to support herself, even working in a store or a hotel. But she had her uncle to think of. She could never take care of him on a working girl's wage.

Ellie had to hold on to Magnolia Grove. Somehow.

She slipped her hand into her skirt pocket and touched the note Lilah May had brought her just after she and Miss Ophelia came downstairs. Joseph wanted her in his office first thing this morning—alone. With no idea what that could mean, Ellie both longed for and dreaded this meeting. Had he discovered some loophole, some restriction that could set her free from this burdensome loan? Or had something worse come upon her that she knew nothing of?

She heard Graham trot down the stairs, no doubt tired of waiting for her to come up, his familiar running-down-the-steps gait taking her back eight years. They'd spent as much time in each other's houses as they had their own, especially that last summer. And she'd noticed how things had begun to change between them, to get sweeter and softer, with innocent yet intentional touches of the hand, the face…

And she'd cut it off.

Even now she still felt the pain, the remorse of refusing him. It had been the right thing to do, but hard. So hard…

And so lonely after he left.

"All is well with Amos." Graham pulled out a chair and sat with them at the table. "He accepted me as your new broker."

Her uncle liked her idea of Graham being their broker—and he hadn't forbidden their supposed courtship?

"That's wonderful news!" Ellie sprang from her chair and flung her arms around his neck.

He tensed and then patted her back, his hand awkward. "Wonderful."

Ellie pulled back. What was she thinking? About the past, that's what. She was thinking too much about the past. She returned to her chair, her face flaming. "I'm sorry, Graham, Miss Ophelia. I forgot myself."

"Think nothing of it," Miss Ophelia said. "I'm an advocate of young love."

"But not young foolishness." Ellie cleared her throat and fanned her face.

"Speaking of love," the older woman said, "I have a solution to your courtship problem."

Ellie's gaze darted to Graham. She knew their arrangement?

"As I told Graham, Susanna Martin came to me with a story about the two of you riding out to Magnolia Grove together. It's causing quite a stir on Pearl Street."

"Susanna causes trouble everywhere she goes," Ellie said.

"True, but you must protect your reputation, especially if Graham is going to try to become a broker in this town. People must know they can trust him. My solution is to accompany you on your daily excursions."

Graham took Ellie's hand in a convincingly romantic fashion. "I'll leave the choice up to you. Having another person along will hamper your work at Magnolia Grove. If you decide to risk being the object of gossip, we will continue going alone. I'm sure I can manage to get enough work as a broker to support all of us, even if I don't get as much as I would otherwise."

"That's true, but you deserve so much more." Ellie turned to Miss Ophelia. "Thank you for wanting to help us. I gratefully accept, starting this afternoon."

"Not this morning?" Graham asked, brows raised.

She slid him the note from Joseph. "I have to meet my attorney at nine."

Ellie could tell when Graham came to the line asking her to come alone. He stiffened in his seat. "Alone? No. I'm coming anyway."

"I'll be all right. It's probably nothing." But as she said the words, she knew Joseph would not make this request without good reason.

Things were about to change. She could feel it.

Chapter Fourteen

"Ellie, I've never had to do anything like this in my life, let alone to the niece of one of my best friends." Ellie sat with Joseph in his office ten minutes later, his face drawn and rather pale for this time of year. He toyed with the stack of papers in front of him, his gaze downward. "It's bad news."

Ellie dredged up a smile she didn't feel. "I'm not sure how things could get much worse. Tell it to me all at once."

"It's not that easy." He handed her a paper. "This document shows the transfer of the Louisiana–Texas railroad from Robert Fitzwald to Edward Anderson."

She scanned the document, her eyes tearing up at the sight of her father's signature. "I own a railroad."

"Since your father's demise, technically, yes. It is in your uncle's name until such time as you marry, and all your profits go into a trust fund that you can access only after your marriage."

A railroad. A successful railroad that hadn't helped Mother while she was alive and couldn't help Ellie now. She jabbed the paper with her finger. "Then why did my mother and I have to beg for food? Why did we live in a sweltering little room above a saloon in the New Orleans French Quarter? Why did she, a Stanton, have to serve whiskey in that establishment while I spent every evening alone? What kind of a man was my father?"

Joseph heaved the sigh of an old man. "It's not as it seems. He started gambling as a lark, a young man's diversion, but he wasn't very good at it. Your grandfather paid his gambling debts for several years, but as the stakes got higher and higher, so did the losses. Finally your grandfather had to cut him off."

"Then what happened?"

"Your father was married by then, and you'd been born. He always felt he had to play one more game, try to win a huge pot, and then he'd stop. But, as you can see by this railroad deed, he never stopped. Notice the date, dear. Your father passed on just three months after he acquired the property."

She didn't want to see it, but she had to look. November 29, 1849. "You're right. We didn't see him after that. I remember because we had a long, lonely Christmas just before he died."

"Here is a copy of his obituary." Joseph handed her a newspaper clipping. "He was on his way to California to prospect for gold when he got into a gunfight and died."

Ellie closed her eyes without reading the clipping. "A fight over a card game?"

"Yes."

She should have known. She shoved the paper toward Joseph and pushed back her chair. Joseph had promised bad news, and he had kept his word. A railroad, worthless to her since she couldn't sell it, and the worst possible news about her father's death. She wasn't even sure why she needed to know that. Life would have been easier without it. "Keep it in your files, please. I don't ever want to see that piece of paper again."

Before she could stand, Joseph touched her elbow, then pushed another newspaper article toward her. "Stay seated, Ellie. You haven't heard the worst yet."

She closed her eyes and pressed her fingers against the throbbing that was starting in her temples.

"Your father won that railroad from Robert Fitzwald in a card game."

Ellie lifted her head. She'd been right. Leonard wanted that railroad back for spite.

"You said you wanted me to tell you the bad news all at once, so I'm going to do that now. The worst news is that Leonard Fitzwald has instructed me to tell you that, if you refuse his offer of marriage, he plans to make that knowledge public and claim that the game was rigged."

The cooing of a mourning dove wafted through the window, and Ellie felt like crying along with it. "Let him do it. I'm going to pay that loan and get out from under his threats. Once I'm out of his debt, he can't do anything more to me."

"That's not exactly true. First, the chances of paying the loan are as slim as they get."

But he didn't know about her secret stash of cotton.

"And if he spreads the rumors about your father, it will damage not only your reputation, but Graham's as well. I don't know his plans for the future, but both Ashland Place and his father's plantation, Ammadelle, are gone. He needs a livelihood, and he needs a good reputation if he's going to continue to live and to work in Natchez."

It couldn't be. "He's going to be a cotton broker." Her voice sounded small, even to her ears.

"Not in Natchez. Not if this happens," he said more

forcefully. "That is why I asked you to come alone. You need to evaluate your courtship with him and determine whether it will stand this test before he finds out about it."

Joseph had no idea how unnecessary that was. But Miss Ophelia had said something to the same effect about gossip. Except that she had referenced something much more benign than this. "Leonard served a confiscation notice to Miss Ophelia."

"I know." Joseph scowled as she'd never seen before. "He pulled some of his late father's strings in Washington and got a Freedmen's Bureau appointment. There's no limit to his malice."

A sinking feeling came to Ellie's middle. "What should I do, Joseph?"

"Find a way to pay that loan, although I don't know anybody in Natchez with the money to help you out, other than Fitzwald. I'd pay it for you myself if I could. Then marry Graham as fast as you can arrange it."

"Joseph, no..."

"Don't argue. You know how Natchez is. Rumors such as this carry twice the weight if their subject is unmarried. Four times the weight if both parties are unmarried. A quick wedding and the protection of Graham's name are your best defenses."

Marry Graham. No, she was going to deal with this on her own. Her father may have been a gambler, and her mother may have had to beg for their food, but Ellie was going to take care of herself and prosper in the process.

"I'll be back here in two weeks, Joseph." She stood, and her attorney followed suit. By no means would she let Graham or anybody know that her father was a gambler and a cheat. She'd close Leonard's mouth by giving him the money. If she could, she'd give him the railroad too. "The next time I come into this office, I am going to hand you thirty thousand dollars to give to Leonard Fitzwald, and then I'm going to Magnolia Grove to throw the biggest party Natchez has seen, before or since the war."

"As your mother used to say, you can do anything you set your mind to," he said in his fatherly tone. "I advise you to go home and plan what you're going to wear."

That had to have been the longest hour of Graham's life.

As the landau pulled up to the carriage house, Graham sprinted out the door toward it. Honoring both Joseph's and Ellie's wishes and staying home this morning had been almost more than he could take. Now he couldn't wait another minute to find out what the attorney said and why Graham wasn't welcome for the saying of it. Whatever it was, he had to know now, so they could plan their next step.

Ellie bounded out of the landau the moment it stopped moving. She caught sight of him and waved. "Come into the parlor. I'll change clothes and meet you there. We need to get to Magnolia Grove and see how many new workers we have."

"Aunt Ophelia will be along in a moment. If we need to discuss your meeting with Joseph in private, this is our only chance."

A cloud passed over her eyes, and she nodded. "Most of our business will be the mundane, but we can't say anything in front of her that we wouldn't say in front of the entire town—the county."

They hastened to the house and the parlor. "I do own the railroad, but my uncle has it in trust." Twisting her mother's pearl ring, she whispered so Uncle Amos wouldn't hear. "Leonard is determined to have my land and the railroad, and he'll do everything he can to get them. I have to ship the first load of cotton as soon as I can. When will you start working on selling it?"

"I'll go uptown and send some wires as soon as you give me the buyers' names and addresses."

She started for the stairs. "We'll do it this afternoon when we get back from Magnolia Grove, so we can be home in the heat of the day."

"I'll go outside and help Aunt Ophelia into the carriage when she gets here."

"You can put Sugar in too."

A half hour later, Graham stopped the carriage in front of the big house and took in the sight of about two hundred men, women and children on the lawn. "I knew you'd get a lot of workers, but I never dreamed of this."

Ellie bounded out of the carriage, again without Graham's help, and reached back in for the giant ledger she'd brought from home. As soon as he had the back door open for Aunt Ophelia, Sugar jumped out and took off after her mistress.

"Come up to the house, everyone, and we'll take care of business." Ellie and Sugar hastened to the house, the curving arch of the centuries-old oak framing its front gallery.

Graham stayed behind to help his aunt across the uneven lawn and toward the cistern house. There she said she intended to draw some cool water to serve the children in the gathering while Ellie worked. Within minutes, the crowd formed a line out the front door and across the yard.

Inside the great hall, Ellie sat at her small rococo entry table with her book and pen, Sugar lying at her feet. Ellie took down each name, explained the terms, and shook each hand.

Amazing. It wasn't enough people to pick twenty-five

hundred acres of cotton, but it would help. Because of Ellie's crazy plan.

He greeted each potential worker and introduced himself as the planter's broker and fiancé. He had to admit, it sounded good, even though it was a ruse. And even though, as a child, he'd dreamed of being the planter. Certainly never the planter's intended.

He stopped that thought cold. The dream of planting died years ago, and he had refused to let himself think about it. Too bad it had to pop up now.

By noon, Ellie had the workers catalogued and was closing her book when one more man strode through the door. His gait was the familiar limp of a man with an artificial leg, and he steadied himself with a sturdy cane. He removed his well-brushed hat and smoothed down his strawberry-blond hair. "Miss Anderson, thank you for helping my family last night. Have you need of an overseer?"

"What a pleasant surprise." She offered her hand, and he took it like a gentleman. "Colonel Graham Talbot, this is Mister Myron Sutton, Lydia's husband."

Graham shook his hand, noting a strong grip. That was a good sign. He pulled up two chairs from the row against the wall. "Please be seated. You don't seem like the kind of man to work outdoors."

"No, sir, but war changes things. I was the manager of Rosemount Plantation before the war. The owner lived near Beaufort, South Carolina, and inherited the property. I was in charge of everything—supervised the planting and harvesting, bookkeeping, upkeep, the help—every aspect of running a cotton plantation." Myron took his seat next to Graham, across the table from Ellie. "I understand you manage your own land, ma'am. But I have a wife and child to support. I know the job of the overseer, and I'm not too good to do the work."

"I already have a competent overseer." Ellie tapped her pen on the table for a moment, her gaze far-off.

Mister Sutton's jaw clenched like steel. "In that case, I'm not too good to pick cotton."

"Let me think a moment…"

As usual, Graham could tell when her idea came to her. Her eyes brightened as always, and he braced himself for the plan.

She bounded to her feet. "Mister Sutton, would you excuse Colonel Talbot and me for a minute?"

Mister Sutton hastened to rise as well, clearly surprised by Ellie's sudden movement. Graham, on the other hand, was used to it, and got up more slowly.

In her uncle's library, Ellie closed the door and pulled Graham to the other side of the room. "We would be fools to let a man with his knowledge and experience pick cotton."

It was coming. He simply had to wait and let her get to her point.

"Last night, I had another idea. Until you get more clients, you'll have a lot of time on your hands."

"True."

"So let's plant some ground for you to manage and for Mister Sutton to oversee."

He struggled and failed to keep up with her. "All of your ground is planted in cotton."

"Not my ground. Yours."

Had the strain been too much for her? "Ellie. I have no ground."

"Yes, you do. I realized it last night. I know your father's plantation has been sold, but Ashland Place, your ground, has not. It's lying fallow, overrun with weeds."

Her words came out faster, her eyes shining like the gold she seemed to think he was going to earn from ground he didn't have. "You don't understand—I can see it in your face. Think about it. That ground might sit there for a hundred years before anybody buys it. Thousands of acres all around Natchez are lying fallow because they've been confiscated but not sold. What's to keep you from farming it anyway?"

That did make a little sense, but not enough. "The cotton season's over. We could think about it next year—"

"Plant peas."

He blinked. Opened his mouth to speak, but he had no words.

Graham closed his mouth and gazed out the window at the men and women still milling around the lawn. Two hundred cotton pickers and a manager—or overseer, or whatever Sutton was. Twenty workers already here before this day. Mouths to feed at both their homes—and she wanted him to plant peas.

He turned to face her. "Honey, I think the pressure has gotten to you. Let's go on home and—"

"I am not losing my mind. I've thought this through, but I didn't know how to go about it until now." She grabbed his arm and pulled him toward the desk. There she snatched a book and opened it to a page she had marked with a slip of her plum-colored note paper. "Look at this. I've been reading about increasing cotton production. Some agriculture experts think we need to plant a different crop after the cotton harvest and then work those plants back into the soil. It's supposed to put nutrients back into the ground."

She hadn't come up with that on her own? He pulled the book closer and read the lines she indicated. Sure enough, peas were supposed to help the soil. And they would grow in the late summer and early fall, after the cotton was harvested.

He closed the book. "That's fine for next year, but we don't have the money to plant peas and then till them under at season's end."

"Of course not. We'll harvest the peas and sell them. That's what I'm going to do, and we'll plant them on your thousand acres at Ashland too. We'll hire Mister Sutton to be overseer out there. Until we plant, he can supervise the movement of cotton from the barns to the river." A smile of confidence and buoyancy broke out over her face. "You'll get a good fee for selling the cotton. Use some of it to buy pea seed. Then Mister Sutton can move to Ashland and oversee the field preparation and planting."

"I'd have to sell the peas—mine and yours. Who's going to buy thirty-five hundred acres' worth of peas?"

"You're the broker. Figure it out."

Well, if he could sell cotton, he could probably learn how to sell peas too. And it would mean Ashland would be—could be—a working plantation again. Of course, there was always the chance that someone would buy it, even right before the pea harvest.

But until and unless that happened, he would be a planter. Within a matter of days. Could he do it? "I don't know. This is moving too fast for me."

"Graham, these are times of change. Nothing will ever again be like before. We have to change too. And sometimes we have to move faster than we want to," she persisted, not knowing she'd dangled his dream before him.

He'd left that dream behind once, along with Ellie. Two dreams busted in one day was more than he could handle. And he'd run away. Like a coward. Like Leonard Fitzwald had on the battlefield.

Maybe he should have stayed and tried to find out why she'd refused him.

Maybe he should find out why she still refused him now.

That thought hit him hard in the chest.

He hadn't wanted to know before, hadn't wanted to endure the added pain of hearing what she despised about him. And that proved all the more that he was a coward.

But maybe it wasn't him. Perhaps something else was happening to her, something so painful that she couldn't tell him about it. She hadn't married in all the years he'd been gone. Why was that? And why had it never occurred to him to find out?

If he hadn't run off like a scared boy, he might have been able to help her, as a gentleman should. And if he didn't now, he wasn't a gentleman.

This idea of planting peas might be the most foolish thing he could do, but it was time to reclaim his dream of planting. And if he could do that, perhaps he could also claim his other, more important dream: Ellie's heart.

It was time to take the first step.

"Hire Mister Sutton. We are branching out into the pea business."

Chapter Fifteen

Graham never dreamed he'd share his library with a dog and a baby. Those two created a homey setting that completely took his focus off his work that afternoon, but having them there softened a bit of the hardness that had become a part of him these past years.

In a way, he needed that diversion while he used his father's library as his own for the first time. Father should be the one to work here, not Graham. But it seemed foolish to rearrange another room to accommodate him when there was every chance that Father would never work here again. As it was, his father sat alone in the myrtle garden, next to the statue of Rachel at the well. When Graham had tried to engage him in conversation that afternoon, the older man had simply muttered something about Daisy and the good dog. If only he were able to come out of this melancholy or whatever it was. Graham could sure use his help.

Betsy crawled off her blanket and chased Sugar on all fours. Her laughter brought a sort of pleasant ache to his chest. *God, thank You for letting me be the one to shelter this little girl. Please help me not to fail her.* Giving her a happy life would be worth any sacrifice he had to make.

The baby crawled toward Sugar and then sat down. The dog turned and raced to her, licked her toes and ran around the chair. Amidst Betsy's howl of laughter, Sugar skidded to a stop in front of her and licked the baby's toes again.

It looked as if the game wasn't going to end soon. Pleasant as this was, he would never get his work done at this rate. And he had to get these telegrams written so he could send them to the cotton buyers today.

Now Sugar joined in the noisemaking with a sharp bark each time she circled the chair. Maybe Ellie's idea of leaving the dog here to entertain the baby wasn't such a good one.

Graham glanced at the walnut mantle clock. Noreen and Aunt Ophelia wouldn't return from the Sutton home for another half hour. He should have known they would head over there, carrying a ham from Noreen's smokehouse and new potatoes from the garden. But he needed them here now.

He did have one other source of help...

Graham picked up the baby, who screamed her protest against having her game interrupted. Then he carried her upstairs and set her down on the floor of his room. He glanced at the pen barrel outside the window. No time to write a note. Instead, he hung his old white handkerchief, the same one he'd used the day he arrived home, on the wire "flagpole" outside his window.

If anyone at Ellie's house looked outside, he'd have help within minutes.

Just as he had Betsy downstairs and settled on her blanket again, the back door opened.

"Graham?" Ellie called. "I saw your signal."

"I'm in the library, held captive by a cute baby and a renegade dog." He could hear her tinkling laughter and her light footsteps as she crossed the center hall. He pictured every step she took. She'd been here so much, she was part of this home. It was incomplete without her.

The thought both warmed and terrified him. His pardon hadn't come, and he hadn't yet earned a dime for his family. He had to keep that in mind and not let his thoughts wander too far where Ellie was concerned.

When she stepped into the office, her honey-colored hair shining in the sun that streamed through the window, she took his breath. She'd changed from her businesslike black dress to a soft gray homey one with narrower hoops and a pretty band of lace at the hem. And when she picked up Betsy and snuggled with her, his heart nearly stopped.

"Is this sweet baby keeping you from your work?"

That baby was no longer his biggest distraction. "I'm trying to get my telegraphs written, but these two are making a commotion. A pleasant commotion, but a commotion nonetheless."

"Are the women of the house gone?"

"You know those two. As soon as I told them about Lydia, they headed over there with armloads of food."

Holding the baby with one hand, Ellie grabbed Sugar's collar with the other. "I'll take charge of these two. Do you want me to try to keep them quiet here in your house, or should I take them to mine?"

No question there. "If you don't mind, take them to the parlor. I like the sound of them playing. Just not right under my feet."

Within a half hour, he had all his telegrams written, along with one to General Lee to tell him they had found Father. Graham had been right. Having a little happy noise in the house had helped him concentrate. He gathered his notes in his portmanteau and stopped in the parlor on his way out. "Do you mind staying until Noreen gets home? If I send these telegrams now, I might get an answer by the end of the day."

"Go ahead." Ellie looked like the mistress of the mansion, sitting beside the window, the baby on her lap and her dog at her feet.

Graham expelled a forceful breath. Things were changing in his heart. Fast. They needed to talk, and soon.

Betsy was pulling at Ellie's hair now, messing up her carefully arranged knot, and the wayward strands made her look even more adorable than before.

Best he get himself out of there before he started spouting everything in his heart.

Two hours later, he left the telegraph office with his portmanteau stuffed full of documents and with Ellie's cotton sold. He breathed a silent prayer of thanks. He could now provide for his family, he'd begun an interesting new business venture and he'd even started sorting out his feelings for Ellie. How could things get any better?

Well, they'd get a lot better if Father recovered, if Leonard Fitzwald somehow fell off the planet and if the Yankee president sent Graham a pardon. But even those challenges didn't seem as bad as before.

When he stepped onto the Commerce Street sidewalk, Leonard Fitzwald stopped his surrey beside him. "Doing business, Colonel?"

"My business is none of yours, Fitzwald." Graham continued in the direction of his home.

"Tell Ellie—"

"How many times do I have to tell you to call her Miss Anderson?" He retraced his steps and stopped at the weasel's carriage. "I don't want to hear you speak her name again."

Fitzwald laughed. "Before long, I'll be her husband, and then I'll decide who calls her what."

If Graham didn't get out of here now, he'd drag the good-for-nothing out of that carriage and show him who'd do the deciding around here. He turned and started across the street.

"You and Ellie will want to attend the planters' meeting tonight at my home."

"What planters' meeting?" Something in Fitzwald's tone bothered Graham. He took one step toward the weasel.

"The Natchez Planters' Alliance. The meeting in which we will decide the wages we pay the laborers. And the one in which we'll decide the consequences for any planter who doesn't join the Alliance."

"You're not a planter. Why are you going?"

"I'm attending as a broker, since I took over my father's business."

"You don't know anything about the brokerage."

"I know this—your aunt already made the whole town aware of your plan to become a broker. If you and Ellie don't join the Alliance, you'll get no business from our planters. They're all plenty upset about Ellie's business practices."

"What business practices?"

"Several members have lost their laborers to Ellie because they can't pay the wages she's offering. The purpose of the Alliance is to keep all the wages the same. No one planter will offer more than the rest—or pay the workers before the crop comes in."

Graham tightened his grip on his portmanteau. He'd known Fitzwald would make things worse for Ellie, but he hadn't foreseen this. "Bullying is your idea of doing business?"

"It's not bullying. No one is forcing Ellie to join or to adjust her wages. We merely give planters an incentive to think of the community as a whole."

"Why don't you leave Ellie alone? She's made it clear that she doesn't want to marry you."

"Fact is, I have no plans to leave her alone." Fitzwald made a huge show of lighting a cigar he'd produced from some recess of his coat. "I'm sure you claim to love her, but so do I. Now that the war is over, I need to settle down, raise a family. I'm the right man for her."

He was delusional. The war must have addled his brains. "Why do you think that?"

"I always have, since before she moved to Natchez."

"You didn't know her then."

"But my father did." Fitzwald's eyes turned hard. "He owned that little railroad line we're disputing about now. Worked hard to build it up. But he lost it in one night."

Graham had heard stories like this before. "He gambled it away."

"Exactly. To a cheating cardsharper." Fitzwald puffed on his cigar. "His name was Edward Anderson."

Ellie's father—a cardsharper?

"I can see your surprise. She kept that little secret from you, didn't she? It's understandable that she didn't want you to know, since gambling is a rather unsavory way for a woman's father to make a living."

Ellie... His heart ached for her. What a heavy burden for her to carry. "Does she know?"

"According to Joseph Duncan, she does, and is quite distraught at the news."

So she hadn't known until now. And this weasel had made sure she found out. "She could have lived a happier life never knowing that. If you loved her as you say, you'd have found a way to keep it from her."

"Look at me!" Fitzwald shouted as he ripped the black patch from his right eye. "Can you honestly tell me I have a chance with her?"

Graham couldn't help staring at the empty socket, the long scar, the smooth spot where half his eyebrow should have been.

"No. But because of who you are, not because of what your face looks like." A little sick to his stomach at the sight, Graham finally looked away. "I'll talk to Ellie, and maybe she'll agree to sell you that railroad, as soon as we can find a way. I'm sure she'd give it to you to pay off the loan."

Fitzwald slid on the eye patch again. "That's not good enough. Ellie is the woman I want."

"Why don't you court Susanna Martin instead? She'd marry you in an instant, and she's pretty enough."

The weasel laughed. "She has her cap set for you. And, as Ellie spends time with me, she'll learn to love me."

Now that Fitzwald had his patch back on, Graham's sympathy for him disappeared. Sure, he was wounded, missing an eye, but he was trying to make life unbearable for the woman Graham loved—

The thought cut through him like a saber, sharpening and clarifying all his feelings about Ellie. Was she the woman he loved? Had he allowed himself to fall in love with her again? He paused, savoring for a moment the joy of discovery. Yes, he loved her—and he wasn't going to stand here and watch Fitzwald ruin everything for them. "I'm not letting her marry you and be miserable for the rest of her life. Take the railroad and leave her alone."

"Remember that night eight years ago, when we both went to Ellie's house? I went there to propose marriage to her. So did you, and you ran me off."

"I'm doing it again now."

"Yes, yes." He blew a puff of smoke right into Graham's face. "You're trying to do that. But the fact is, Ellie refused you that night. That's why you left town and never came back."

"I'm back now. I'm going to marry Ellie, and you're going to stay away from her." And at that moment, Graham knew it was true. Marrying Ellie was what he'd wanted as long as he could remember.

"When, Colonel? I've heard nothing of a date. I don't believe she consented this time either."

"We don't have a date yet, but we will." As soon as possible. As soon as he could court Ellie the right way, from his heart instead of trying to figure it out in his head. And as soon as he could get this weasel out of their lives. "Either get out of that buggy and we'll settle this like soldiers, or drive it away from here and leave Ellie alone. Those are your choices."

Fitzwald tamped out his cigar. "We're not doing it your way, Colonel. Ellie won't make that payment, I'll start foreclosure proceedings on Magnolia Grove, and she'll marry me in order to keep it and to support her invalid uncle. It's that simple."

The look he gave Graham with just one eye chilled him even more than General Sherman's cold, hard glare.

Graham had always known Fitzwald had a well-developed dark side. But until tonight, he hadn't realized the wickedness of the man's heart.

He had a feeling that, in the coming days, he would see even more darkness there.

* * *

"You never had that talk with Lilah May."

Uncle Amos's words brought Ellie's head up from the ledger she was working in after supper that evening. She'd both anticipated and dreaded the talk, and so she'd put it off. And she didn't have time now, since she had to determine how much money she'd need from the sale of last year's cotton. By the end of August, they'd be harvesting, and she'd be paying extra wages. But judging from the way her uncle fidgeted with his pillows and bedsheet, she needed to have the talk, for his sake if for no other reason. "Lilah May, are you busy now?"

"Huh. The way this man's been eating, I'm busy cooking all the time. But I can spare a minute or two."

Since Miss Ophelia had convinced her uncle to sit in his bedside chair every afternoon, his improved appetite made more work for Lilah May. But what a relief to see him getting better. If only his memory would do likewise. "Let's go downstairs to the parlor. Uncle Amos doesn't want to listen to women's talk."

And besides, that way she could see when Graham returned from sending his wires to the cotton buyers. She closed the ledger and took it with her as she and Lilah May headed for the parlor.

Once there, she invited her maid to sit next to her on the deep blue couch. "Uncle Amos wants you to talk to me about romance and courtship."

"He wants me to tell you more than that."

Ellie glanced out the front window. Perhaps Graham would come home soon and relieve her from what would surely prove to be an embarrassing discussion.

"He asked me to tell you his story."

At that, Ellie turned her attention to Lilah May. "I didn't know he had a story."

"It's not a happy one. I remember when he first started courting."

Uncle Amos—courting?

"He has loved one woman his entire life."

That couldn't be. But she'd never known Lilah May to make up stories. "Who is it?"

"Ophelia Adams."

"Miss Ophelia!" Ellie leaned forward to catch every nuance of this suddenly interesting conversation. "But she married Willis Adams. What happened?"

"Mister Willis went to war in Mexico. He was in love with Miss Ophelia and wanted to marry her before he left. But her parents, Mister Graham's grandparents, wouldn't let her. She was only sixteen."

"That's not so young to marry."

"No, ma'am, but Miss Ophelia's mother thought it was too young to be a widow. So she and Miss Ophelia's daddy made them wait and forbade Mister Willis from having contact with her while he was away."

"They thought they were insulating her from pain, didn't they? But I can imagine that it didn't work out that way."

"It worked out fine for Miss Ophelia. Mister Willis courted her through the mail, sending his letters to Mister Amos to give to her. He also asked Mister Amos to squire his girl around town to make it look like she was courting with him instead of Mister Willis."

All at once, Ellie saw what was coming. "And my uncle fell in love with her."

"He never told her. But he never found another woman, and now that Miss Ophelia is a widow, Mister Amos is sick and can't court her." Lilah May ran her hand down her skirt, smoothing it. "Usually, when a man and woman spend that much time together, one or both of them fall in love. Mister Amos is afraid you'll fall in love with the colonel, and you'll get hurt."

A tight laugh erupted from Ellie's throat. "I'm not falling in love with him. And he certainly isn't in love with me."

"I got eyes," Lilah May said with that you-can't-fool-me look of hers. "Neither one of you has any experience in love, except that time before he left for West Point. So you don't know how to hide your feelings. I can see you're in love."

"No, you're wrong." Wasn't she? "We were children when he went away. As for now, yes, Graham is a handsome man—and strong and gentle and dependable and honorable, but anybody can see that. It doesn't mean I'm in love with him."

Lilah May wasn't convinced. Ellie could see it in her eyes. "You're right. But what happened to you eight years ago, the day he went away?"

Ellie expelled a sharp breath, remembering how she hadn't come out of her room for four days. She'd cried until she'd feared her heart would break, and then she'd feared it wouldn't and she would continue to live. Ellie had numbed since then, had pushed the memory so far back in her mind that it frightened her to recall it now. Those dark days and tormented nights had been far worse than even the day her mother died. At least Mother was out of her misery. With Graham, there'd seemed to be no release from it.

She clawed her way out of that memory and back to the present. When Lilah May passed her a handkerchief, Ellie realized her cheeks were wet with tears. At the time, she'd seemed to have no choice but to refuse Graham. She couldn't have been wrong, could she?

"How would a person know for sure?"

"I don't know about that. But it seems to me that if you imagine what your life would be like without him, and you can't stand the thought of it, that would be a clue."

Graham strode up the walk then. His posture, his gait, told her something had changed—something big.

Lilah May glanced out the window too, and then she stood and started upstairs. "There's one sure way to know."

"What's that?"

"When you give away money you need so someone else can live his dream of being a planter, you're in love."

The little snoop. "You looked over my shoulder when I was figuring the cotton sale in Uncle Amos's room."

"I did, but I didn't have to. You were muttering the whole time you were figuring."

Ellie had to break that bad habit. "How does Uncle Amos bear not having the woman he loves?"

"Same way you do. He pretends it didn't happen. It worked until this courtship thing came up with you and the colonel. He's perturbed about it because it makes him think about his past." Lilah May scurried up the stairs.

Imagine what your life would be without him. What would she do if Graham left again? Never to see him again—what would her life be like?

She opened the door. He met her on the gallery, his eyes gray in the softer light, his face strong with a shadow of evening beard, his bearing solid and gentle. *Life without him—*

Her breath caught at the thought.

"Ellie? Are you all right?"

What had he seen in her face? She shook off the thought and scrambled to think of something that would take the focus from her discomfort.

"You sent the wires?" Having finally come up with a

conversation topic, she breathed deep of the sweetness of relief. "What have you heard in return?"

He gestured at her dress. "I assume you want me to come in and tell you, but I doubt I could get past those skirts."

She moved inside so he could pass through the doorway, unhindered by hoopskirts. On second thought, she needed to examine these new emotions of hers before she could trust herself to be alone with him and not blurt out something silly. The front gallery would be safer, out in public as it was. She waved her trembling hand at him as if shooing a fly. "There's a nice breeze. Let's sit outside."

He hesitated. "We don't want anyone to overhear. I have some rather private things to tell you—"

"Go, go!" She pushed at his shoulder.

"Ellie, what is the matter with you?"

So much for not sounding silly. "It's just that…I want so much to sit outside."

Graham shook his head, his unbelief all over his face. For a moment, she thought he was going to say something, but he merely stepped back and gestured for her to come outside.

"I sold the cotton to Mister Owen Bradley of San Antonio." He held out her chair and then sat next to her—a little too close, to her thinking. He handed her a small paper sack. "For a modest celebration."

She opened the sack. Pralines.

He remembered.

"They used to be your favorite."

"And they still are. I haven't allowed myself the luxury in a long time." She selected one for him, then reached in again for hers. She took a nibble of the nutty, creamy confection. "It's even better than I remember."

Graham ate half of his in one bite. "We used to think

nothing of buying a sack of these every day. Now it's a treat. Things have changed in eight years."

Yes, they had. "I don't mind, though. Sometimes life seems sweeter when we have to do without. We appreciate the treats more."

"You're going to appreciate my news too. We're putting the first load of cotton on a steamboat at seven tomorrow morning, and the next one at noon. We have to ship as much as the boats can hold every day in order to empty the barns for the new crop." He ate the rest of his candy. "The cotton will travel to New Orleans via steamboat, then the Louisiana–Texas Railroad—your railroad—will take it to Mister Bradley in San Antonio. From there, Bradley will transport it to Mexico."

"Fine." She struggled to stay focused on his words. What had possessed her to have such a conversation with Lilah May right before Graham got back? But who would have known their talk would affect her as it did? She needed time to think.

"I'd say it's more than fine. I haggled for a great price."

He was right—this news was more than fine. And Ellie had to leave behind this foolishness. She drew a great breath and tried to clear her mind. "What price did you get?"

"Forty-two thousand for the whole lot."

She clapped her hands together like a child. "I couldn't have gotten that much from him. He's the shrewdest of all the cotton buyers. You'll have plenty of money for pea seed."

"When I went by Myron Sutton's place and told him we needed him to start work in the morning, he said the baby is much better today."

"You're full of good news tonight."

"And some not so good." Graham paused. "The planters in the area aren't happy with us. Seems some of them have lost their workers to us, and rumor has it that more will come tomorrow."

She took another bite of her praline. "We expected that."

"Yes, but we didn't expect the planters to band together to set wages for the laborers. That's what they're doing tonight. They wanted us to attend, but we need to stay out of it."

"I agree. Why would we attend a wage-setting meeting? They can do whatever they want among themselves, but we'll set our own wages. It's the only way I'll be able to make my payment to Leonard."

At the sound of Leonard's name, Graham tensed his right hand into a fist, a cold gleam of anger sharpening his eyes. "I'm glad you think so. I have no intention of playing his game."

There was more to this than he was telling her. She could see it in his eyes, hear it in his voice. "What else does his game involve?"

He hesitated. "Fitzwald is a gambler—has been since we were boys. He bluffs and then cries when he loses."

A gambler...like his father. Like Ellic's father. A cold realization of Leonard's true character and the extent of his greed shot through her like ice. What chances would he take to get what he wanted? "I wish I could give him that railroad. I don't care a smidgen about it."

"I suggested that to him this afternoon." Graham's voice lowered, took on a dark tone. "He's not interested. He's risking everything for the big pot."

"What do you mean? What's he risking?"

"He wants it all. Railroad, Magnolia Grove—and you."

She cast a glance at Graham, his chiseled profile, his sturdy frame. Leonard was the only one gambling here. Even though Ellie's father was a cardsharper, she didn't believe in chance. God was on her side, she was sure of it.

By no means would she fail to pay that loan. Losing everything would kill Uncle Amos. And marrying Leonard in order to keep their property would mean losing Graham, even before he was truly hers.

No, she wasn't going to fail.

Chapter Sixteen

"Miss Ellie, I never saw you look so beautiful. It's true what they say—you are the belle of Natchez."

"Lilah May, you exaggerate. That's a sin." But as Ellie sat at her dressing table the next evening and watched her maid arrange her hair for another party in Graham's honor, she realized Lilah May was right. Not that she was the belle of Natchez, but that she looked prettier than she ever had. Lilah May had taken extra pains with her hair. Her blue silk gown fit just right, and it deepened the blue of her eyes.

But there was something else, something she couldn't define...

"You got the look of a woman in love."

Oh, dear. Not Lilah May too. "Uncle Amos told me the same thing at supper."

"You might as well admit it. And the colonel's got it as bad as you."

Ellie wasn't so sure.

"You got a few minutes to rest before he gets here." Lilah May stood back to admire her work. "Mmm-hmm. You look just right."

"I don't know about that, but I don't feel very good."

"You sick?"

"My stomach is turning, my jaw is quivering, my hands are shaking—"

Lilah May reached over with her pretty brown hand and patted Ellie's. "That's because your woman's wisdom is telling you that everything is changing. Your heart knows it, but your body don't know what to do with itself. You'll be all right after the colonel gets here."

No, she wouldn't. Her heart was going to give out before he got Handsome Boy hitched to Miss Ophelia's runabout.

Lilah May closed the door as she left, and Ellie felt more alone than ever in her life. How could she know what to do about Graham? She had to be honest, to admit she loved him.

No, that wasn't honest at all. She had to admit that she still loved him. Still. After all these years.

Lord, what now? You know how it was when Father stayed away from home, no doubt gambling every night.

"I was hungry, God. Hungry!"

She fought her tears, not wanting a red and splotchy face for the party.

"When I was small, I used to get so hungry, my stomach hurt," she whispered to the heavens. "I thought I was sick. Mother always made me drink medicine, but it was nothing but sugar water. That was all she had to give me."

Ellie tried to imagine the pain of hearing one's child cry with hunger and having nothing to give her but sugar water. What if little Betsy was hungry, and Ellie had no food? And Betsy wasn't even her child.

What if she married Graham, and they had a child, and she couldn't feed her—

Lydia had run a mile looking for Ellie, so she could get medicine for her daughter.

"Dear Jesus, I'm so scared. What do I do?"

Of a sudden, she recalled Lilah May's words of yesterday. *Imagine what your life would be without him.*

Well, she'd done that, and she hadn't liked what she'd imagined. Hadn't liked it one bit.

At the very least, the man deserved to know she loved him. If he brought up the subject. If Lilah May had been right about his feelings.

If Ellie didn't lose her nerve...

"Miss Ellie," Lilah May called from outside her door. "You have a gentleman caller."

Gentleman caller? Why did she say it like that? Surely it wasn't Leonard. Lilah May would run him off in less time than it would take to swat a fly.

Ellie raced to the door and opened it. "Who is it?"

Her maid looked at her as if she'd lost her senses. "Colonel Graham Talbot from next door. Remember him—muscular man with dark hair and green eyes?" she said with the bite of sarcasm. "Who did you think?"

Ellie turned back to the dressing table and snatched her fan—the one with the crape myrtle blossoms painted on it. Somehow, having her myrtle fan with her tonight gave her a measure of comfort.

She descended the stairs with trepidation at first. Halfway down, she caught sight of Graham. Standing by the door, he held her gaze as she slowed her steps even more, wanting to prolong the moment. That first sweet moment when she saw him as the man she loved.

She'd missed seeing him in his uniform. Everything about him—his stance, the set of his mouth, his sturdy hands—radiated strength mixed with gentleness.

And oh, sweet myrtle, he was handsome.

Then he smiled. One of the few true smiles she'd seen since he'd come home. It brought out the dimples in his cheeks and made him irresistible. Her heart pounded as she came closer, touched his arm.

"You're beautiful."

She saw it in his eyes as his smile faded to a look of awe. He did have feelings for her. But was Lilah May right? Was it love?

Ellie swallowed hard and ran her hand down his arm, caught his hand. She smiled and blinked, trying to keep her sudden swell of tears from obscuring her vision of him.

"I thought we'd walk tonight," he said, but she feared her heart might burst from the exertion, as hard as it pounded now.

As they left the house, the sun began to set in a cloudy sky, casting a rose-colored glow on the white columns of Graham's house next door. The faintest breeze wafted and blew little tendrils of her hair across her cheek, tickling it.

Graham cleared his throat, his arm tensing a bit under her hand. "Ellie, I can't go to that silly party. We need to talk." He stopped in the middle of the brick sidewalk. "But we can't go to my house because Aunt Ophelia will ask a hundred questions."

"Lilah May would do the same at mine." She thought a moment. "Our old hideout?"

His flicker of a grin told her she'd chosen right. "It's still there?"

"I invited you there the first day you were home. Remember?"

"So you did. In your note."

She sensed that he was struggling with his thoughts, and so she held her peace as they approached the river bluff. They strolled up the uneven, weedy brick walk to the abandoned Reynolds mansion and then to the backyard.

Their cast iron bench, the black paint now chipped, still sat in the middle of the marble-slab arbor floor. Wisteria vined all around and formed an outdoor room that sheltered them from the neighborhood's eyes and ears.

Graham sat next to her and pulled a small sack from his pocket. He opened it and offered her a praline, then ate one himself while gazing off toward the river. "This river is one of the few things that hasn't changed."

"We've had four hard years of war." She bit into her candy, savoring the sweetness.

"It's more than that. Over the past few days that I've been home, everything has changed for me—in my heart, my mind. Life has begun to make sense again. I don't know how my whole world changed so fast, how I healed so quickly. But I know you were a part of it." He angled a little, moving slightly closer. His eyes turned smoky as he cupped her cheek with his hand.

He kissed her then, entwining his fingers in her hair, smelling of a woodsy cologne and tasting of sweet pralines and comfort and security...

But they had no security.

She kissed him back anyway, tried to push aside her fears until the warmth of his touch collided with a cold place within her—a place she'd kept guarded, protecting herself, for more years than she could count.

She pulled away and saw the questions in his eyes.

He did have feelings for her. Lilah May was right. But she'd been wrong about one important matter: Ellie was not the only one who would get hurt by this imaginary courtship.

"What is it?" As he clasped her hands, his voice deepened, dropped to a near whisper. "Tell me what's wrong. I know you care for me, Ellie."

"It's true. I do. But everything in our world has changed." Her words came fast and shrill. "I never would have believed Lydia Sutton would not have the means to buy food and medicine for her child."

"It's happening all over the South. It's unfortunate, but people have to move forward, go on with life, with—"

When he paused, she looked up at him, the silence poignant as she sensed he wanted to say *with love.*

"Tell me what you're holding back from me, Ellie."

"I don't know what I would do," she said, her voice tremulous, "if I had a child and couldn't feed him."

"The war is over now, and by the time you have a child, the economy will have leveled off."

"What if it doesn't? What if I can't feed my own child?" She tried to blink away the tears threatening her eyes. Tears were the last thing she wanted, but for some reason, she couldn't control them. "The night of Miss Ophelia's party, you asked me why I would never marry. I've been hungry as a child, Graham. My father did not provide for us." She saw the comprehension dawning in his eyes. "The reason I won't marry is because I'm afraid it will happen again—to me and to any child I might have. I've got to provide for myself."

Graham paused, frowning at her words. "There's a better chance that you'd marry a man who would make sure he provided for you and the child."

Myron Sutton's words came back to her in a flood. *I'm not too good to pick cotton.* Graham was right—some men would do anything in order to care for their families.

She shook off the thought. "But it could happen—"

"Think this through, Ellie. You don't refuse love just because you're afraid. What if someday someone gives you a child who needs you, like Noreen was given Betsy? Will you let that child go hungry because you won't take her in? Or all of us could die, and you'd have to take care of Betsy. Are you going to stop loving her because you're afraid you might get hurt?"

"I'm not afraid I'll get hurt. I'm afraid the child will." *Just as I was.*

"I think you've been fooling yourself. You're afraid of your own suffering, not the child's."

Could that be true? Graham knew her better than anybody. Did he see a part of her heart that she'd hidden from everyone else, even herself?

With a flash of clarity, she knew he did.

The truth hit her in her middle. Graham was right, and she'd never seen it. She'd let her past determine what she'd do with her future. She covered her mouth with her hand, taking in the reality of her own falsehood. The years of deceit—when had they started, and why? With her father's betrayal? Her hunger? Her mother's passing?

Perhaps Graham recognized her lie because he'd seen it in her eyes the day she refused him. And still saw it today.

She may never understand how this change had come to her, but somehow she needed to bring it to an end, to learn to live without the lie and the fear.

Change was the one thing they could count on. Natchez—the whole South—was trying to adjust to their new way of life. The old was never coming back. Even her comfortable self-reliance and fear would have to die.

And as much as she hated to admit it, she needed help to make the first steps. "Graham, I need you to pray for me to change that. I can't do it on my own."

"I will. And you'll overcome it. You've never failed to meet a challenge."

"But I've never had a challenge this hard before. The fear has become so much a part of me, I don't know how to let it go without losing my sense of who I am."

He pulled away at last and caught her hand, his eyes taking on a faraway look. "It's hard to adjust when God puts His finger on a part of your life that He wants you to surrender to Him. I felt the same way, coming home from war. Before the surrender, I felt like the war would never end. I couldn't imagine ever returning to any sort of normal life. I had gotten so used to the darkness of battle, I didn't know what to do when I came back to the light of peacetime living."

Peace—what an appealing prospect. To be free of her fear of the past repeating itself… Ellie couldn't even imagine it.

Jesus, I confess I'm not willing to lay my deepest fear before You yet. But I'm willing for You to make me willing…

Dear God, please watch over this ship and its cargo. Everything depends on it.

On the river bluff with Ellie the next morning, Graham watched their first load of cotton start south for New Orleans.

Ellie's face glowed like the sunrise. He could watch her rapt expression all day as she enjoyed the sight of her cotton ready to float down the river.

If only things were different. At the moment, Graham's biggest challenge in life was waiting for God to build trust in her. And for his circumstances to change.

Almost as hard was knowing the sweetness of Ellie's kiss and holding himself back from it. Loading all those cotton bales himself, singlehandedly, would have been easier.

While everything else in his life was changing fast, he had to go slow with Ellie. She was right that he had no ability to provide for her. Just as she feared.

And what was he supposed to do about that? If only he were loading cotton of his own alongside Ellie's. That would make all the difference. But perhaps this shipment would make everything else start to fall into place. As soon as the buyer sent the payment to Ellie's bank in a couple of days, she'd have money to pay her loan to Fitzwald. And with his cut, Graham could buy seed for Ashland Place. "It feels good to see this boat off, knowing it's full to capacity with your cotton."

"It's going to work out, isn't it?" she said in a tone that made him wonder if she was stating a fact or asking a question. "If it doesn't, what will you do? Will you regret trying to help me?"

Was she thinking of Fitzwald and his threats? If so, she needed to stop, now. "You've helped me more than I've helped you. When I came home, I was strung as tight as your secret-message pulley. Without you to help me make the change from officer to civilian, I'd have been a mess."

"You were a mess." She smiled. "What about regrets— if it doesn't work out?"

"Everybody has them. If we can't make it with cotton, we'll make it another way."

But he didn't have another way. Fitzwald was bound to make sure Graham didn't work in Natchez. And what else could he do besides his brokerage? What a time for him to fall in love.

He glanced at Ellie in her pretty white dress, charming as a bride. If only she could rid herself of her fear, Graham could tell her how much he loved her.

Then again, how would merely saying the words *I*

love you make anything better as long as he couldn't support a wife?

He rubbed his temples. How had everything gotten so complicated? What had happened to the days when a man and a woman fell in love, declared that love and got married?

"Are you all right? You have that frown on your face." As always, she looked straight through him to his heart.

"I'm fine." He offered her his arm. "We'd better get home before Aunt Ophelia discovers we sneaked out here alone."

As they turned to start toward Pearl Street, Joseph's brougham pulled up. His driver stopped the oversize carriage alongside them, and Joseph leaned out the window. The grim look on the attorney's face brought a sinking feeling to Graham's stomach.

"Graham, Ellie, I'm glad I found you. We have to talk."

"What now?" Ellie already had enough trouble. Graham reached for the door handle and helped her in, then seated himself beside her.

Joseph tapped the roof with his cane, and they started up the street. "More bad news, I'm afraid."

Ellie's eyes grew wide. "From Leonard, no doubt."

With an air that seemed involuntary, she leaned a fraction closer to Graham, keeping her gaze on Joseph. Graham took her hand and held tight to it, willing his encouragement to her—encouragement she'd never seemed to need before. Or perhaps she'd simply kept it hidden until now.

Joseph handed him a long sheet of paper. "This is being distributed about the state today. A copy will be in this afternoon's *Courier*—and every other newspaper in the area."

Graham scanned the document.

Sheriff's Sale July 11, 1865
Ashland Place, Cotton Plantation, 1000 Acres
Greek Revival Home Built 1839

Ashland, for sale. All Graham's hopes sunk like a burning steamboat.

"Not this," he managed to say, his mouth suddenly dry. He passed the flyer to Ellie, not wanting to read the description of the outbuildings and riverside setting.

Ellie took it from him, her hand shaking. Within a moment, she turned to him, her eyes filled with tears. "Graham, no..."

The catch in her voice nearly did him in. He hadn't seen her cry over her own troubles, so by no means would he allow her to see how much this news affected him. "It's all right. We'll think of something, or we'll just let it go. Lots of people are losing their land these days."

"Joseph, we were going to plant Ashland, hoping no one would buy it," she said, her little finger wiping the corner of one eye.

Graham took the flyer from Ellie and gave it back to Joseph. "Maybe nobody will, and we can go ahead with our plans."

"It won't work." Joseph reverted to his lawyer voice. "Leonard Fitzwald is going to buy Ashland Place at that sale. It's nothing but spite."

And it was working. The ache in Graham's chest threatened to smother what little optimism he'd held on to since coming back to town. He would never have a cotton crop at Ashland Place. He'd never even have a pea crop. "What can I do, Joseph?"

"Get a lot of money together in a hurry. The bank won't finance more than 50 percent of the buying price."

The only person Graham knew of in this town who had that kind of money was Fitzwald himself.

"This doesn't make sense to me. Fitzwald has never been interested in land." Not until Graham came back to town.

Then he realized the true motivation of Fitzwald's heart. He wanted everything Graham wanted: Ashland Place and Ellie. "He's doing this for revenge."

Joseph gave one slow nod. "That's what I think."

"Where can I come up with half the money to buy back my own land?"

Ellie tapped his knee with her parasol. "Your brokerage. You need more work. Since Leonard's father passed on, all the planters in town need a new broker. If they don't hire you, they'll have to go all the way to New Orleans to find a competent one. Everybody knows Leonard never learned his father's business."

"I'll need to find work right away—for this crop. That's going to be hard, if what Fitzwald said is true." Graham turned to Joseph. "According to him, all the members of the newly formed Natchez Planters' Alliance vowed never to hire me if Ellie kept her promise of wages to her workers. Do you know if that's true?"

Joseph slid the flyer back into his portmanteau. "Many of the planters have expressed that to me. Not everyone."

"Who didn't?" Ellie asked.

Joseph's gaze shifted to the right for an instant as he ran his fingers over that magnificent moustache of his. "A Yankee who owns land south of town, for one."

"But who?" She leaned forward a bit. "Graham could contact them today and offer his services."

"I agree. He should do just that, and I'll make a list for him as soon as I get back to my office." Joseph gave

Graham's forearm a fatherly pat. "Even if Ashland Place is lost, you'll make a way for yourself. And who knows? The two of you might save the plantation after all. Talbots don't quit, and you're a Talbot."

But Graham and his father were the first Talbots ever to lose as much as an acre of family land. "All the same, I'm not buying that pea seed until after the sheriff's sale."

"Graham," Ellie said, a frown on her face, "I have cotton stored at Ashland Place."

A sinking feeling hit him in the gut. "How much?"

"Over a fourth of what I kept back from last year's crop. We have to get it out of there today. Let's use that cotton as our afternoon load."

It might've already been too late, since Fitzwald had probably been snooping around out there. "If it's a fourth of the entire lot, it's too much for this shipment. The steamboat doesn't have enough room." Graham paused, thinking. "We can move some of it to the barn we emptied this morning. Where can we put the rest?"

"I have one more barn at Magnolia Grove, but it's so remote, I didn't want to use it. The ground is still muddy after the rains last week."

"We'll get it moved today."

The carriage came to a gentle stop in front of Ellie's house. When the driver opened the door and Ellie turned toward it, Joseph mouthed the words, "Come back."

Graham nodded, exited the conveyance and turned to help Ellie out. What more could Joseph have to say, which he clearly didn't want Ellie to hear?

Having received her promise to come to his house after she checked on her uncle, Graham strode back to the brougham and climbed in. He was in for more bad news, no doubt, but he was thankful to get the telling of it over with now rather than later. "What else, Joseph?

Say it quickly, because Ellie is eager to get going. She's worried about that cotton, and to be honest, so am I. We need to get it on steamboats in a hurry."

"Upon my word, I'm ready to give up this profession. I've been in the business of delivering bad news for the past fifty-seven years, but this whole situation wears on me."

Come to think of it, Joseph looked a bit pale, as if all his energy had drained from him. Graham owed it to him to make this as easy on the elderly man as he could. "Go ahead and give it to me. As you say, I'll be all right."

Joseph's steely gaze did nothing to reassure Graham. "It's about the planters who have not joined the Alliance."

Graham sweated through the weighty pause.

"There are two of them. They're the only ones Fitzwald has no leverage over. The rest still owe him a commission from last year's crop, and Fitzwald has threatened to foreclose on their plantations if they use you instead of him as their broker."

Two? He wasn't kidding when he said he was the deliverer of bad news. "Only two planters in all of Natchez are willing to hire me as their broker?"

"I'm afraid so. I wanted to tell you in private so you could decide whether to tell Ellie."

"I don't want to add to her worries."

Joseph turned his gaze in the direction of Ellie's home. "Ellie's a good girl, Graham, and she's been put to the test. Through this war, her uncle couldn't have gotten by without her, even before his apoplexy. She's been like a daughter to Noreen too."

That much Graham already knew. And he needed to get out to Ashland Place. "I've never seen you dance around an issue like this. Tell me what's on your mind."

"All right, I will." He leaned forward and impaled

Graham with his gaze. "I don't like it when young couples in love keep secrets from one another."

First Amos gave them romance advice, and now Joseph, who had been a widower for forty years? "I'm not sure why everyone has so much to say about our courtship."

"I can tell you why I do. For one thing, I've known you since before you were in short pants. For another, when Ellie came to live with Amos, he named me her guardian in case of his demise. And for the third, I don't think people should tamper with love."

Had he been talking to Amos about them? Did he know they'd fabricated this courtship? "What do you mean by tampering?"

"Keeping secrets." Joseph spoke slowly as if Graham were the one in his eighties—and senile. "In love, complete truth is the only way to go. Don't keep secrets."

It was a little late for that.

"It might be a good idea to marry her right away, Graham."

"How in blazes can I marry her—" The kindness in his old friend's eyes stopped the tirade Graham felt coming on. He lowered his voice. "I have nothing. I can't support her, let alone her uncle. I'd hoped to make it as a cotton broker, but it doesn't look as if I'm going to get much work in this town, if any. And I haven't heard a word about my pardon. I can't buy or sell until—unless—I get it. Even if I could scrape up the money to buy Ashland Place, it would have to stay in Noreen's name until I get the pardon—if I ever do."

"Nevertheless, a hasty marriage might help your reputation in this town. And you two belong together. You always have. Don't let anything stand in your way."

"Ellie's not ready to set a wedding date."

"You'll have to persuade her to."

Of course, the real reason Joseph wanted them married so soon was because if Ellie figured out she was the reason Graham wouldn't get work, she'd never agree to it. But Joseph didn't know she wouldn't marry him anyway.

Graham needed to talk to each planter in the Alliance and see if he could convince them to hire him. Once he knew whether this brokerage idea could work, he'd know better what to do.

He stood and reached for the door handle. "I appreciate your concern. You've always been a good friend to me and my family."

"I'm not speaking to you as a friend now. I'm speaking to you as your attorney—and Ellie's. There's more happening than you are aware of."

"What do you mean by that?"

Joseph pointed out the carriage window. "Here comes Ellie. Talk to her—today. Don't let another day go by."

With those cryptic words ringing in his ears, Graham stepped from the carriage. Joseph tapped the ceiling with his cane, loud enough for Graham to hear it from the outside, and the barouche took off.

Could the elderly man have a few secrets of his own?

Chapter Seventeen

"I haven't seen you this quiet since the night we stole a whole pecan pie from Lilah May and hid from her in the stable." Ellie glanced at Graham as he turned the landau west into Ashland Place's lane, his frown once again as pronounced as the day Betsy arrived.

He hesitated as if he'd been lost in thought and had to catch up with the conversation. "Lilah May was a formidable foe in those days."

"I can imagine how hard it is for you to come here, knowing it's going to be sold. You don't have to go with me. I've got Sugar for protection."

At the sound of her name, the dog opened one eye and then went back to ignoring them from her spot at their feet.

"Even if we didn't have Fitzwald to beware of, I would still need to come here one last time."

"Maybe it doesn't have to be the last time."

He groaned. "Don't tell me you have another plan you haven't told me about yet."

"I wish I did." For a moment, Ellie allowed herself the luxury of imagining herself presenting Joseph with all the money they needed to keep both Ashland Place and Magnolia Grove. Then their lives would change. Graham would be free to court her in earnest—if he loved her. Maybe she could even turn loose of her fear of losing everything, of being hungry, of depending on someone else to survive.

Graham drove by the white plantation home without seeming to look its way.

Ellie laid her hand on his arm. He needed more than a new plan from her. They both needed God to intervene on their behalf, and they both knew it. Ellie breathed a silent prayer, about the hundredth one that morning, for Him to do just that. And although she still had no answer or plan, she chose to believe He would guide her.

"We still have a chance," she said, willing herself to believe it.

He closed his eyes for a moment, almost as if offering a seconds-long prayer. "Joseph gave me some advice today, and it's going to be hard to follow."

"What was it?"

They stopped in front of the most remote barn at Ashland. Ellie scrambled out then took Sugar by the collar and helped her to the ground.

"It's a new plan, all right." Graham's mouth tightened at the edges. "Joseph wants us to—"

Sugar's growl cut him off as she stood before the barn's double doors.

"What's the matter with her?" Graham asked as the dog paced in front of the entrance.

Ellie grabbed her collar again and pulled her close so Graham could open the doors. "This is the third time I've heard her growl lately."

Then Ellie noticed white puffs of cotton lying in the

road before the barn, and her heart lurched. "Graham, the cotton—on the ground…"

He glanced around, clearly catching the sight, and flung open one door. "No, Ellie—the cotton…"

Ellie knew what she'd see—an empty barn, the cotton gone. Her legs suddenly weak, she lifted the back of her hoopskirt and sat down hard on the ground. "How could he?"

Sugar had never growled at anyone except Leonard, the night he and Joseph came to her home. But on Sunday, she'd also growled at the barn that had held the cotton they loaded onto the steamer not two hours ago.

Leonard Fitzwald had been there, and he'd been here. Sugar could still smell him.

And he had effectively shattered her hope.

"It had to be Fitzwald." Graham turned from the empty barn. He should have seen this coming, should have stayed here last night, guarding the cotton. Then again, Ellie had cotton hidden in five separate spots over thirty-five hundred acres, so he never could have kept it all safe.

He took a moment to form a plan. "We need to get the sheriff. On the way, we'll stop at Magnolia Grove and have your overseer and new manager keep watch over the other barns."

Surprisingly, Sugar had stayed near them and followed Ellie into the landau. "Well, there are only the two of them, and I have cotton hidden in three more areas. They'll have to go together because Mister Sutton would never find them on his own."

"Why not? Barns are hard to miss."

"I used only two barns—this one and the one that held

the cotton that sailed out today. That's why I wanted to ship this load next."

"Where could you put cotton bales besides in a barn?"

She let him help her into the conveyance for a change. "I have some in an abandoned house, some in a boarded-up church and some scattered in outbuildings at Mill Creek Plantation. The main house there burned two years ago, and the family moved to Baton Rouge. The whole plantation is grown up in weeds. I wanted to keep it in places where the Yankees wouldn't think to look."

Well, she'd certainly accomplished that. Graham would never have looked for cotton in those places either. He spoke to Lucy and Buttercup, and they started toward Magnolia Grove.

"My mistake was using your barn. It was too obvious—to Leonard, at least. My plan didn't work."

For once, Ellie's smile was gone. She'd tried so hard, and seeing her sit there with her shoulders slumped was almost more than Graham could take. "We can still do it. We'll work together—"

"I can't get by without that cotton. Even with it, I probably couldn't have made it until we get paid for this year's crop."

"You don't mean that. I'll help you."

Ellie shook her head, silent.

What was wrong with her? "This isn't like you. You always think of a way to make things work out."

"Maybe that's the problem. Maybe I put too much stock in my own mind, my own reasoning." She hesitated, wrinkling her brow as if in deep thought. "Do I try to control things too much? Is God disciplining me?"

Graham had to think hard about that. Since he hoped to marry Ellie one day, if she'd ever have him, he had to be careful to give her wise counsel. *Is that how You see it, God? Is this Your discipline?*

Immediately, he thought of the things Ellie had tried to control. She'd tried to make an honest living for herself and her invalid uncle. She'd offered jobs at higher wages than anyone else in the area would pay. She'd offered Graham a job so he could provide for his family. She'd even tried to help him get rid of all those girls when he'd needed quiet time to think.

"No, the things you did are not the fruit of a wicked heart but a generous one, so I don't think this is God's discipline. I think it's the result of a greedy thief who wants to ruin your life so you'll come running to him to rescue you."

"I'm not so sure." She turned her head, her gaze seemingly on the Queen Anne's lace by the roadside. Was she wishing they were still children, picking wildflowers and having no cares? "Maybe I was wrong to start this imaginary courtship."

Her listless tone—one he'd never heard from her before—sent a jolt of fear through him. Thus far she'd fought her way through this mess like the bravest soldier. What had changed?

"What did you start to say about Joseph earlier, when Sugar growled and interrupted you?"

Now, what did that have to do with it? He considered brushing it off, but Joseph seemed to think he needed to deal with the issues right away. "Just that he thinks we should stop keeping secrets from each other."

Her eyes flew wide open, her distress spilling out like a waterfall. "Secrets?"

Graham's heart caught at her whispered word. "Joseph thinks I need to tell you that Leonard has threatened to force the Natchez Planters' Alliance to blackball me as a cotton broker."

Ellie whirled around, her eyes blazing. "He can't do that."

"A lot of the planters still owe his father commission on previous years' cotton. He's going to foreclose on those men's properties unless they hire him as their broker."

"So you won't get any work in this town." The fire died down in her eyes, leaving behind a sort of defeated chill.

"Maybe, maybe not." How vague should he be? "A few planters don't owe him money."

"How many?"

He'd apparently dodged the issue with the skill of a hedgehog. But he'd decided to take Joseph's advice, so he might as well follow through to the finish. "No secrets. Two."

As they drove up Magnolia Grove's lane, Ellie's sharp silence frightened him more than her lethargic tone had earlier. "Ellie, what aren't you telling me?"

She shook her head, pressing her fingers against her eyelids.

"Ellie!" He snatched her hand and held tight to it, his sudden self-doubt as heavy as this weighty silence. "You can't pull back from me like this."

She opened her eyes and then pointed toward the house. "It's Leonard. He's here."

Graham shot his gaze over to Moses and his dogtrot-style home between the main house and the house servants' quarters. There Fitzwald stood beside his surrey, his puny arms bent as he shoved his fists onto his hips like a girl.

The coward. Afraid to face Graham, he'd come to intimidate the help instead.

Graham should have tried to get Ellie to stay at the house so he could face the weasel alone. It was too late now, so instead, he barreled down the dirt lane and came to an abrupt stop, dust billowing up around them. He leapt from the landau, his heart pumping hard.

"Stay in here, Ellie." He was at Fitzwald's side within seconds.

Ellie paid him no attention, clambering from the landau as fast as he had.

"Moses, you'd better go in your house."

"No, sir. I'm the overseer here, and I'm bound to stay beside you."

Was nobody going to do as he said today? "Here's a man as brave as Ellie. Fitzwald, you could learn from both of them."

"Don't use that tone with me, Colonel. I'm soon to be the master of this plantation."

Fitzwald's raspy voice cut through Graham like a rusty bayonet. "There aren't any plantation masters anymore. Didn't you hear that we lost the war? And if there were, you'd never be the master here, even if you steal every fiber of cotton on the place."

"That's slander, Colonel." His voice raised in pitch until he sounded like a woman.

"You wouldn't say that if you hadn't stolen Ellie's cotton."

Even though Graham had lived with soldiers for the past four years, he cringed inwardly at the level of foul language spewing from Leonard's mouth. "Ellie and I have wedding plans to discuss, and they don't include you."

"Get out of here, Fitzwald." Graham kept his voice low, menacing.

Fitzwald's face turned red around that macabre black eye patch. "You're a hothead, just like Ellie's father."

"I am when you threaten her. That's not going to change."

"I'm doing you both a favor. Ellie will marry me and keep her property and the money she owes me. In return, I'll cancel the planters' debts to my father and give them permission to hire you. Since you're not marrying Ellie, the news of her father's gambling habit won't hinder you," Fitzwald said loudly enough for anyone outside the cabins to hear, and maybe some of them inside. "I'll even postpone the sale of Ashland Place until you can buy it. Everybody gets what they want."

"What about what Ellie wants? You've gone crazy, Fitzwald. You need to leave, now."

"Graham, stop."

Stop? He swung around, his thoughts a tangled mess.

"Leonard, I must return to town. Will you excuse us?"

"Certainly." Quick as a snake, he snatched Ellie's hand and kissed it.

Her eyes flashing fire, she jerked it back and rubbed it on her skirt. She opened her mouth, surely to shout some sense into him, but then she closed it again.

Well, if she wouldn't, Graham would. He grabbed the weasel's shoulder and spun him toward his carriage. "Don't touch her again."

Sugar, at their side in an instant, bared her teeth and growled at Fitzwald as if she'd like to take out his other eye.

He muttered the worst of profanities as Graham escorted him to the surrey. "Get out of here before you get hurt."

When Fitzwald had driven off down the lane, Graham helped Ellie into her carriage. For once, she didn't protest or try to do it on her own.

He opened his door and stepped aside as Sugar hopped in. Then he swung the horses and landau around. As they passed the big house, he turned to Ellie, trying to think of something to say—anything that might take the pain from her eyes.

"Ellie…" He reached for her hand, the same one Fitzwald had assaulted with his thin little lips.

As she held on to his hand, she blinked, fast, as if holding back tears.

"Don't cry, sweetheart. I'll make sure he never does that again."

She wiped her eyes and turned in the seat to face him. "Leonard is using the planters' loans to force them to use him as their broker."

He slowed the horses to take the turn onto the road. "That's about right."

"If I don't marry him, you won't have work. You won't be able to support your family, and you won't be able to buy Ashland Place."

Was that what she was upset about? "Don't worry about it. I'll find something else."

"Like what?"

What did it matter at this moment? "I haven't considered other options yet because until now, it was already settled."

But from the look on her face, she didn't consider it settled. Not at all.

"Joseph talked to you about secrets. You tried to tell me about yours on the way here, and now you know mine."

He drew a deep breath. "Honey, you're going to have to come right out and say what you mean, because I'm as confused as I've ever been in my life."

"Your secret was that you won't get any work from the local planters." She spoke slowly, as one would with a child. "Mine was that my father was a gambler. He won that railroad from Leonard's father—in a card game."

"That's half true. I admit to keeping that secret from you. But I already knew how your father got that railroad."

She frowned. "How did you know?"

"Leonard told me."

"He'll ruin your life just as he's ruined everything else." She held his hand against her cheek, her tears warm against his skin. "I can't let you lose everything because of me."

"I'm not going to. But even if I did, you couldn't do anything to stop it, and it wouldn't be your fault."

As he said the words, he realized why she was upset. His military career had come after she refused his proposal eight years ago. And now most, if not all, of his problems had their roots in his West Point past.

She thought all his problems were her fault.

"Ellie, sweetheart, I know what you're thinking. But it isn't true. I made my own decisions, and you weren't to blame."

"You left for New York the day after I refused you. Now I realize I encouraged Leonard back then. I never meant to, but it's still my fault that he hates you."

She reached up and brushed back a lock of his hair. Something in her touch—or was it her expression?—held a note of sadness, of finality, and it sent a chill through him that the hot Mississippi sun couldn't banish.

"Graham, our pretend courtship is what's stirring Leonard up. We can't continue with it. If we do, you won't be able to provide for your family. You'll never have your plantation."

No, she couldn't be saying that. His pulse raced as it had when she refused him the first time. "You're upset now, and I understand—"

In his desperation, he'd spouted the first thing that came to mind. But he needed time to think, to convince her how wrong this was, how right they were together. He'd never have a chance if they stopped spending time together.

"We have to end the courtship."

"You don't mean that. You don't want it—I can tell. I know you better than anyone."

The anguish in Graham's voice could have changed Ellie's mind in an instant if doing so wouldn't ruin his life. Graham did know her better than anyone, it was true, and he was right that she didn't want it. "Think of little Betsy—and Noreen. They depend on you. They don't have anyone else."

"No, we both still need the fabricated courtship. That way, we can still spend time together, working to sell your cotton, without hurting our reputations. And then I can stay close by to protect you from Leonard. We'll find a way—"

It was cruel to let him think she might reconsider. "If we continue, neither of us will have anything. We'll lose a lot more than your brokerage. Both my homes will be gone, I'll have no way to earn a living for myself and Uncle Amos, and you'll never have Ashland Place. You'll probably lose Noreen's home too, because she won't be able to pay the fall taxes. Where will we all go?"

"Ellie." His voice deepened, husky. "Do you care for me?"

She hesitated. It was the same question he'd asked eight years ago. This time she was powerless to laugh it off as before. Care for him? She was in love with him. Uncontrollably, undeniably, get-weak-in-the-knees-when-he-looked-at-her in love with him. Eight years ago—and now. Even though she never allowed herself to admit it back then. And that was why she had to do this.

"Because if you care for me, even a little, this makes no sense at all."

When did love ever make sense? Had it made sense to her mother? Until this moment, Ellie thought she was doing the right thing. But now, seeing the way he stood his ground, waiting for the answer he already knew, a pang of doubt overshadowed her. Was there another way?

"You're worth more to me than all the plantations in Mississippi. We'll make it work somehow," he said, his voice gravelly. "I promise."

Promises. Why were they so hard to keep? "Yes, I—care for you, but I don't have a solution this time. I can't—"

Her throat suddenly tightening with unshed, silent tears, Ellie bounded from the carriage, the door banging, metal against metal.

She'd been a fool. Since her mother's death, she'd promised herself she wouldn't fall in love. Now she fled from the one man who had begun to still those ancient fears and draw her heart to himself in ways she'd only dreamed. Of course it had to be this way. How could she have let herself fall in love with him—again?

She tried to shut out the sound of his voice calling her name as she sprinted across the yard. Her skirt whirled around her legs, threatening to throw her off balance, until she caught sight of Susanna Martin in her own yard across Washington Street.

Susanna rushed across the street and caught Ellie's

hands. "Whatever has happened? You're racing about as if your house was burning down."

"My house is fine." Her heart was the only thing falling to pieces.

Susanna sidled up close to her. "Did you and the colonel have words?"

The familiar glint in Susanna's eyes showed that she sensed a morsel of gossip. Maybe the girl was Ellie's best ally at the moment. She would spread the news of the courtship's end faster than Ellie could, and the sooner Leonard found out, the better.

However, then Ellie would have no chance to change her mind…

The slam of Graham's stable door drew her attention. She turned to see him mounting Dixie. Then, his back perfectly straight, he barreled up Commerce Street without glancing her way. Leaving again. Just like before.

Graham…

She had to do it now, or she never would. She drew a deep breath and silently prayed for strength.

"We are no longer courting."

Her words sounded cold and hard, but in reality, they burned fire in her heart. She heard other words too— Susanna's insincere words of consolation, Graham's words of pain and, loudest of all, Uncle Amos's dire prediction: *Somebody's going to get hurt. I think it's going to be you.*

How right her uncle had been. And how foolish she'd been to ignore his advice.

Chapter Eighteen

Graham pushed Dixie as hard as she could go on the busy street, his mind racing faster than the horse's hooves as he headed for the sheriff's office. Last time, he'd run away from Ellie's rejection. This time, he ran toward the solution to their problems—at least, he hoped his ideas would solve them. For the first time, he was the one with the plan.

Five hours later, he burst through Ellie's back doorway, unannounced and without knocking. "Ellie?" His voice boomed across the center hall and echoed off the front door. "Ellie! I know you're upstairs. Come down here and talk to me."

Lilah May scurried into the hall. "What you doing, nearly busting that door off its hinges? And lower your voice. Miss Ellie's upstairs with a sick headache."

"Get her down here, unless you don't care whether or not we save Magnolia Grove."

The maid's eyes widened for a moment, and then she made for the stairs.

"What are you bellowing about?" Ellie's hushed voice drifted down. "Lilah May, please check on Uncle Amos and make sure he didn't hear the commotion."

As Ellie's light footsteps sounded on the steps, Graham moved farther into the hall and to the bottom of the staircase. Long and narrow, its twenty-six steps looked more like fifty today as she moved slower than Joseph ever did, even at his age.

Then as she drew nearer, Graham saw the reason for her hesitation. Red-rimmed, puffy eyes and tearstained cheeks told their story. His heart clenched at the sight. She'd admitted she cared for him, and now he saw that she did. But could she love him? During his frantic pace of the afternoon, he'd tossed that question about in his mind until he had to hand it over to the Lord. When he had, only one thought had come to him: love doesn't fail.

He edged closer, choosing not to remark on her appearance, especially since the tears made her even more beautiful.

"I meant what I said." Ellie stood on the last step, clinging to the newel post.

"So did I. That's why I've been busy all day, putting my plan in place." He swept off his hat and gestured with it toward the library. "Allow me to report to you, Miss Anderson."

She frowned. "Why did you call me that?"

Graham started toward the back of the house and the library. "I'm not your beau anymore. I'm merely your broker and you're my client, so I addressed you as such."

"You're not my broker anymore. I fired you this morning." Despite her bold words, she trailed him to the library, as he knew she would.

"I obligated myself to ship last year's cotton to the buyer in New Orleans. I'll never get any work in Natchez if you don't let me follow through with that."

When they were seated at the round library table, Ellie pulled the bell cord near the corner bookcase.

Lilah May entered the room almost immediately. No big surprise that she was lurking nearby, but Graham hadn't heard her come down the steps. Then again, she'd always been stealthy.

"Would you please serve refreshments to my broker and me?"

At the phrase "my broker," Lilah May narrowed her eyes at her employer. "Fine. You want lemonade with the lemon or without, like you been drinking it all afternoon?"

"With lemon, please."

Poor Ellie, with her downcast eyes and little-girl voice. She was in over her head, and she knew it. If Graham accomplished nothing else in his lifetime, he was going to make sure she kept her land and home. Even if he never had the right to take her in his arms and comfort her as he wanted to now. "You still drink sugar water when you're upset?"

"Sometimes." She shifted slightly in her chair. "Tell me your plan, Colonel."

So that was how she wanted to play it. That was fine, since he'd instigated the formality. "First I went to the sheriff's office to report the theft and file a complaint against Fitzwald. We can't do much on the mere evidence of a dog's growl, but Sheriff Tillman knows Fitzwald, and he's going to keep an eye on him."

He hadn't expected much enthusiasm about that bit of news, and he didn't get it. "I also moved the shipments of cotton forward. We load the bales in the church tomorrow morning and the rest in two days. I would have loaded them all today if there'd been room on the ship."

Lilah May came in then with a pitcher and glasses on a tray. But she didn't use Ellie's mother's crystal this time. As Ellie poured and the maid left the room, Graham prayed for wisdom. More than anything else, he wanted to be the man to step in and save the woman he loved. But there was a good chance that she would veto his whole plan. And it would be a lot harder to put into place without her cooperation.

God, help me to understand more than my eyes can see. He sipped his lemonade, trying to discern the best way to address the rest of the plan. "I also visited the two planters who didn't owe Fitzwald any money, and they want to hire me as their broker. Then I called on four more planters in the Alliance, and one of them engaged my services. Another said he'd consider it."

"Three clients and a possible fourth that's impressive." Her bright eyes confirmed her growing enthusiasm.

"I then went to Barkley's print shop and ordered handbills advertising my new brokerage, and I took out an ad in the *Courier.* I also ordered a sign to post at our house: Graham Talbot, Cotton Broker." He didn't tell her he'd sold his West Point class ring to pay for it all. His thumb brushed the bare third finger of his left hand, where he'd worn the ring for five years, even through the rigors of battle. Never having dreamed of parting with it, he nonetheless gave silent thanks for the sale.

"But the most important thing I did today was to call on Mister Sutton and your overseer. We're going to camp out at the spots where you hid the cotton, and Moses is going to get as many workers as he can to help. We're not letting anything happen to the rest of the crop."

"You thought of everything." For the first time during this conversation, Ellie's eyes warmed with a little half smile. A smile of hope, of trust.

"And that's not all." Graham leaned close and brushed his fingers along her jaw, her cheek. "Today is the last day that weasel Leonard Fitzwald will control any part of our lives."

"But what if he—"

Graham held up one hand, stopping her. "He doesn't matter anymore. I'm going to deal with him." He paused, moving even closer until her face was so near he could feel her light breath on his skin. "I'm the one with the plan this time, and I've put all of what little I have left into it."

Her wide eyes and reddened cheeks told him he'd made his point clear. Now all he had to do was make the whole thing work. Starting tonight, guarding Ellie's cotton.

And he would do that if it took his last breath.

God, did I do the right thing?

Just before dusk that night, Ellie sat propped up in her bed, ready for her nighttime prayers, and watched Graham's window. He had his gaslight up high, and she could see his silhouette at the window desk where he always sat to read his Bible. He must have decided to take a moment with the Lord before heading out to Magnolia Grove. But having him within her line of vision tonight somehow made this whole day seem even worse.

Lord, I was foolish to get my hopes up after hearing Graham's plan. Now, alone in her room, it seemed she and Graham had traded roles, with him getting a great idea that probably wasn't going to work out. She released all her disappointment in a deep sigh. If only Uncle Amos hadn't borrowed that money. If only Leonard hadn't come back to town. And Graham—if only they hadn't shared two perfect kisses...

Those two kisses would be all the romance she'd have for the rest of her life. She certainly wouldn't have that feeling with Leonard. The peck he gave her hand today was so cold and dry, it could have come from a chicken's beak. How would she tolerate marriage to him?

Ellie sat straight up in bed. She didn't have a choice. If Uncle Amos, Noreen, Graham's father and Betsy were to have roofs over their heads, Ellie had to follow through with the decision she'd made just after Graham left. She had to marry Leonard. She had to leave the past—and her love for Graham—behind.

The night's heat and stickiness did nothing to help her sleep. She got up and poured water from her pitcher into her bathing bowl and carried it to one of her open windows. Setting the bowl on the windowsill, she hoped it would cool whatever breeze might blow in.

As she stood there in the light of the just-waning moon, she caught sight of the pulley and the twine that stretched between her window and Graham's. Now that she would soon be engaged to Leonard, this message system was certainly not appropriate. It had to go. On impulse, she grabbed the pulley and tugged on it until it wrenched away from the house. Then she sent it flying across the yard, twine and all.

Only it didn't bring finality to her romance as she'd hoped it would.

Instead, Ellie should have done what Graham was doing—reading. She lit her own gaslight and flopped onto her bed. Then she pulled out her Bible and opened it to a random page.

She read Joshua 8:1 out loud: "'Fear not, neither be thou dismayed.'"

The problem was that she was both dismayed and afraid, and those feelings probably would not go away anytime in the near future. Neither would her love for Graham.

Maybe a different verse would give her a new perspective. She picked up her Bible and started to open it to another page by chance. But then she heard her mother's voice in her mind, warning her against using that method exclusively when seeking an answer from God.

Do You have a special verse for me tonight, Father?

Mother's favorite Bible verse came to mind, and she turned to Philippians 4:13 and read it aloud. "'I can do all things through Christ which strengtheneth me.'"

Ellie twisted Mother's pearl ring on her right hand. *You can do anything you set your mind to.*

Had Mother done what she'd set her mind to? Ellie had been her one concern in life, and Mother had certainly raised her to love God, as she'd set out to do.

And, come to think of it, Ellie had set her mind to holding on to Magnolia Grove, as well as this house, throughout this entire war. And she'd done it, against all odds. So why back down now, just because things looked impossible?

She cast her gaze toward Graham's window again. He'd spent everything he had, believing God would help him. He'd prayed, gotten direction from God and put a plan to work.

So why didn't Ellie do the same? Would she turn coward now, when they might win this battle with Leonard— when she and Graham might soon be free to love? Perhaps God was giving her a chance to trust Him with all that was dearest to her.

Leonard was the coward. Her father was the gambler. Ellie was neither. She was a woman in love, a woman who trusted God.

Lord, I'll keep trying. If I fail, then at least I'll know I did my best. I'm counting on You to guide us through these next days.

Ellie looked up and saw that Graham's room was dark. She closed her Bible just as Dixie's hooves sounded on the packed dirt of Commerce Street.

Just after dawn the next morning, Graham sneaked in the back door of his home, hoping not to raise the family. As soon as he'd cracked open the door, he smelled ham and biscuits.

Aunt Ophelia. That woman had made herself a blessing in their home. He headed to the dining room and found her in a bright pink dress, pouring coffee for Father.

"You're both up early."

"And you're slipping in at first light for one of my biscuits." Aunt Ophelia made for the sideboard, where she poured another cup and handed it to Graham.

He reached for the steaming cup and sipped the brew. "I just stopped in to borrow Father's old boots, but I don't mind having a bite before I head back out. About two o'clock this morning, I heard something in Magnolia Grove's cypress bog, and when I went out there to investigate, I slid into the water. My feet have been wet ever since."

"Ellie's light was on late last night." Father looked up from his plate and, for the first time since he came home, made firm eye contact with Graham.

"Father…are you well?"

Aunt Ophelia pulled Graham to the side as his father turned his attention back to his plate. "He's coming and going this morning," she whispered. "But he's better than he was. He keeps talking about Ellie's light, but at least he hasn't mentioned Daisy during breakfast."

Did his father sense Graham's turmoil, and had he somehow rallied himself to help? Time would tell, but for now, Graham would take any good news that came his way. Maybe if he continued discussing the topic of Father's interest, the older man would progress even more. "I saw it too, Father. She's struggling. I prayed for her through the midnight hour."

"As did I, son. Do you have the mind of the Lord in the matter?"

Graham swallowed hard, the lump in his throat barely allowing him to breathe. How many times had he heard his father say those words? And now he was coherent enough to say them again and, best of all, to recognize Graham as his son. He glanced at Aunt Ophelia, who also caught the significance of the statement, judging from the tears she suddenly wiped from her eyes.

He cleared his throat. "Yes, Father. I believe I do."

"Then act on it quickly."

"I intend to." Graham seated himself and, after silently thanking God for the food, he ate his breakfast more hurriedly than the fare deserved.

A quiet tapping sounded at the back door.

"Who would call at quarter past six in the morning? Whoever it is, it must not be an emergency. He didn't knock loudly enough for that." Aunt Ophelia stopped fussing at the sideboard, which again contained a little gold, thanks to the sale of Graham's ring, and hastened to the door.

Moments later, Ellie crept into the room, her light blue skirts rustling less than usual with her careful gait. Her blue eyes shone in the morning light, making him catch his breath. Was she always this lovely so early in the morning? It was a look he would never tire of waking up to—every day of his life.

"Is Betsy up? I don't want to awaken her."

Graham and his father stood, then Graham seated her next to himself.

"Betsy has been mercifully sound asleep since four o'clock, and so is Noreen." Aunt Ophelia hastened toward the butler's pantry and returned with a plate and silver service.

Ellie accepted it with thanks and helped herself to a ham biscuit, her face alight. "I have an idea."

Graham should have known. That's what that look always meant.

"Your light was on late last night," Father said, no hint of expression on his face.

Ellie's bright smile made up for it. "You're right, Colonel. You must be feeling better."

"But your light was on late last night," he said again in an insistent tone.

"I'm all right now. I had things to think about."

"Including your new idea, no doubt." How crazy would it be? But she was here, and she was making plans. That meant she hadn't given up.

God, You've been good to us. And Graham's renewed prayer life was not the least of His blessings. No longer did his prayers seem to vanish as soon as they left his mouth.

"Miss Ophelia, there's going to be a whole passel of men out at Magnolia Grove guarding my cotton for the next three days. They need a woman on hand to cook for them." Ellie sipped the coffee his aunt set before her. "I need Lilah May to stay here to help take care of Uncle Amos. Would you be interested in the job? I'm running low on provisions, so we'll serve ham from my storage room and vegetables from my garden. That should hold us over until my payment for the first cotton shipment comes in."

"I've replenished our coffee, sugar and flour with the little money I came home with, so we can contribute some of that, as well," Graham said.

Aunt Ophelia gave her a saucy grin. "I'll start getting things together right away."

For a change, Ellie's plan wasn't bad.

He stopped the thought cold. In the past, he'd grown accustomed to her ideas bringing nothing but chaos. But her recent schemes had worked out for their good. Mostly. Perhaps he needed to change his attitude toward them.

But something told him he would always groan a little when hearing her announce a new plan.

Chapter Nineteen

"Ellie, I've never seen anything quite so unconventional." Miss Ophelia's stage whisper surely carried all the way across Magnolia Grove's backyard as she and Ellie stood on the gallery just before dusk that night.

Ellie cast her gaze over the twenty or so workers striding from the cabins toward the house after a hard day of hoeing cotton. They propped their hoes against the side of the house, stepped onto the back gallery and entered the great hall. Sugar followed and flopped down in the middle of them.

"I agree, but these men are risking their own safety to help me. I wanted to have prayer here in my house, in the home where I spent much of my childhood and made some of my best memories."

They went inside, where the workers, Moses, Mister Sutton and Graham doffed their hats and bowed the knee. As Graham began his prayer, Ellie also dropped to her knees, her gratitude for this moment clouding her vision. Each man here had volunteered his help, refusing pay. Such loyalty was worth more than piles of gold or barns full of cotton.

Graham ended his prayer for protection, wisdom and insight by opening his Bible. "Remember Philippians 4:13: 'I can do all things through Christ which strengtheneth me.'"

After the final "amen," the workers filed out the front door, Miss Ophelia following. Graham hung behind with Ellie.

"Sutton and Moses are in charge of guarding the abandoned house and outbuildings. I'll be just up the road at the chapel, close to you. As I hope always to be." His voice was now barely a whisper. "I know what you said and I know what you meant, but that's not the way this will end. I'm going to defend your property, I'm going to see your cotton onto the ship, and then I'm going to come back and say a few things to you that have been on my mind. No matter what."

This man—this warrior—kindled her hope in ways she hadn't dreamed. "You can do anything you set your mind to."

Graham leaned down and dropped the lightest of kisses onto her lips—a kiss of anticipation, of promise, like a vow. She brought her fingers to his cheek, brushing them against the evening stubble there. His lips tasted of coffee and cream as he kissed her again, stealing her breath. Then he broke away, gazing at her with those beautiful green-gray eyes.

"I have my mind set on one thing." Graham touched his finger to her lips for an instant. Then he set out, looking every inch the colonel.

If Leonard came here tonight, he'd face a fiery opponent.

As Ellie took a moment to catch her breath, Miss Ophelia sailed into the great hall. "I take it the courtship is resumed."

Now, how did she know what had been going on? "Perhaps, in time."

The older woman's laughter rang out like the dinner bell. "If that's what you want me to think, then that's what I'll think. But it's a good thing I came along to chaperone."

It was past time to change the subject. "There's a breeze tonight. Would you like to sit on the widow's walk and cool off? This room is sweltering."

They extinguished the gaslights and headed upstairs to the second-floor great hall, Sugar trailing behind them.

"This is my favorite place in the house," Ellie said as they reached the homey room at the top of the stairs. "Since all the bedrooms open into it, Uncle Amos, Lilah May and I used to sit here in the evenings, talking and reading. I miss those days."

They coaxed Sugar up the narrow, enclosed stairs that led to the roof, then settled into comfortable rockers. The moon hid behind a heavy bank of clouds and did not reveal even the privy or the two cistern houses twenty yards from the back gallery.

"I have good memories in this house too," Miss Ophelia said, rocking gently. "Your uncle and I have always been dear friends, you know."

How well she knew of the courtship this woman and Uncle Amos had fabricated long before Ellie was born. Too much of Miss Ophelia's life paralleled Ellie's own, a fact that still frightened her if she allowed herself to think about it.

"I visited Amos before we left for Magnolia Grove. I think much of his illness is caused by his anguish over the war, and I told him so."

Ellie wasn't alone in her opinion? The fact brought a measure of comfort.

"The stroke of apoplexy certainly caused his paralysis, but he could still be productive, still live, if he'd exert himself a bit. Before I left, he asked Lilah May to send for Roman to help him downstairs. He wants to move his bedroom down there."

Uncle Amos—going down the stairs? "Is that wise? The doctor hasn't said to move him."

"He'll die in that bed if he doesn't get out of it. That's what I told Amos."

Ellie could hardly argue with that.

The light breeze and gentle humming of cicadas enticed Ellie into laying her head against the back of the rocker and closing her eyes.

She drifted in and out of sleep until Sugar's low growl raised her from a light doze. Sitting up slowly, she looked in the direction the dog faced and heard the four-beat gait of a horse walking up the lane. Graham?

"Miss Ophelia, someone's riding toward the house." She touched her shoulder.

The older lady roused and leaned forward in her rocker, peering over the railing. "Can't be important. He's riding too slowly for that."

The sound of hooves came closer to the house, and the shadowy figure of man and horse appeared. The man dismounted, and Sugar growled again, louder this time.

Ellie sucked in a sharp breath. "It's Leonard. He's the only person Sugar has ever growled at," she whispered.

Miss Ophelia shaded her eyes as if that would help her see him better. "A dog's growl isn't the most reliable way to identify a man."

"In this case, it is." Without a sound, Ellie moved to

the railing for a closer look and saw a square can in the man's hand. "What's that he's carrying?"

When the figure moved onto the front gallery, Sugar's growl intensified. Then a sloshing noise—and the odor of kerosene. A flash of orange light and the roar of flames.

"He's setting the house on fire—"

Ellie clambered to the staircase, but Sugar beat her to it.

"God, have mercy!" Miss Ophelia's shrill prayer fueled Ellie's silent one as they raced to the ground floor. Her thoughts rolled like smoke as they burst into the great hall downstairs.

Eerie orange light illuminated the room through the fanlight and sidelights of the front entrance, dancing on the walls and ceiling. Sugar ran from the front to the back door, her barking muffled by the sound of the crackling fire.

Ellie threw open the back door. Sugar bounded out ahead of her and dashed around the house.

Stepping from the back gallery to the yard, Ellie caught sight of the tools the workers had left propped against the wall. She grabbed the longest hoe and rushed to the front, Sugar's growling bark loud in her ears. She had to stop Leonard. If she didn't, he'd set the back gallery on fire too, and if he guessed where she'd hidden the cotton, he'd do the same to it.

Reaching the front of the house, she slowed and peered around the corner. The fire's light revealed a spindly form with an eye patch as the man tried to escape the dog's attack.

Leonard. The man of her nightmares.

Sugar nipped at Leonard's right leg, and Ellie saw her chance. She stole up to his blind left side and lifted the hoe as high as she could.

Kicking toward Sugar but missing, and dodging her teeth to his right, Leonard pulled his sidearm from its holster.

The anger that shot through Ellie fueled a sudden strength. "Don't you ever hurt my dog!"

He swung toward her, his one eye wide.

She brought the hoe down hard on his head.

Graham and his half dozen field hands sat crouched like infantrymen in the thick stand of pine east of the chapel. The cicadas must have outnumbered the leaves on the trees, judging from their deafening racket. He took out his handkerchief and mopped his damp face and neck in the stifling heat and humidity. After all those years of war, who'd have thought he'd spend another night out in the open, waiting for an enemy to cross into his territory?

He pushed back his hat, scanning the road and the overgrown yard around the chapel. Of a sudden, the cicadas hushed. Not a sound whispered from the road, the woods.

Something had changed. He sensed it as always before battle. His heartbeat filled his ears as he rose silently to his feet, grasped the handle of his sidearm.

Gunshots—six of them in succession—then the clanging of a bell.

Magnolia Grove's dinner bell.

Ellie—

"Fitzwald must be at the big house. Everybody move out!" Graham raced toward Dixie, hidden along a footpath a good twenty yards into the woods. What could be happening there? Who fired the shots?

He flung himself onto the horse and thundered down

the road. He should have stationed a man at the house. Should have given Ellie a weapon—

Rounding the bend, he caught a whiff of burning wood.

Surely that weasel hadn't set something on fire…

He spurred Dixie to top speed. When he reached Magnolia Grove's lane, he saw orange flames leaping up to the gallery's ceiling. In the glow, someone sloshed a bucket of water into the fire, her hoopskirts billowing with her effort.

As Dixie galloped up the half-mile-long lane, Graham scrambled to sort the facts in his mind. The woman with the bucket had to be Ellie. She turned and rounded the house, no doubt heading toward the two cistern houses, fighting the fire with his elderly aunt.

Nearing the brick structure, he scanned the area illuminated by the fire. If Fitzwald had set it, where was he?

Graham jerked Dixie to a stop and hitched her to a low-hanging magnolia branch. Approaching on foot, he passed an inert form lying in the grass inside the circle drive. For an instant, he took in the sight of the hoe and the man lying facedown on the ground, his head in a puddle of blood.

Ellie's dog stood, growling, over the body.

It had to be Fitzwald. But what had happened? "Sugar, stay."

The fire still crackled, flames licking at the second-story gallery now. Graham made for the cistern house in back. In the darkness there, a slight body rammed into his chest.

Ellie. She held two buckets of water, much of which sloshed out with the impact and soaked his pants and boots.

"Was it Fitzwald?" Graham shouted, holding her upper arms.

"I think I killed him—" Her voice choked as with tears as she screamed her answer. "He's in the front yard."

The air filled with the sound of men running, yelling. Graham grabbed the buckets from Ellie. "Where's Aunt Ophelia?"

"Cistern house. Pumping water."

He set down one bucket and pulled out his gun. "Find her and give this to her. Tell her to guard Fitzwald and use the gun if she needs to. Then get some more buckets."

As she ran toward the dairy, Graham's men poured into the yard. Moments later, Myron Sutton thundered up the lane, his black gelding's hooves pounding the dry ground.

"Fitzwald set the fire, Sutton," Graham hollered over the din of men's shouts and the crackling of the fire. "Get Sheriff Tillman, fast."

Finally, after what seemed like hours, Graham emptied two buckets of water onto the last embers. Then he bent over, hands on his knees, and drew a long breath of less-smoky air. After a few moments of rest, he hastened to the front of the house.

There in the circle drive, Aunt Ophelia stood guard over the motionless form, which now lay under the nearest live oak. A gun in each hand, she pointed both at Fitzwald's chest. Someone, probably one of the workers, had bandaged his head with coarse cloths and stopped the bleeding, and someone had propped his legs on a sack of grain from the stable.

"He's still alive," Aunt Ophelia said, "so the men dragged his sorry self over here, out of their way. Sugar and I are making sure that, if he wakes up, he doesn't go anywhere."

"Where's Ellie?" Graham glanced around, thinking to see her helping to guard Fitzwald.

His aunt peered about as well. "Why, I don't know. I've been keeping both eyes on this—this—"

Her hesitation made Graham eager to hear what his refined yet unconventional aunt would think of to call Leonard Fitzwald now.

"—this outsider."

Graham worked hard to keep from chuckling. Yes, "outsider" was the worst possible name Aunt Ophelia could call a born-and-bred resident of the town she loved. "So you no longer consider him one of our own?"

"Don't be cheeky. I'm armed, you know."

"Yes, ma'am."

"I'll gladly turn these weapons over to you as soon as you find Ellie and make sure she's all right."

"I'm on my way." He started toward the back of the house and the dependencies but stopped as Ellie rushed toward him.

"The fire's out, honey," he said, taking in her beautiful sooty face and soggy, dirt-smeared dress. "We did it. We saved the house."

Without so much as a nod of apology to Aunt Ophelia, she wrapped her arms around his waist. "Miss Ophelia and I—we tried, but we couldn't have done it alone."

He laughed and held her and smoothed her hair, which had come loose from its knot and hung down her back in a pretty, tangled mess. Then he pulled one arm away and pointed at Fitzwald, leaving the other around her shoulders. "Looks to me like you did a good job."

"I was afraid I'd killed him."

Her voice sounded so small, so tinny, that it shook him a bit. "Are you all right?"

"I just wish he was gone."

Graham looked at Ellie and then at the weasel. "He'll be in jail soon. Tonight you have effectively prevented Fitzwald from causing any further problems for a long time."

Now if Graham could only solve a few more big problems in his life...

I almost lost it.

The place Ellie loved more than any other, the home where she felt comfortable and relaxed, where she'd spent happy childhood days—might have burned to the ground tonight. With no near neighbor to see the fire, her dear Magnolia Grove home would have been gone before help could come.

She ambled to the kitchen dependency and filled the coffeepot with water, then added grounds. It wouldn't be as good as Lilah May's or Miss Ophelia's, but making coffee was the least she could do for the men who'd saved her home.

After she served the workers, she made another pot, carried it to the front lawn, and sat next to Graham and Miss Ophelia in the dew-dampened grass. The torch one of the workers had brought from his cabin cast a pleasant glow on the lawn. She poured a cup for Graham and added a splash of cream as he liked it. Then she gave a heavily sweetened and creamed cup to Miss Ophelia and poured a sugary one for herself.

"I sent Sutton for Sheriff Tillman, and the men back to guard the cotton in the old church, in case the weasel had others working for him." Graham took a long swig of his coffee.

"You're staying here?" Miss Ophelia asked, laying her hand over her huge yawn.

"For the rest of the night."

"Can we sleep inside the house?"

"Too much smoke. The fire burned through the downstairs door and into the great hall. Fitzwald was trying to burn the house from the outside in." His voice sounded husky, probably from breathing too much smoke himself.

"I'm glad you were here to take over. I couldn't have kept pumping water much longer." Miss Ophelia's fatigue sounded thick in her voice.

"You were a hero as much as the men were, Miss Ophelia." Ellie turned to Graham. "She not only pumped water, but she also rang the bell and fired Leonard's gun in the air to call you."

Sugar ambled over and flopped down at the older woman's side. She scratched the dog behind the ears. "We're all heroes—especially Sugar."

"She sure is. She stood here beside Fitzwald and made sure he didn't wake up and try to escape," Graham said.

"Yes, and she did more than that. I saw the whole thing…"

As Miss Ophelia related the details of the evening, Ellie lay back in the grass as if she was a young girl again, without a care in the world. However, she wasn't. She was a grown woman with the cares of family and business on her shoulders. With the help of God and her friends and workers, she'd avoided this catastrophe. But now she had the added expense of repairs on the house, and she owed these men a bonus for their part in saving her home.

If only they could get rid of Leonard for good—

She cut off that thought, remembering how she'd felt when she thought she'd killed him. No, she didn't want that. All she wanted was for him to leave her alone. To go somewhere far away...

An idea hit her like a bucket of cold cistern water. "Graham, he'll go to jail, won't he?"

"Leonard? Of course, even with his political pull. That kerosene can has his name on it, and you and Aunt Ophelia both saw him set the fire."

Her heart raced as fast as her mind. "Can he make me pay the note while he's in jail?"

Graham's head shot up and he hesitated a moment. "He can't initiate legal proceedings when you miss the payment, and he has no relative to do that for him. Joseph is still his attorney, but rest assured that he won't file the complaint."

"That means I won't have to pay that loan until he gets out of jail."

"If you have to pay it at all."

That statement brought all kinds of possibilities to Ellie's mind...

Miss Ophelia made two attempts to get up off the ground before Graham had a chance to come to her aid. He hoisted her to her feet, and she patted her hair. "Everything's going to work out, dear. I think I'll retire to that rocker on the widow's walk where I had a nice nap this evening, before a rude person interrupted it." She glowered at Leonard.

"Will you be all right by yourself, or shall I come with you?" Ellie asked, hoping she'd decline.

"I will chaperone this party from the rooftop." She smiled and winked at Graham.

"I'll come up as soon as I've spoken to the sheriff, Miss Ophelia."

Once they were alone, other than the unconscious

Leonard, Graham reached for Ellie's hand. "You're free now. Your home and cotton are safe."

"Do you think he was going to burn this cotton instead of stealing it?"

"I made a ruckus in town about the stolen crop, so Fitzwald probably thought he was less likely to get caught this way."

Ellie couldn't help the prayer of thanks welling up in her heart. "What about the cotton in the abandoned house and the outbuildings?"

"All safe. He probably intended to torch the house and the outbuildings at Mill Creek Plantation next—if he knew you had some of your bales there."

It was over. Leonard had no further hold over her— over them.

"Now that he's out of our lives, I need to ask you a question." His voice thickened, as if her answer would matter even more than Leonard or the cotton. "Why did you refuse me eight years ago?"

She owed him an explanation. Pulling in a deep breath, she focused on the sight of the burned gallery and the smell of smoke and kerosene. "I've told you about my fear of not being able to feed a child. My mother used to beg for our food. Father was always off somewhere, gambling and drinking. And when Mother died, I was hungry for days. When the police finally found me and sent for my uncle to collect me, I decided I would never rely on a man to provide for me."

"Not even me, Ellie? Have I ever let you down?"

"I thought I had to live as a spinster, never have a child I might not be able to feed. That's why I spent so much time learning from Uncle Amos. I knew it would be up to me to provide for myself—to run that plantation— when he was gone. And when he took ill, it was time for me to start. I did a good job until Leonard came home and called in that loan." She sloshed some of the strong, almost thick coffee on her dress as she swirled it around the cup. "I admit that I still struggle with that."

Graham took the cup from her and set it on the ground beside him. "You're saying you don't trust God to provide for you."

"I can't see how the two are related."

"Well, I can. You think this plantation can save you. And for some reason, you think you can't have both it and love. But that's wrong. You can have both."

It made sense—in a way. Above all else, she did not want to be guilty of not trusting God. But now she could see Graham was right about that. *Forgive me, Lord. Help me to turn from that great sin.*

But one thing still bothered her. "Miss Ophelia lost her plantation—and her home."

"Yes, and unlike you, she did nothing to try to save them. But does she seem happy now? Does she like living with us?"

Ellie had to admit she did.

"Don't you see? She didn't give up anything. She hated living alone in that big house. The only time she was happy was when she was giving parties and having company. All my life I've heard her quote Luke 15. 'Use your worldly wealth to gain friends.' That's what she did. And she's happy now because she feels we need her, which we do."

Ellie could have it all—love and security? She ached to believe that.

The rattle of a wagon drew her attention to the drive. "The sheriff."

With a grunt, Graham stood. "Sutton's riding behind

him. Don't take your eye off Fitzwald while we talk to him."

Ellie sighed but took Graham's hand and let him help her up. Although she could have done it as quickly herself.

Turning reluctantly to Leonard, she realized he could merely be pretending to be unconscious, lying there listening to them until he found an opportune time to escape.

Apparently he was, since he cursed and sputtered as Sheriff Tillman, Graham and Mister Sutton began tying his hands and feet. When they had him in the back of the wagon, Ellie gave the sheriff her story.

The sheriff frowned and shook his dark head. "In the morning, I'm going to remove your plantation from the sheriff's sale, Colonel. I have a feeling Mister Fitzwald won't have any political clout in this state after tonight. I'd sure like to see you pay the taxes and buy that place back."

Graham gave him a half smile, half frown. "I'd like that too, but I can't because I haven't received my pardon. No buying, no selling of ground until that comes."

Mister Sutton leaned against the side of the wagon, perhaps to rest his bad leg. "Well, since you're getting married soon, why not put the land in your wife's name? Wouldn't be the same, but it'd be better than not having it at all."

"In Ellie's name—and plant it right away?" He looked off into the distance, toward Ashland Place. "I never heard a better idea."

As the sheriff climbed into the driver's seat, Ellie turned to Graham, heavy loads lifted from her mind and heart. "He's right. Now that Leonard can't collect from me, I can pay the taxes and get your ground back for you."

Watching the wagon pull away, Ellie gave thanks that she'd never again need to deal with Leonard. "Mister Sutton, you'll have a sizeable bonus tomorrow."

"No, ma'am," he said with his usual businesslike expression. "You've done more for us than I've done for you."

"But you helped save my home, my cotton."

"I did, but you helped save my daughter. That's not even close to a fair trade." He tipped his hat as he mounted his horse. "We'll always be in your debt."

As he rode down the drive, Ellie took in all Mister Sutton had said. He was right. A plantation was nothing compared to a child.

"Forgive me for speaking the obvious, Ellie," Graham said, "but you gave Mrs. Sutton your last gold dollar in order to provide for her child. If you can do that, you'll always be able to provide for your own child. Even if you have to rely on others, as Mrs. Sutton did."

He was right. She'd provided for little Annie—maybe even saved her life.

"You did it for love, and you received love in return. The Suttons would do anything for you now."

Then the nearly full moon peeked out from the clouds, and its cool light cast a grim reality on the gallery and what could have happened that night. Graham extinguished the torch and they strolled into the backyard, away from the charred wood and heavy smell of smoke.

They stopped to sit on a bench under a crape myrtle, the moonlight now spilling out around them. Ellie arranged her skirts, then realized how silly that was, considering their wet, dirty condition.

"You're the most generous, loving person I know."

Graham took her hand and brushed his fingers over her wrist, his eyes a deeper green in the moonbeams. "That tender heart of yours is what made me fall in love with you."

And she still loved him after all this time. Not merely with the love of her former days, a young love that longed for a life of fun and adventure with him. No, the years and hardships had aged and matured her feelings for Graham into a lasting devotion. A sweet blend of the joy of youth and the stability of years. "I've loved you since we met. Since long before that night. But…"

"What is it, Ellie?" He met her gaze, his heart in his eyes as she'd seen it all those years ago. "We've always been right for each other. We belong together."

They did—he was right. "But what if I rely on you and something happens and I lose you—just as I did when my parents died?"

"Then you'll go back to the way you live now. You'll hold things together as you always have. And you'll have the memory of a happy life filled with love."

He made it sound so simple. "If things turned out that way and we were together, I could still take care of the plantation?"

"Honey, it wouldn't work if you didn't. It doesn't have to be you providing or me providing. Why can't we be partners instead? Look how well we worked together tonight. Without both of us, this place would have burned to the ground. What's wrong with each of us doing what we do best?"

That made more sense than anything she'd ever imagined. She wrapped her arms around his neck. "That's a great plan."

"I never thought I would find love again. How could I when I never stopped loving you?" She wasn't prepared for the emotion, the vulnerability, dawning in his eyes. "Maybe I'm fooling myself now, but I thought you might want to…"

"I do, Graham." She laid her hand over his heart. "I always have."

His heart pounded under her hand. "We complete each other, Ellie. You give me lightheartedness and fun. As long as we've been apart, I haven't had that."

"And you bring me stability, solidness. I'm not as flighty as I used to be."

"You're still flighty enough to be interesting." He stood and plucked a white myrtle blossom from the tree. A full smile dimpled his cheeks as he handed the flower to her. "Will you marry me, Ellie? Right away?"

She took in his stunning eyes, his strong jaw. And now the dimples. He'd changed, as had she—and she found she liked it. Liked it a lot. She breathed in the bloom's scent. "I will. Right away."

"Ellie, I'm a gentleman, and I've never broken a promise to a lady. But I'm breaking one now."

Breathless, she slipped her hand onto his arm. "What promise?"

And then, with his tender touch sweeping away a tiny bit of her fear, he drew nearer. "To keep this courtship a counterfeit."

Then she kissed him, but not a light, gentle kiss like he gave her in the great hall that evening. No, this was a kiss of commitment, of a deeper promise than she'd thought possible. She wrapped her hand around the back of his neck and felt him pull her closer. A man like Graham, needing her to complete him—the thought brought tears to her eyes. And she needed him too, more than she'd known before this moment.

Finally, she broke away. Her cotton payment would

come tomorrow, and they'd have enough money to have the reception she'd always wanted—at Magnolia Grove. "I'll marry you, Graham. The day after tomorrow."

Chapter Twenty

Two days later, Ellie awakened to a thunking sound against her windowpane.

She sprang from her bed and drew the pen barrel inside. Graham must have affixed the secret-message pulley to her window frame yesterday while she delivered her wedding invitations. She untied the crape myrtle blossom from the vessel and held the white flower to her nose. A faint, sweet scent, subtle yet enduring.

When she had extracted the message, she returned to her bed to read it.

> Wake up, sleepyhead! In two hours, I'll be at your house to beau you to church. And this time, you'd better have your bridal veil, not your grandmother's old hat.
> Your soon-to-be husband,
> Graham

Smiling at his little references to the note she'd sent him just days ago, she grabbed a sheet of her plum-colored stationery and jotted a note in return.

I'll be ready before you are. The race is on!
Your loving, faithful, devoted intended. And this time, that's no joke!

She hastened to the window, then caught her breath. At least a dozen blue handkerchiefs flew like flags from the windows of his house.

Blue flags—an invitation to an adventure.

She grabbed the twine and sent the missile sailing above their lawns. "I'm pleased to accept your invitation, Colonel Talbot!"

Later that morning, Colonel and Mrs. Graham Talbot exited the crowded church amid a flurry of rice. Even Father joined in the custom, a smile in his eyes for the first time since he returned from war.

As the two families drove to Magnolia Grove, Ellie's face shone bright as the morning sun. "I don't care if Miss Ophelia sees me kiss you now, husband." She edged closer and did just that, a warm, gentle kiss that made all their struggles worth it.

Graham laughed, his tone as light as his heart. "She's in the carriage that went north to your house to get Lilah May's pies—and Sugar—and we're going south to Magnolia Grove. So if you meant to shock her with that kiss, it didn't work."

"However, your stepmother is in the backseat of this buggy," Noreen said amidst Betsy's chatter. "But she isn't shocked. In fact, she approves."

"So does your father."

Graham felt his eyes fill, his heart nearly bursting with the blessed changes in his life and family.

When they drove down Magnolia Grove's dirt drive, past the cypress bog and then under the canopy of live oaks, Ellie kept her gaze straight ahead as if memorizing each detail. "Pretty soon, the whole yard will be full of carriages and wagons. Miss Ophelia will love that."

"The gallery looks lovely, Ellie," Noreen said as they drew closer to the house. "I didn't expect you to get it fixed in time."

"Graham did that. He gave all the workers the option of either hoeing cotton or cleaning, painting, mowing, weeding, repairing the gallery and helping him install a new door. They all chose to work here."

The house didn't look as festive as it would have, had they married before the war and the hardships it brought. But the vases of crape myrtle blossoms on the outdoor tables looked more beautiful to Graham than bushels of orchids.

When they stopped in front of the house, Graham got out to help Ellie. Father also hastened around to the other side to assist Noreen and Betsy.

Yes, change had come to the Talbot and Anderson families.

Noreen headed straight for the kitchen dependency to check on the food and help the women Graham had hired to cook. She had barely left his sight around the house when the first carriages started down the lane.

Susanna Martin and a Confederate lieutenant she'd found somewhere greeted them first. "I declare, Colonel, I can't keep up with you two. Just days ago, Ellie told me herself that your courtship was over."

Her petulant tone grated against Graham's nerves, but it didn't seem to bother her escort, who turned a haughty smile on her. "You know how these affairs of the heart are, dear," the lieutenant said. "Here today and gone tomorrow."

At the man's words, Susanna looked so disappointed that Graham almost felt sorry for her. Nevertheless, he couldn't allow the soldier to cast a shadow on Ellie's day—and his. "Not all romances are that way, Lieutenant. It depends solely on the hearts behind them."

Guests continued to arrive and mingle, and just as Noreen whispered to him that the meal was ready, a carriage came racing down the drive.

It looked like Ellie's landau. Was Ellie's household not here yet? He glanced around for them. "What on earth—"

Some calamity had to have happened for Roman to drive in such a manner. Graham ran to meet the carriage as it ground to a stop amid a whirl of dust.

"Graham!" Joseph bounded from the carriage as if he were thirty years younger. "A letter—from President Johnson—"

If he said more, Graham didn't hear it. He gave only a glance to the envelope's return address: 1600 Pennsylvania Avenue, Washington City…

He ripped it open and pulled out a huge sheet of paper, folded in fourths.

"ANDREW JOHNSON
PRESIDENT OF THE UNITED STATES OF AMERICA
TO ALL TO WHOM THESE PRESENTS SHALL COME, GREETING:
Whereas, Graham P. Talbot of Adams County, Mississippi, by taking part in the late rebellion against the Government of the United States, has made himself liable to heavy pains and penalties…"

* * *

His voice cracked, and he realized he'd been reading it aloud. He tried to keep reading, but his throat tightened and nothing came out but a croak. No. It couldn't be. Was this a warrant for his arrest? That seemed ridiculous, but what else could the document mean? "My pardon has been denied..."

Ellie took the paper from his trembling hands and scanned down the page until she let out a cry. "You didn't read far enough. Listen—

"Now, therefore, be it known that I, Andrew Johnson, President of the United States of America, in consideration of the premises, diverse other good and sufficient reasons me thereunto moving, do hereby grant to the said Graham P. Talbot a full pardon and amnesty for all offenses by him committed, arising from participation..."

She shoved the paper back into his hands. "It's your pardon!"

Pardon. It couldn't be. He skimmed the words that now blurred on the paper in his hand. "Where does it say that? I want to see the word *pardon*."

Ellie poked the paper. "Right below the spot where you stopped reading." She eyed the page again. "You'll have to read the whole thing later, because it has instructions about taking the oath of loyalty and responding to the pardon."

And there it was. His pardon. *Thank You, God.*

He pulled Ellie—his wife—close as the gathered crowd clapped and shouted their congratulations. Then he had to take a moment to wipe his soggy eyes before he could continue. He looked around at the family standing about him—Noreen, Father, little Betsy and Aunt Ophelia, who looked a bit disheveled but pink-cheeked after the whirlwind buggy ride. His new family, Ellie and Amos, who looked dapper with Aunt Ophelia at his side. Roman and Lilah May, who muttered about her pies being ruined during that wild ride. The tables laden with food. His neighbors and friends. Joseph, who brought the good news. Even a string orchestra to entertain them.

He didn't deserve this. How had his life turned out so good? He'd never know, but he intended to give thanks to the One who'd orchestrated it all.

He turned to their minister, standing beside him, no doubt waiting to be called upon to ask the blessing for the food. "Reverend Gifford, I hope you'll forgive me for the unconventional deed I'm about to do. According to tradition, the minister should pray over this meal, but I have much to thank God for, and I can't let another man do that for me."

With Reverend Gifford's blessing, Graham glanced around the lawn at their guests, each bowing the head or knee. "Father, you've overwhelmed me with Your goodness. I did nothing to deserve all this, so I give You thanks. Your hand brought all this blessing to me, and I thank You in the name of Your Son, Jesus. Amen."

"Meh-men!" Betsy's little voice rang out next to him, and he kissed her soft hair.

"Ellie, you said you would throw the biggest party Natchez has ever seen, before or after the war." Joseph held up his cup of icy Chatham Artillery punch—without the liquor, of course. "And you've done just that. Congratulations on outfoxing a weasel, and best wishes on your marriage."

Amid shouts and well-wishes, Miss Ophelia insisted Graham and Ellie serve themselves first, and to appease her, they did. Their plates loaded with turkey, étouffée, ham and just about every vegetable he could name, they settled in at the table nearest the house.

"Before we eat, I want to give this to you." Ellie held out a small box.

Oh, no. A wedding gift. "Ellie, I'm sorry. I didn't think to get you anything."

"You did. Your mother's ring. It's precious to me and I love it, so just open the box."

Graham lifted the lid, and his class ring glittered inside the case. How had she done that? He slid it onto the third finger of his left hand, where all West Point men wore them. Then he gave her a quick hug. "That's the most perfect gift you could have given me. How'd you know where to get it?"

"Joseph told me who you sold it to."

Graham had a feeling his wife would be one step ahead of him for the rest of his life. And to be honest, that felt pretty good.

As they began their first meal together as a married couple, the orchestra played the opening notes of "Aura Lea."

"Aura Lea—the maid with golden hair." He touched one of her curls.

"I don't know what Aura Lea did, but this golden-haired maid couldn't be any happier." She paused and frowned. "Except for one thing."

Then she got that look in her eye. She was thinking again…

"I want to live here, Graham. This is my favorite spot in the world, much homier than our house in town."

"That's the only thing I haven't figured out yet—where everybody is going to live," he said. "We have six adults, one baby, one maid, one groom and four houses between us. How is this going to work?"

Her smile glistened in the afternoon sunlight. "Don't worry. I have a plan…"

* * * * *

If you loved this story, pick up these other emotional tales of counterfeit courtships:

ACCIDENTAL FIANCÉE
by Mary Moore
THE ENGAGEMENT BARGAIN
by Sherri Shackelford
THE TEXAN'S ENGAGEMENT AGREEMENT
by Noelle Marchand

Available now from Love Inspired Historical!

Find more great reads at www.Harlequin.com

Dear Reader,

Thank you for reading my first book with Love Inspired Historical!

Finishing the first draft, I didn't know how Ellie would overcome her greatest fear. Then I remembered my father always telling me, "You can do anything you set your mind to." These words helped me through RN training, Bible college and twenty-seven years of marriage and ministry. Thinking of this, I knew Ellie's mother had encouraged her the same way. This early teaching, coupled with Philippians 4:13—"I can do all things through Christ which strengtheneth me"—helped Ellie achieve her goal.

I hope that, like Ellie and me, you have someone who encourages your dreams. If not, Jesus promises to be that strength for you.

I'd love to hear from you! Please contact me through Love Inspired, at https://www.facebook.com/christina linstrotmiller, or on Twitter @CLMauthor. See my Sugar, on whom Ellie's dog is based, at https://www.facebook.com/SugarDogMiller.

Christina Miller

REQUEST YOUR FREE BOOKS!

2 FREE INSPIRATIONAL NOVELS
PLUS 2 *FREE* MYSTERY GIFTS

Love Inspired® HISTORICAL

YES! Please send me 2 FREE Love Inspired® Historical novels and my 2 FREE mystery gifts (gifts are worth about $10). After receiving them, if I don't wish to receive any more books, I can return the shipping statement marked "cancel." If I don't cancel, I will receive 4 brand-new novels every month and be billed just $4.99 per book in the U.S. or $5.49 per book in Canada. That's a saving of at least 17% off the cover price. It's quite a bargain! Shipping and handling is just 50¢ per book in the U.S. and 75¢ per book in Canada.* I understand that accepting the 2 free books and gifts places me under no obligation to buy anything. I can always return a shipment and cancel at any time. Even if I never buy another book, the two free books and gifts are mine to keep forever.

102/302 IDN GH6Z

Name _____ (PLEASE PRINT)

Address _____ Apt. #

City _____ State/Prov. _____ Zip/Postal Code

Signature (if under 18, a parent or guardian must sign)

Mail to the **Reader Service:**
IN U.S.A.: P.O. Box 1867, Buffalo, NY 14240-1867
IN CANADA: P.O. Box 609, Fort Erie, Ontario L2A 5X3

Want to try two free books from another series?
Call 1-800-873-8635 or visit www.ReaderService.com.

* Terms and prices subject to change without notice. Prices do not include applicable taxes. Sales tax applicable in N.Y. Canadian residents will be charged applicable taxes. Offer not valid in Quebec. This offer is limited to one order per household. Not valid for current subscribers to Love Inspired Historical books. All orders subject to credit approval. Credit or debit balances in a customer's account(s) may be offset by any other outstanding balance owed by or to the customer. Please allow 4 to 6 weeks for delivery. Offer available while quantities last.

Your Privacy—The Reader Service is committed to protecting your privacy. Our Privacy Policy is available online at www.ReaderService.com or upon request from the Reader Service.

We make a portion of our mailing list available to reputable third parties that offer products we believe may interest you. If you prefer that we not exchange your name with third parties, or if you wish to clarify or modify your communication preferences, please visit us at www.ReaderService.com/consumerschoice or write to us at Reader Service Preference Service, P.O. Box 9062, Buffalo, NY 14240-9062. Include your complete name and address.

LIH15

SPECIAL EXCERPT FROM

Love Inspired® H I S T O R I C A L

*With her uncle trying to claim her ranch, widow
Lula May Barlow has no time to worry about romance.
But can she resist Edmund McKay—the handsome
cowboy next door—when he helps her fight for her
land...and when her children start playing matchmaker?*

*Read on for a sneak preview of
A FAMILY FOR THE RANCHER,
the heartwarming continuation of the series
LONE STAR COWBOY LEAGUE:
THE FOUNDING YEARS*

"Just wanted to return your book."

Book?

Lula May saw her children slinking out of the barn,
guilty looks on their faces. So that's why they'd made such
nuisances of themselves out at the pasture. They'd wanted
her to send them off to play so they could take the book to
Edmund. And she knew exactly why. Those little rascals
were full-out matchmaking! Casting a look at Edmund,
she faced the inevitable, which wasn't really all that bad.
"Will you come in for coffee?"

He tilted his hat back to reveal his broad forehead, where
dark blond curls clustered and made him look younger
than his thirty-three years. "Coffee would be good."

Lula May led him in through the back door. To her
horror, Uncle sat at the kitchen table hungrily eyeing
the cake she'd made for Edmund...and almost forgotten
about. Now she'd have no excuse for not introducing them
before she figured out how to get rid of Floyd.

"Edmund, this is Floyd Jones." She forced herself to add,
"My uncle. Floyd, this is my neighbor, Edmund McKay."

As the children had noted last week when Edmund first

stepped into her kitchen, he took up a good portion of the room. Even Uncle seemed a bit unsettled by his presence. While the men chatted about the weather, however, Lula May could see the old wiliness and false charm creeping into Uncle's words and facial expressions. She recognized the old man's attempt to figure Edmund out so he could control him.

Pauline and Daniel worked at the sink, urgent whispers going back and forth. Why had they become so bold in their matchmaking? Was it possible they sensed the danger of Uncle's presence and wanted to lure Edmund over here to protect her? She wouldn't have any of that. She'd find a solution without any help from anybody, especially not her neighbor. Her only regret was that she hadn't been able to protect the children from realizing Uncle wasn't a good man. If she could have found a way to be nicer to him… No, that wasn't possible. Not when he'd come here for the distinct purpose of seizing everything she owned.

The men enjoyed their coffee and cake, after which Edmund suggested they take a walk around the property to build up an appetite for supper.

"We'd like to go for a walk with you, Mr. McKay," Pauline said. "May we, Mama?"

Lula May hesitated. Let them continue their matchmaking or make them spend time with Uncle? Neither option pleased her. When had she lost control of her household? About a week before Uncle arrived, that was when, the day when Edmund had walked into her kitchen and invited himself into her…or rather, her eldest son's life.

"You may go, but don't pester Mr. McKay." She gave the children a narrow-eyed look of warning.

Their innocent blinks did nothing to reassure her.

Don't miss
A FAMILY FOR THE RANCHER
by Louise M. Gouge, available August 2016 wherever
Love Inspired® Historical books and ebooks are sold.

www.LoveInspired.com

Love Inspired

Love the Love Inspired book you just read?

Your opinion matters.

Review this book on your favorite book site, review site, blog or your own social media properties and share your opinion with other readers!